GOLD

Joe Kinney

authorHOUSE®

AuthorHouse™
1663 Liberty Drive
Bloomington, IN 47403
www.authorhouse.com
Phone: 1 (800) 839-8640

Published by AuthorHouse 12/23/2015

ISBN: 978-1-5049-6896-6 (sc)
ISBN: 978-1-5049-6894-2 (hc)
ISBN: 978-1-5049-6895-9 (e)

Librray of Congress Control Number: 2015920790

Print information available on the last page.

CHAPTER
1

lice Muller looked at the bridge. It was maybe fifty feet long and it stretched across the river. From the looks of it, it should have fallen down years ago. It was one of those bridges that did not have any legs supporting it. There were two ropes along the top, one on each side and she guessed two along the bottom the ends of all four of them anchored at both sides of the bank of the river. The top ropes were held in place by four boards standing vertical and sunk into the ground in deep holes. The bottom ropes were tied to the base of the vertical poles. There were a lot of ropes strung vertically between the top and bottom ropes and then someone had placed some boards across the two bottom ropes to walk on. The bridge was about four feet wide. The whole stinking thing looked rotten, like it was ready to fall down. If it fell it was into the river ten feet below. She did not know the name of the river, but it was running fast and she knew just by looking at it if someone fell in they would drown, and that was not part of Miss Muller's plans, to drown in some unknown river somewhere in northern Mexico. She looked to the other side of the bridge and saw Hansen standing there, his horse and three mules tied to some scrub bushes. One of the four professional gunmen she was riding with.

"Let's go Muller," She said to herself, out loud, "if you fall in you will find the Promised Land and according to all those preachers it has lots of gold. The streets are made of it." She swallowed hard and took the first step onto the first board. The boards were uneven. Over the years some of the boards had broken and been replaced by newer ones. So some of the boards were thicker then others making them higher by an inch or two and still others were not as wide as the originals, so there were spaces between the boards, some spaces wider then others. If you did not watch your step your foot could go through the larger spaces. She was frightened and having a hard time moving forward. She had taken only a few steps and now the horse was pulling on the reins, not wanting to cross the bridge anymore then she did. The three mules would be the same way, but she kept pulling. She looked down through the spaces between the boards as she moved and saw the rubble floating in the river. She stopped and froze. She was twenty feet out and could go no further she was so frightened. She could not go back because the horse and mules were there. The mules were tied with their reins to the tail of the mule in front. The first mule was tied by a rope to the saddle horn on her horse. She could not take her eyes off the river. Blind terror gripped her which is why she froze. The terror that gripped her would not let her move forward or backward. She was going to die. The bridge was falling and she was going into the river. Her left arm hurt from squeezing one of the vertical ropes supporting the bridge. Her right arm hurt from squeezing the reins of the horse. Her, the horse, the three mules were all going to die because they were going to fall into the river.

Muller never heard him coming across the bridge, even though he ran. She first knew he was there when he punched her arm loose that was holding the rope on the side of the bridge. She looked up and saw Hansen, he was saying something, but she did not understand. "I am going to fall in!" she screamed. She saw it coming before she felt the punch. Hansen's right fist slammed into her stomach and she doubled over as her lungs expelled every ounce of air. As she fell forward Hansen bent over and caught her over his left shoulder. She was still looking down and still knew she was going to fall into the river no matter what Hansen did.

"Come on animals." She heard Hansen yell at the horse and mules, as he pulled the reins of the horse. She was bouncing from being carried over his shoulder and her stomach hurt where Hansen had hit her. She was still terrified and trying to catch her breath, but now she was moving and she knew Hansen was not going to let go of her until he reached the other side. She watched as the end of the bridge got closer and she realized that Hansen was running. How he could do that was beyond her. Carry her, lead the four animals and run at the same time across this piece of junk someone had called a bridge. She was looking at everything upside down and she was going to throw up very shortly. The river was still there and she could see the debris floating in it. Muller closed her eyes, she did not want to see herself plunge into the river. She wanted to scream and she could not control herself. She would have too except that suddenly she was dumped very unceremoniously onto the ground. Her head hit the sand with a thump and she opened her eyes in time to see the horse, then the mules trot by. She laid on the ground closed her eyes and started to cry. She felt two hands grab the front of her shirt and pull her to her feet.

"Stand up and clean up your face." Hansen said to her. "You're over the bridge and you didn't fall in the river and die." He turned away to watch the next man start to cross leading his horse and mules.

Muller took a minute to compose herself and then looked at Tucker leading his horse and mules slowly across the swinging, wobbling, bouncing, squeaking bridge. She moved to beside Hansen and said, "Thanks for helping me. I was..."

"I don't want to hear it, you're across and that's it." He stated flatly, never taking his eyes off Tucker, who was now half way across.

She waited a minute watching Tucker pull his horse and mules, then asked Hansen, "How could you run on that thing?" she pointed to the rickety bridge.

Hansen turned and looked down at Muller, "Lady, the only person more scared on that bridge then you, was me. Now forget it.' he turned back to watching Tucker. Wilson started across. Muller watched Tucker as he exited from the bridge.

He walked up beside Hansen, looked at Wilson leading his animals across the bridge and said in a hurt tone of voice, "Jeez Al, I feel bad. You didn't carry me across the bridge." Hansen just turned and looked at Tucker. "Is it because my man boobies are not big enough?" Tucker asked and having said that he pushed his breasts up while pushing his chest out. Hansen laughed, and turned his attention back to Wilson, who was now almost across.

As Wilson walked past Tucker and Hansen he asked Hansen, "How come you didn't carry me across, Al?" the same hurt tone of voice as used by Tucker.

"Your tits ain't big enough." Tucker said and walked away leading his horses and mules. Hansen shook his head, smiling, Wilson looked confused and followed Tucker. Muller saw Wilson say something to Tucker. Tucker answered and Wilson burst into a fit of laughter. Muller knew they were laughing at her and she swore to herself, standing opposite Hansen, that she would show them. She swore she would never loose her nerve again.

Farmer was half way across the bridge when Muller looked back. He was having a hard time with his animals, but they were moving. She wondered if he was as afraid of crossing as she was. Half way across one of the mules sat down, the second mule in line.

"Charlie?" Hansen yelled at Farmer.

Farmer turned and looked at Hansen and waved, "No problem Al, it'll be up in a minute." He yelled back and moved past the horse and first mule. Muller watched as he spoke to the mule and suddenly the mule stood and Farmer moved back to the front and picked up the reins of the horse and calmly lead the horse and mules the rest of the way across. Farmer stopped as he reached Hansen and Muller thought to herself, here comes another remark about big tits.

She watched Hansen look at Farmer as Farmer said, "You just got to know how to talk to the women folk to get them to do what you want." and he walked on followed by the horse and mules.

"Charlie, do me a favor and take the point." Hansen said. It seemed strange to Muller that Hansen never gave a command, he gave them alright, but it was always in the form of a request, never a direct order.

"Yea," was all Farmer said.

Muller and Hansen looked at each other and Hansen shook his head. "Mount up we're moving on."

CHAPTER 2

The sun shone down on the five people. There were no clouds in the blue sky, only the sun, the merciless sun. The temperature had to be one hundred and twenty in the bottom of the wash where they were walking on foot leading their horses and their three mules. Everything was burnt or dying or already dead. There were no trees for shade. No abandoned buildings to go into to get out of the sun, there was just the shale rock and sand. The shale rock was broken, small broken pieces lying on top of other small broken pieces two, three, sometimes four layers deep. The blowing sand acted as a lubricant so the shale would slide more easily and did often under the horses hoofs or the walkers boots. The sand was just as dangerous as the shale. The ever present wind gently blew it into holes and cracks, filling them in so the man or animal would step on them and twist or break an ankle or leg. A twisted or broken ankle or leg meant death, a slow painful death unless one used his own gun on himself.

Water was the most precious commodity in this part of Mexico. Men killed for it to stay alive, and men died without it. Muller looked again at Hansen's mule loaded down with water bags. Each person had six water bags plus six canteens. Muller also had several bottles of booze. One could never tell when the occasion for a drink of something a little stronger then water may arise.

She looked again at the sun and felt the oppression of the heat. It was like a weight on her shoulders pushing down, bending her, trying to break her. Her head was drooping and she did not know how much longer she could keep walking when she felt someone next to her. She made an effort to look to her right and Tucker was walking along side her.

"Pick up your head and straighten your shoulders. You walk like you're giving up, like you're beaten, like you're ready to quit." He spoke quietly and Muller knew no one else heard him. "You're tougher then the sand and the rock and the sun and heat. If you were not tough enough to make this trip you think Hansen would have signed on. You think Farmer would be out there?" It was poised as a question, but Muller knew it was a statement. "Those two guys know people and they knew you were one of a tougher breed put on earth to do this sort of thing. You ride with Hansen, Tucker, Farmer, and Wilson and you ride with the best. Someday after we get the gold and are rich and living in luxury you will pick up a newspaper and there will be an article about the Hansen gang and how they went to Mexico and took all this gold and brought it back when nobody else could do it. And somebody will ask you about it and you will remember just how tough it was and you will try and tell them, but it just won't be the same as being here. It won't be the same as walking on this lousy rock and having sand in your boots and in your hair. Hardly being able to breath because it is so hot. Always being afraid somebody is going to shoot you. This is what some men and some woman were born to do and you are one of them. So stand tall and walk straight, you're doing fine." Tucker finished and Muller felt better, stronger. She straightened her shoulders and picked up her head and felt some inner strength flow through her.

"Thanks Ace, for the talk, I think I needed that." She said sincerely, looking at the man walking next to her.

He looked back and smiled at her. "Good, now give me a belt from that hip flask you're carrying."

Muller burst out laughing and handed Tucker the flask. Tucker took a long pull and handed the flask back to Muller. She put the cork back in it and put it back inside the waist ban of her pants. She straightened her shoulders and started to walk more briskly.

"Good girl." Tucker said, then slapped her on her rear end and laughed as he let her get back in line in front of him.

CHAPTER 3

It was dusk now and Muller looked out across the wide open spaces and wondered how anyone could possibly live in these conditions. Sand, dust, so hot during the day you could not stand it, so cold at night you had to light a fire and wear a coat and you still shivered, the gentle breeze continuously blowing the sand. The sand was into everything. It was in the water, in the food, but worst of all it got under your clothes. It always felt as if something was crawling on you. Then it rubbed your skin raw and it just hurt. If there was a hell it would have to be here. She looked back at the three men sitting around the fire drinking coffee, men that were tough, tough as leather. The first man was Albert Hansen, tall, maybe six foot two inches and well built maybe carrying two hundred and twenty pounds, but no fat or flab, just muscle. She had picked him as the leader because the old marshal had said to. He had been to Mexico before, maybe even to where she wanted to go. She noticed Hansen had removed his gun belt and had laid it on the ground next to where he was sitting. To Hansen's right sat Charlie Farmer. Farmer was lean, and unlike Hansen he never took his gun off. Maybe he was being hunted, or maybe he just felt insecure without it. She did not know and did not care. Hansen had said he was the best cold blooded killer anywhere and she had come to trust Hansen. The third man was Ace Tucker. Tucker had to be in his forties and was given to fat. He was soft around the middle and he would tell you how good he was with a gun anytime you asked. He must have been pretty good because he was still alive at his age, besides Tucker was a real clown and they would need a little humor on this trip. There was a fourth man, boy really, his name was Harry Wilson. He was in his early twenties, not more than twenty-two. Hansen had said he was very good with a gun and that is what Hansen had told her she needed for this trip. Then she had seen Wilson in a gunfight and she knew what fast was.

This trip, the be all and end all for Alice Muller, Alice Muller, con artist, thief, and prostitute from Wichita, Kansas. She had lived by her wits since her family had thrown her out twenty years ago after finding out she had seduced the fourteen year old neighbor boy. She was thirty-five and knew this was the biggest and best job she had ever tried to pull off, to say nothing of the most dangerous. She had stolen a map off a man in his hotel room and from the moment she saw it she felt it was a good map. You could buy treasure maps for ten cents apiece, but this one was different. It was old and burned along one edge. She had taken it to a friend of hers, the old marshal, and he had told her he was too old to go, but he had told her about Hansen. The old man had also lent her the three thousand dollars she used to hire the four gunman she was with now. The deal was this. She would lead them to the treasure and they each got ten percent, plus the five hundred dollars cash money up front. She also supplied the fifteen mules they had. Each person had three mules, one to carry their supplies and two to carry the gold back that they were going after. She would get sixty percent, the old man would get half of her share. She had left the map with the old man, she could remember the way. If she carried the map there was the chance one of the men could steal it and then why would they need her. She had also made it plain to all four men that if she did die on this trip and the old man found out that she had been killed by one of them he knew enough people to have them hunted down and killed. Each and everyone of them. Muller figured that was as close as she could get to a guarantee that they would not kill her after they got the gold.

CHAPTER
4

Muller remembered the night she had been working in the saloon in Wichita. The man had started drinking and he had plenty of money. It was the job of the girls to get the patrons to spend as much as they could in the saloon, and the girls did a good job of that. Anything they made in the rooms upstairs afterward was split between them and the owner. Anything they could steal off a drunken customer was theirs. It was the stealing off the customer that landed Muller where she was now. He had passed out on the bed and she had searched his pants and jacket and found his wallet, more then four hundred dollars in it. What a fool for carrying that much money into a saloon and getting drunk and then going to bed with one of the saloon girls.

She had thrown his wallet down and gotten dressed and then looked back at the jacket and had seen the map sticking out of a hidden seam in it. She had reached and taken the map opened it and looked at it. It was burned along one edge and faded bad, but still readable. There was something about the map that drew her attention to it. In the upper right hand corner was some kind of little devil like character with his spear pointing toward some mountain. She did not understand what it meant and she knew if the guy woke up and saw her with the map he would probably beat her up or worse, so she folded the map back up, stuck it down her cleavage, which was more then ample to hold it, and went to her room. She remembered changing clothes and putting on jeans and a button up the front shirt and boots. She was going for a long ride. She climbed out the back window of the saloon and down the ladder like the thing used to hold the flowers in the summer. She ran to the livery stable and snuck in the back door. She picked what looked like a good horse, saddled it, and lead it outside. She had folded the money she had stolen from the man in the saloon and put it in her pants pocket. She took it out, removed one hundred dollars and stuck it on a nail that was sticking out of one of the boards of the stall the horse was in. She mounted up and headed south for Texas where she knew a man, maybe the only man she could trust, with her new found secret. The man was old, maybe sixty, an old lawman, but a good friend. That is where Alice Muller headed that fall night she rode out of Wichita, Kansas with three hundred dollars, a stolen treasure map, and a fast horse.

CHAPTER 5

Muller remembered walking into the saloon and looking around. She knew she would be blind for a few seconds because of the bright sunlight outside and the semi darkness inside the saloon. She waited while her eyes became accustom to the darkness, then she walked to the bar. There were not many customers and only one bartender and two girls working the floor. Two card games were going on, the craps table and the other four card tables were empty. There were three men at one card game and four were at the other.

"We ain't hirin', Lady. The owner says we got enough girls." The bartender spoke and his voice startled her.

Muller turned and looked at the overweight man, "I'm looking for a man named Al Hansen." She said quietly.

The bartender pointed at the three man card game, "He's the big guy, with his back to us."

Muller did not wait for the bartender to say anything else, like he would get Hansen, She simply walked over to the table and approached Hansen from his left side. She stopped when she was within two feet of his side. "Are you Al Hansen?" She asked boldly, this was no time for the shy type girly tone of voice.

He turned and looked up at her, he had a square jaw, brown eyes and what looked like about a three days growth of beard, "That's me." He said smiling up at her.

"I would like to talk to you outside for a minute." Muller said, trying not to stare into his eyes, this guy was a looker.

"Sure." He said, standing up. He was a big man and with a barrel chest, arms like telegraph poles. She noticed as he stood up he unlatched the hammer hoop on the pistol he was wearing. "There is a room in the back we can use." He added as he took her left arm and steered her toward a door at the end of the bar away from the saloon entrance. He guided her none to gently across the floor and through the door which he opened an instant before she would have walked into it with him pushing her. The room was lit by a single oil lamp on a table in the center of the room.

Muller heard the door close behind her and she tried to tare her arm loose from his grasp, but he held it, "You can let go now, I promise not to beat you too badly if you do." The sarcasm in Muller's voice could not be missed. He let go of her arm and in the process turned her around. This guy was not only big, he was strong as a bull, thought Muller. "What's with the strong arm stuff?" She asked, rubbing her arm.

"What do you want?" He asked, ignoring her question.

He was looking directly at her and she felt uncomfortable. "I have worked a lot of saloons..."

"Lady I don't do the hiring and firing around here, I just keep it peaceful." He interrupted her.

"Let me finish." She almost yelled back, he was good looking and big, but he was starting to get on her nerves,

"Get to the point." He said.

"A man named Sam Jones said I should talk to you about a deal I am putting together." She answered, "He said you would be the man I needed to see to get a couple of men together to do what I want to do."

"What do you want to do?"

"What's with you, you have a hot hand in that poker game out there." This time Muller did yell.

"Last night I threw a guy out and he said he and his friends would be back to see me. And in my line of work I don't trust anybody." Was his answer.

13

"Sorry." Muller said, looking at him, "I'm not here to help settle anyone else's score. I'm here to ask you to help me get to Mexico and find a stash of gold."

Hansen looked astonished, his eyes got big and his mouth dropped open, then his face turned from surprise to a smile, "You're kidding me."

"I'm not, and Jones is a good friend of mine and he didn't think it was such a wild idea or he would not have sent me."

Hansen thought about it for a few seconds and then looked at her, "Okay, if Jones says it's a good deal, I'll listen."

Muller told him about the map, naturally omitting the part about how she stole it. "Jones says it looks real enough and he is willing to take a shot at it."

"He ain't going?" Hansen asked.

"No" She said, "He said he would, but he's too old and tired. What he did do was give me a big stake. I have money enough for a lot of supplies and whatever else we need." Muller paused strictly for effect, "Plus you get five hundred bucks right now if you decide to go." She watched at the look of surprise on Hansen's face.

He turned around and looked at the door, then turned back. "I get the five hundred now?"

"We just have to get to my horse." She answered.

"You buy everything?"

"I buy everything."

"You're on, Lady. Which brings up another point, what's your name?" He asked.

"Alice Muller." She answered, taking the extended hand.

"I'm glad to know you and your money, Alice Muller." Hansen said, smiling.

CHAPTER 6

A day later and twenty miles south Hansen and Muller dismounted from their horses and walked into the boarding house. It was a run down place and Muller was glad she did not have to come in here by herself. She had lived in some pretty sleazy places, but this was lower then anything she had ever lived in. Hansen walked to the front counter and the man behind the counter looked up from sitting in the chair reading the paper. "What?" he asked as they approached the counter. The top of the counter was dusty and had a lot of circles where people had put bottles and glasses that had been damp. The floor could almost pass for a dirt floor it was so flifty and had not been swept in so long. The only way Muller knew it was a wooden floor was the sound their boots made as they walked across it, and the cracks in the dirt where it fell through the spaces between the floor boards, which were many.

"I'm looking for Ace Tucker." Hansen said in his quiet, deep, voice.

"You mean a kind of older guy, kind of like fatty and good with a gun?" The clerk asked.

"That's him." Hansen answered.

"I don't know nobody like that." He answered, going back to his paper.

Hansen smiled at the clerks answer, nothing like a good smart answer, he waited. The Clerk looked up again from the paper, "What?" Again the question.

Muller wondered how Hansen would handle this without getting into trouble with the law in this town where he did not know anyone. Let's see what kind of a man Jones picked to help me, and she watched. She had her answer in seconds.

"I'm lazy and doing anything I don't have to just pisses me off." Hansen said to the clerk who was back to looking at the paper. "So it would piss me off to have to walk all the way around the counter to break all your fingers until you tell me what room Ace is in."

Muller could not believe how fast Hansen leaped over the counter and was standing in front of the clerk who had just looked up from the paper. The register book had fell to the floor, the ink pot lay next to the book, the ink splattered against the back wall where the keys to the empty rooms lay.

"Get back on the other side of the counter, buster. Ain't nobody but me allowed back here." The clerk said looking up at Hansen towering over him.

Hansen reached down and grabbed the clerks left hand, he removed it from the paper and snapped the little finger. Muller heard the crack in the silent lobby and was shocked by the scream of the clerk. Hansen clamped his left hand over the clerks mouth to silence him. He held it there for only seconds, then said quietly to the clerk, "Give me the room number or I will break the other four, then your hand, then your other hand, and so on until I work my way up to your neck." He removed his hand from the clerks mouth.

"Two eleven." The clerk said, his voice trembling with a combination of fear and pain.

"Now understand this, if you try something when the lady and myself turn our backs, I will kill you. You will be dead." The threat in Hansen's voice was terrifying, even to Muller. The clerks' eyes bulged as he nodded yes in understanding, rapidly, again and again.

Muller watched as Hansen turned and walked to the end of the counter and started for the stairs. She followed and because he was so much taller then her and his legs longer she almost had to run. He turned left at the top of the stairs and walked almost half way along the hallway until he stood in front of room two eleven. He knocked loudly on the door, almost pounding with his right fist. The flimsily door shook with the power of the blows. There was no sound from inside the room, so Muller watched as Hansen took a step backward and kicked the door in. The inside of the door frame shattered and the door opened with a bang as it crashed into the wall behind it. He walked in and Muller followed. She could not believe what she was looking at. Along the wall to the right was a bed with a man and a woman in it covered by a sheet, she assumed they were naked. The floor had at least ten whiskey bottles lying on their sides, empty and at least six more standing on the dresser, those also looked empty. Muller had been on her share of drunks, but this was too much. Clothes and dirty glasses were scattered everywhere. The room had the same amount of dust and dirt as the lobby of the boarding house. Spider webs were everywhere, between the walls and ceiling and on the windows. God, I hope I never end up in a place like this, Muller thought.

"You Tucker?" Hansen asked the man lying in bed, passed out. The man did not answer, he simply laid there unconscious, his mouth open and his eyes closed. He was snoring his lips flapping every time he exhaled, and for some reason Muller noted he needed a shave The woman opened her eyes and blinked.

"He Tucker?" Hansen asked the woman.

"Huh?" She asked, having no idea what was going on. Hansen walked to the dresser and picked up the water pitcher, checking to make sure it was full. He walked back to the bed and poured the contents of the pitcher on the man lying in bed.

Some of it splashed on the woman and she yelled, "Hey, what the hell you doin'?!"

The man was choking on the water Hansen had poured into his open mouth. He had started coughing and gagging. He rolled out of bed onto the floor, rolling in the sheets as he did so, leaving the woman in bed uncovered and naked. Muller would be willing to bet the woman was addicted to alcohol and opium. Hansen turned to the woman and said, "He Tucker?"

"I think so, he said something about Ace. I don't really know. We been drunk for the last three or four days." She said, making no move to cover herself.

"Get out." Hansen ordered her. She slid out of the bed and stood up.

She stepped next to Hansen. She put her right hand on his left shoulder and asked, "Why don't you get rid of her and let me show you a good..."

That was all she said before Hansen pushed her so hard she stumbled out the door and ran head first into the wall on the opposite side of the hall. She fell to the floor unconscious. "Throw her clothes out and close the door." He told Muller who promptly threw out a dress that was lying on the floor, picking it up using only her finger tips and closed the door. Hansen none to gently leaned over the man who was just coming to and slapped him twice across the face, "Wake up."

The man opened his eyes and looked at Hansen standing over him. "Huh?" was his reply.

"You Ace Tucker?" Hansen asked the man lying on the floor, wrapped in the sheet.

"I was when I started drinking a couple of days ago." He answered. Muller smiled, knowing what he meant, having been on a few binges in her past.

"Get up and get dressed, I have to talk to you." Hansen said stepping away from Tucker.

"She ain't your wife is she?" Tucker asked, looking at Hansen, referring to the woman Hansen had just thrown out of the room. Muller could not help herself at the expression of fear Tucker's face and the question, she erupted in laughter.

"No, she ain't" Hansen answered Tucker.

"She your wife?" Tucker asked, looking at Muller.

"No." Muller answered.

Tucker had been looking at her and he asked, "You wanna' get married."

"Get up, ain't nobody getting married this morning." Hansen said.

Five minutes later Tucker was finally dressed. He was still pretty drunk and would not stop talking. Finally Hansen had enough and told him to shut up and get his stuff together.

"We going somewhere?" Tucker asked trying to button his pants.

"Yea."

"Where?"

"I'll tell you later."

"She coming?" He looked at Muller.

"Yes." Muller answered in a voice so quiet Tucker could hardly hear her.

"Ill go."

Tucker picked up his pistol and holster and his hat as he staggered around the room looking for whatever he thought was his.

"Sure you don't want to marry me?" Tucker asked Muller as they left the room.

CHAPTER 8

Muller walked behind Hansen, she was followed by a still drunk Tucker. He had asked her to marry him at least six times so far and they had walked only three blocks. She wondered where Hansen was taking them when they walked around the corner and there was a huge tent, the different sections alternately colored red white and blue. Muller heard a lot of shouting and wondered what was going on. She saw a large group of men standing off to one side of the tent and she thought it must be a fight, a boxing match. She hoped it was a good one, she enjoyed a good fight. She was not tall enough to see. Then everything went quiet and a second later she heard a gunshot and instantly the yelling and shouting started again. She and Tucker followed Hansen as he pushed his way to near the front of the crowd. She could see a boy really, he could not be more then twenty standing on a chair. He was wearing a red shirt and white hat and blue jeans, black boots that were so well polished they were shining in the sunlight. He was wearing a black gun belt with a matching cutaway, fast draw holster. A nickel plated revolver rested in the holster that was tied to his right leg, the white handle of the pistol standing out starkly against the black holster. The nearest edge of the group of men was a good ten feet away. There was also an opening in the crowd, a passageway that was maybe twenty feet wide facing away from the tent. Muller was no stranger to a good hustle and she knew instantly that was what she was looking at. She looked around and saw the man taking bets and she moved through the crowd until she was standing next to him.

"What's the game?" She asked. He was a fat guy wearing a derby hat to protect his balding head from the bright sunshine. He was wearing a striped suit, white shirt and a black string tie. I wouldn't trust this guy as far as I could throw him, she thought.

He looked at her, his eyes undressing her from her brown hair to her black boots, "This is the game, Honey, I cover all bets. The kid throws a beer bottle up in the air and while it is in the air he shoots threw the little hole you drink out of. He shoots the bottom out without breaking the rest of the bottle. Then he puts his pistol back in the holster and catches the bottle before it hits the ground. How much you got?"

"I got ten says he can't do that." Muller said, not knowing why she did, other then to see the trick done.

"Ten and a roll in the hay with me." The Barker yelled and the men standing around all laughed and yelled even louder.

"Maybe with him," Muller said pointing to the kid on the chair, "but not with you fatso. You probably stink." This brought another round of laughter and cheering. The kid was good looking, tall and slim, The thought aroused Muller and she put it aside. There was at least a million bucks waiting down in Mexico. When she got her share she could hire any stud she wanted. She tossed a ten dollar gold piece to the Barker and waited.

"Miss." The young man on the chair said to her, smiling and bowing while tipping his hat. "Another bottle." He said to the Barker and he tossed an empty beer bottle to the young man. The kid caught it and in the same smooth move tossed it into the air. It turned end over end. It went maybe twenty feet in the air and suddenly there was a gunshot and the bottle seemed to explode. What was left fell and the kid caught it by the neck before it hit the ground. He stepped off the chair and handed the bottle to Muller.

"I bet that's the first time you paid ten dollars for a broken beer bottle." He said smiling at her. He then climbed back up on the chair.

"I'll be dammed." Muller said looking at the bottle. The edge where the bottom had been was almost perfectly flat, as if cut by a knife. Muller still could not believe the kid had done it. She turned and walked through the crowd gazing at the bottle she held in her hand.

"Let me see." Tucker said walking up next to her. She handed him the bottle and turned just in time to see the kid do it again, more cheering and laughter.

"Wow." Was all Tucker said. Muller looked at him and he suddenly looked sober.

The show went on for another hour until the young man standing on the chair told the Barker taking bets he was too tired to shoot anymore today. The Barker told the crowd that the show was over and come back tomorrow and the kid would do it again. The kid put the chair into the wagon which stood nearby and started walking away when a man called to him and the Barker. "Hey kid, I got this beer bottle I just emptied, let's see you shoot this one." saying that, the man threw the bottle at the kid none too gently. Hansen, Muller, and Tucker had started to approach the kid when the man had started yelling at him. They stopped as the kid caught the bottle.

"He only shoots the bottles for money, and besides, he said he was tired and when he gets tired he quits." Answered the Barker.

"He can shoot the bottle, or I can shoot him and then you." The man said.

"Give him his money back, Tony." The kid told the Barker.

"How much did you lose?" The Barker asked, walking toward the man, reaching in his pocket.

The man pulled his pistol and shot the Barker dead on the spot. Muller was shocked, but not so shocked that she missed both Hansen and Tucker pulled their pistols.

"Put the gun away." Hansen said to the man, who looked at both Hansen and Tucker. He must have realized there was no way he could shoot both of them. He did as Hansen ordered. Muller watched as the kid ran to the Barker lying in the street. Knelt next to the fat man and shook his head. Muller started toward the kid when Hansen grabbed her arm.

"Leave it." He said.

"Somebody get the sheriff." Someone yelled.

"He is on his way." Someone else answered.

Muller was still watching the kid as he stood up and looked at the man who had shot the Barker.

"You won't need the sheriff." The kid said quietly. "You need the undertaker." And saying that he turned and faced the man who had shot the Barker, he flicked the hammer holder off the pistol he was wearing and looked at the man, "You got five bullets left in that gun, I bet your life you don't get to use another one."

There was no more then thirty feet between the kid and the man who shot the Barker. Muller saw the man move his right hand towards the pistol holstered around his waist. She thought later, maybe, just maybe, he touched the handle of the pistol before the bullet from the kids' pistol hit him in the chest. He got this shocked look on his face and collapsed to the ground, just as dead as the Barker he had killed only a minute before.

The sheriff arrived seconds later. He was elderly, overweight, and he was out of breath when he got to the scene. "Give me that gun kid." He said and the kid handed his pistol over to him, "Now tell me what happened here."

"He shot Tony and I shot him." The kid said. Muller could see the tears running down the kids face. Her heart went out to him.

"His guns still in his holster and I have seen Pain draw and he was fast." The sheriff said. The kid shrugged.

"It was a fair fight, Sheriff." Hansen's voice startled Muller. "The guy shot the kids friend in cold blood, but the kid gave the guy a fair chance."

"The guy didn't do bad, he came in second." Tucker commented. There was a ripple of laughter from some of the crowd.

Hansen walked the few feet to where the sheriff and the kid stood. "My name is Al Hansen and I'd like to talk to you for a minute." He said to the kid.

The kid turned away and wiped his face on the sleeve of his red shirt. Muller could tell he was embarrassed.

"What's his name?" Hansen asked the sheriff.

"This is Harry Wilson," he said pointing to the kid, "and that was Tony Straight." The sheriff said looking at the fat man lying on the ground.

"This might not be a good time, Al." Muller said, moving next to Hansen.

"We don't have a lot of time." He said to Muller, he turned to Wilson. "We need to talk, Wilson."

"Yea." Wilson said and turned and started to walk away. Hansen followed him. Muller watched as they walked away. She started to follow them when Tucker grabbed her arm and stopped her.

"Let Al handle it. He seems to be pretty good at handling people." He said, and Muller noticed he seemed to be sober now. "Besides, now me and you can be alone." Saying that, he walked to the sheriff, leaving Muller standing by herself in the street. Muller followed Tucker.

"You know, somehow that trick was rigged." Tucker was telling the sheriff.

"I know, but so did everyone else, so people really paid to see it done. Wilson missed every once in a while, but that was just to keep the crowd interested." The sheriff answered.

"How did he do it?" Tucker asked.

"They would not tell anybody, but they made some money and it was kind of honest." The sheriff replied.

Hansen returned to stand next to Muller. "Wilson just wants to stay long enough to make sure his friend gets buried, so we'll be leaving tomorrow morning."

F ive minutes later it was all over. The undertaker arrived and removed the two bodies. He told the kid they would be at his place and he could come and say good bye to his friend.

The undertakers name was Bitters, Walter Bitters. He was straightening out the body of Pain when he heard the door open. He turned and looked, expecting the Wilson kid, but it was someone he had never seen before. It was a big man, soft around the middle, maybe forty years old. He needed a shave and the black hat was dusty, as was the light blue shirt, the dungarees and boots. The pistol he wore was in a cutaway holster and he looked like he knew how to use it.

"Can I help you?" Bitters asked the man.

"My name is Ace Tucker, you ever heard of me?"

"No Sir, I have not." Answered Bitters.

"That don't matter, what matters is I know how you undertakers work. I'm a friend of that Wilson kid and his buddy had a lot of money on him. I expect the kid to get all of it when he comes to get his buddies stuff." Tucker said, the voice threatening.

"I beg your pardon, Sir, just what are you implying?" Bitters put all the injured tone he could in his voice.

"I am not implying anything, I'm saying you undertakers take every dime off the dead guy and then keep a big slice of the money for yourself and then charge the relatives or friends for burying the guy. Just make sure the kid gets all his friends money or I will be back and you and I will have another talk." Tucker said, "You understand?"

Bitters simply nodded his head that he understood.

"Good." Tucker said. He turned around and walked out of the undertakers place, softly closing the door behind him.

Bitters removed the wad of bills from his pocket he had taken off Wilson's friend and put it in the envelope with the deceased other possessions.

CHAPTER 10

The four of them rode to the little house. The ex marshal lived here. His name was Sam Jones. He was old now and he had a lot of things wrong with him from living a hard life, the life of a lawman on the frontier. Jones was sitting on a rocking chair on the front porch, as if he had been waiting for the three men and one woman to come to his house. He sat on the rocker every day, rain or shine and thanked God for this land and the people he knew and loved. He could see the beauty of God's handiwork in the vast land spread out in front of him. The only one of the four people he knew approaching his house was the woman Alice Muller. He remembered the first time he had met her. She had been involved in a bar fight and he had thrown her in jail for a week. They had become friends that week and he loved her as a father loved his daughter. She in turn had returned that love as a daughter would to a father she loved deeply.

Muller lead the four horsemen and she dismounted and ran up to Jones and gave him a big hug and kiss.

"I been tryin' to get her to do that to me for two days." Tucker complained light hearted.

"You need to get a rocking chair, Ace, instead of a horse, then she'll kiss and hug you." Wilson said laughing. He and Tucker had become fast friends the last two days they had been traveling together.

Al Hansen dismounted and while he did it Jones stood up, revealing a pistol that had been hidden under his right leg.

"I found three of the men. That's Al Hansen." She said pointing in Hansen's direction. "The old guy is Ace Tucker." She smiled and said pointing to Tucker still sitting on his horse, "And the kid is Harry Wilson." She finished.

"Where's Farmer?" Jones asked.

"He is supposed to live along the way so I figured we'd pick him up on our way down." Hansen answered.

Jones nodded his agreement. "You can water your horses and wash up around the back of the house." Jones told them. "By the time you get done supper will be ready."

"Can you two take the horses and water them." Hansen asked Tucker and Wilson. The two took the horses and after dismounting walked the horses around the back of the house to the well and the trough.

"Who is the old man?" Wilson asked Tucker.

"You ain't never heard of Sam Jones?" Tucker replied with a question.

Wilson was dumb founded, "That's the Sam Jones. The legend." Wilson still could not believe he had seen the man.

"That's him," Tucker said, "He was busting heads in the cow towns while I was still peeing in my drawers. He is one of the main reasons there is any kind of law and order in this part of the country."

"He's pretty old. I bet he ain't that good anymore." Wilson said.

"You can try him anytime you like. But I will tell you this, you will have a headache worst then I did yesterday." Tucker was referring to his hangover. "Come on, we'll go in and you can try him." Tucker said starting toward the house.

Two minutes later the five people were in the one room house sitting around the table.

As Wilson and Tucker sat down, Tucker said to Jones, "The kid here thinks he's pretty good. Thinks you're old and that he can take you."

"Is that so?" Jones said, looking at Wilson, "Well stand up, you might as well try."

Wilson went to stand up and as he did so Jones pushed the table with such force that he knocked Hansen and Tucker over backwards from the chairs they were sitting in. He pushed so hard and fast that Wilson never had a chance to get his right hand to his pistol before he was pinned against the wall and Jones had a forty-five caliber revolver pointed at his nose.

"The first thing you want to learn about gun fighting, Sonny, is humility. Never, ever, underestimate the guy you're going up against." Jones said, "Now a couple of years ago I would have bobbed you on the head with this pistol and tossed you into the clink. I ain't a lawman no more so I will let you go if you promise not to try that again."

"Yes Sir." Wilson answered. The shock of what had happened still on his face. Jones pulled the table back to where it was and sat back in his chair as Hansen and Tucker stood back up and righted their chairs. Wilson righted his chair and moved back to the table.

"Turn and face that window, youngster." Jones said to Wilson. Wilson did as he was told, "Now let's how fast you are." The boy flicked the hammer hoop off his pistol and faster then the eye could followed the pistol was out and cocked, aimed at the window.

"How accurate can you shoot?" Jones questioned.

"He's accurate." Muller said, looking at Wilson with a smile.

"Well after we get done talking in here, I will take you out back and show you a couple of tricks I picked up over the years." Jones said to the boy, he turned to Tucker, "So I finally get to meet Ace Tucker. I think I chased you a couple of times a few years back."

"Closer to fifteen or twenty, Marshall. Ain't neither one of us getting any younger." Tucker answered.

Jones looked at Hansen, "I picked you to lead this because you're big, strong, and smart. I expect you to bring back my girl here alive and well."

Hansen nodded.

"Okay this is the deal," Jones said, "Alice here found a map and it tells where there is a lot of gold buried. You each get five hundred bucks, three mules, and supplies. You have to supply the guns, ammunition, and courage. The gold is in Mexico in a cave and Alice here knows where the cave is. All you have to do is get her there and back and you each get ten percent of what you bring back. Me and Alice each get thirty percent on account of we figured this whole thing out. Now that being said, let's eat." Jones finished and Muller put out the plates and started serving the food.

CHAPTER
11

Hansen lead, then came Muller, Tucker, and Wilson. Both sides of the trail were almost completely covered by brush, small scrub trees maybe eight feet high. High enough so a person could not see what was on the other side. There was also a slight rise where the brush started so the brush in the back was even taller, giving the small log cabin behind it much wanted privacy. The entrance trail into the ranch was narrow and up the incline. Hansen turned his horse and walked it up the narrow trail and to the top of the rise. The dark green lawn spread out in front of Hansen.

Muller topped the rise and saw the lawn. She had expected the usual land that one saw here, sand and brush. The beauty of what she saw almost took her breath away. The brush at the front along the main trail covered any view of the lawn from the main trail. It was dark green and it looked perfectly flat. Somebody knew how to care for the grounds of this place. She looked past Hansen and the house, a small cabin, maybe twice the size of the cabin Jones lived in. She looked past the cabin and saw the man look up from what he was doing. He was about one hundred feet behind the cabin, two hundred feet from where she sat on her horse. He was holding a pickaxe in one hand as he looked at the approaching riders. As Muller looked she saw he was digging out a tree stump. She watched as he put down the pickaxe and walked a few feet and picked up a pistol and holster. He pulled the pistol from the holster and stood waiting. Muller could not make out his face from this distance. His shirt was wet with perspiration, as were the top half of his pants. His tan hat was crumbled, dirty, and sweat stained.

Hansen had stopped his horse in front of the cabin and had dismounted. Muller did the same, as did Tucker and Wilson.

"This guy is very good and very dangerous, so watch what you do until I talk to him." Hansen said. "On second thought, maybe you three should stay here and let me go by myself." It was stated as a suggestion, but the three knew it was an order, so they stood by their horses watching the man standing in the field watching them.

Hansen removed his gun belt and hung it on his saddle horn. Then he walked out into the field where the man stood waiting.

Hansen approached the man, who looked to be in late twenties. Hansen raised his hands to show he had no gun and had not come to cause trouble. When he got within ten feet of the man the man raised the pistol and pointed it at Hansen's chest.

"You Charlie Farmer?" Hansen asked.

The man nodded yes.

"My name is Al Hansen and I need a good gun for a job in Mexico."

"Who are they?" Farmer asked, motioning with his head toward Muller, Tucker, and Wilson. The pistol was still pointed at Hansen's chest.

"They are the other three that are involved in this deal. They are going and if you come you will be the last one. It is a five person deal." Hansen answered.

"Have them come over here, but their guns stay there." Farmer said, Hansen noted the voice was cold, emotionless.

Muller heard Hansen yell for them to come to where he and Farmer were talking, but to leave their guns.

"I don't like leaving my gun." Wilson said.

"If he was going to shoot us Harry, he would have started doing it by now." Tucker said as he unbuckled his gun belt. Muller looked at Tucker taking off his gun and followed his example. Finally Wilson did the same. All three hanging the gun belts on their saddle horns as Hansen had done.

As they started walking across the dark green grass Muller said to Tucker, "This is so beautiful, I feel like taking off my boots and walking in my bare feet." She reached down and touched the soft grass. Then proceeded to do what she had said and grabbing hold of Tuckers right arm she removed her boots. The grass was thick and plush, like the carpet in the most expensive hotels. She felt it tickle the bottoms of her feet and slide between her toes. "This is great." She told the two men.

They walked to where Hansen stood and stopped.

"Put your boots back on lady, there are a lot of rattle snakes around here." Farmer said.

Muller looked around her on the ground as she pulled her boots back on. "How did you get this grass like this?" She asked, still looking at the ground.

"What's the deal?" Farmer asked Hansen, ignoring Muller's question.

"There is a cave in Mexico and it has a lot of gold in it. We take what we can, or all of it and bring it back. We get ten percent. Muller and the guy backing this deal each get thirty percent. You get five hundred bucks up front if you come. You supply your own guns and ammo."

Farmer looked at Muller, then Tucker, then Wilson. He paused, then slipped the pistol back in the holster, he nodded in understanding. "Who found out about the cave?" he asked.

"I did." Muller said and noted for the first time the cold green eyes looking back at her, "I got a map and it was on the map."

"How'd you get the map?" Came the next question.

"I stole it." She answered. Muller was becoming annoyed at the questions. "And before you ask the next question, I wore the guy out having sex with him in a room above a saloon. When he was asleep I stole the map, his wallet, and a horse from the local livery stable."

"How would you like to try and wear me out?" Tucker asked Muller, smiling. Muller ignored him, she was too busy glaring at Farmer. Wilson burst out laughing and the tension eased.

"Let's take it easy." Hansen said, he too was smiling at Tucker's comment. "You going or not, Farmer?" He asked, looking at Farmer.

"I get the five hundred now." Farmer stated.

"If you're going I will pay you the five hundred." Muller said.

"Fine. I'll go." He answered, "There is one thing."

"What's that?" Hansen asked.

"The woman has to cut her hair short. Those Mexican bandits see her and they will kill us trying to get to her."

"I will tie it up under my hat." Muller answered and turned and walked back to her horse. She was angry because she hated being told what she should do with her body, or parts of it. So just to show this Farmer guy, half way to the horses she stopped and removed her boots. "Him and his rattlesnakes can kiss my ass." She said aloud to herself as she walked to the horses.

"That woman is so fine!" Tucker said, watching Muller walk back to the horses.

"I don't like taking a woman. They end up being nothing but trouble. She will cause friction between us." Farmer said, referring to the four men standing there.

"We have to take her. She's the only one who knows the way to the cave." Hansen said.

"And she has the money." Wilson said.

"Good looking, a body like that and all that money. No wonder I'm in love with her." Tucker said.

"Ace," Wilson said, "You're a man of low moral character."

"Yea," Answered Tucker, "ain't I great."

CHAPTER 12

She looked up as Wilson climbed down from the rocky perch he had been using as a lookout post.

"We got company." He said to Hansen as he approached the fire.

"How many?" Hansen asked as he stood up and strapped the gun belt around his waist.

"Five and they are coming right towards us." Came the answer.

"How the hell did they know we were here?" Tucker asked no one in particular, getting to his feet.

"We probably had a tail and did not even know it." Hansen answered. "We'll have to be more careful from now on. We'll get ourselves killed if we ain't."

Hansen tied the holster to his right leg and looked up at the three men and one woman. They were waiting to be told what to do. Hansen's mind went blank for a second, This is what you are getting paid for, He thought, then his brain started to function and he knew what to do and what to say.

"Charlie," This to Farmer, "You get up in the rocks where Harry was." He turned to Tucker, "Ace you get behind that big boulder over there." Hansen pointed to his left to a huge rock that would be almost directly opposite where Farmer would be. A nice crossfire if they needed it. "Alice, you take all those mules and Horses back around the corner of this wash and hold them there. Leave us two horses and a supply mule so we look real." Hansen waited while Farmer climbed up the steep rock wall of the wash. When Farmer got to the spot he waved to Hansen and only then did Hansen check and make sure Tucker was where he was supposed to be. Tucker was holding his Henry rifle in a relaxed position and Hansen knew he was ready. He turned and looked behind him for the animals and Muller. The last mules rump was just going around the corner. That is good, he thought, we are as ready as we will ever be.

"Harry, get about ten feet to my left and about five feet behind me. If anybody goes for their gun or points a rifle at you or me shoot them. We'll ask questions later." He told Wilson.

"I think you ought to know something Al," Wilson said as he backed up.

"Yea, what's that?" Hansen asked, still looking in the direction of the approaching Mexicans.

"I been down here before and some of these guys might know me."

Hansen turned and looked at Wilson. Wilson pointed toward the end of the wash with his left hand, his right hand was resting easily on the butt of his holstered pistol and Hansen turned and saw the five men two hundred feet away.

The five bandits were mounted on their horses walking them slowly along the floor of the wash. The leader knew there were at least four men, maybe five. The problem was he only saw two. He looked up and down both sides of the wash and then he spotted the third man, behind the boulder to his right. "Hector, one is behind the rock to the right." He told the man riding just behind him.

"I see him now." Hector answered. Hector pointed his rifle towards Tucker and told the men behind him to watch him.

"There is another just around the bend behind them." One of the bandits said from behind the leader. The leader saw Muller peeking out from behind a rock maybe one hundred feet behind the two men in their path. He looked along the floor of the wash, then along the walls and again he saw no one else. "I guess there are four. Any of you see a fifth?" This was a life and death question and the five bandits knew it. They looked around and saw nothing.

"There are only four." Hector said from behind the leader to all the men. The leader looked at the two men standing in their path, one in front and the other behind him and to his left. Just far enough away to make sure that it took time to reaim your pistol, and time is what you don't have in a gunfight. And there was going to be a gunfight. The leader was within fifty feet of Hansen when he stopped his horse. His men pulled up even with him in a line across the wash.

"Hey..." shouted the leader just as he died in his saddle, the rifle bullet from Farmer's 30-30 Winchester smashing into his head. Hector died next, the bullet from Wilson's pistol hitting him in the chest. Hansen shot the man sitting to the leaders left and the man next to him. Tucker fired two bullets into the last man sitting on a horse, but not until that man fired a shot from his rifle. The bullet struck Hansen in the palm of his left hand.

Hansen, Wilson, and Tucker stood where they were as if rooted to the spot. The echoes of the gunfire resounding off the rock walls of the deep wash. In seconds Farmer was down on the floor of the wash heading for the Bandits. Then Hansen moved and the frozen moment was gone forever.

"I need one of them alive, Charlie." Hansen said.

Farmer turned and looked at Hansen then turned back to checking the Bandits. First Farmer made sure they were all dead, and then he started stripping them of their guns and clothes. He was methodical in this operation. He checked the saddle bags, rifles, and water on the horses and lead them back to the boulder Tucker had stood behind and tied them along with the other two horses and mule.

"We may need these." He said, pointing toward the horses.

"I know I shot at least one." Muller said, the excitement in her voice unmistakable as she approached the four men breathlessly.

Hansen looked at Tucker and winked. "I got two." He said interrupting Muller.

Tucker held back a smile and said "I got three."

Wilson could not help but smile and said. "I got four."

Muller got angry at the three men making a joke out of what she said and turned and walked back toward the turn in the wash where she had left the horses and mules. As she walked away she heard Tucker say in a voice loud enough for her to hear, "Charlie must have buried the other five real quick like. Since that totals ten dead guys." She heard them laughing and just kept walking.

Muller walked back to where she had ground reined the mules and horses and lead them back to be with the other animals. She moved next to Hansen and said, "Let me see your hand." He had wrapped it in a piece of cloth. She removed the cloth. The bullet had gone clear through. She got a bottle of whiskey from her saddle bag and poured some onto the wound, it was not bleeding too badly, but it was swelling and bruising already. She then wrapped a clean piece of cloth around it.

"They were all dead." Farmer said to Hansen in answer to Hansen's earlier question.

"How do you know?" Muller asked.

Farmer gave her a questioning look, "'Cause I looked at them."

"You missed the two around the bend where I was." Muller said hooking her left thumb and pointing it toward the bend in the wash, she also squeezed Hansen's hand. Two things happened simultaneously. Farmer started running toward the bend in the wash still carrying his Winchester and Hansen yelled. Muller had squeezed as hard as she could and she knew Hansen would be in pain for at least a couple of hours. "It's not nice to make fun of a Lady." She said to Hansen and got up and walked away. Farmer returned with two more horses, more clothes, and guns. He put these with the other animals.

Muller was standing by herself, away from the horses. Farmer walked toward her until he was just behind her.

"There were two and they were both dead. That was some nice shooting. I'm also sorry I laughed at you." He finished and walked away. Muller turned around, but Farmer was already to far away to say anything. He was still carrying his Winchester. He was also the only one to apologize.

CHAPTER 13

Fifteen minutes later they were moving again. Farmer had the point, he was maybe a quarter of a mile ahead of the other four. He was in sight most of the time. Muller was next, then Tucker, Hansen, and last was Wilson. Hansen slowed his horse until he was even with Wilson, he had to talk to him. He turned to the boy and said with a note of anger in his voice, "I don't like surprises Harry, and you being down here before was a surprise."

"Sorry about that, but I didn't think about the fact that somebody might remember me." He answered, looking straight ahead. He did not want to look at Hansen, knowing he had made a mistake

"Tell me about your last little trip down here." Hansen said looking ahead. The terrain here was treachous. The wash was opening up to a flat plain, the shale rock with a scattering of sand covering it continued. There were large pieces of rock scattered as far as the eye could see over the flat land. Hansen had not been in this part of Mexico before, but he knew what they were riding into. The sand drifted endlessly across the shale rock. It could never accumulate because the wind blew constantly. The rocks free standing had the side exposed to the wind sand blasted smooth and rounded, the other side had a tail of sand where it had fallen protected by the rock from the wind. The wind never blew very hard, but it was blowing all the time. It was enough to drive a person insane if they were exposed to it long enough. The gentle whistling sound as the sand blew over the rock surface could make you crazy.

Wilson too was watching the terrain ahead, guiding his horse carefully over the rocky surface. "I was down here two or three years ago. I was in the army then and there were twenty of us. We were out of uniform, some secret mission. We were supposed to capture or kill some Mexican bandit that operates down here. We looked for about a week and couldn't find him so we went back across the border. We killed a couple of bandits in some town and we even started after the gold when the Captain decided it was a bad idea. He didn't want to get killed down here and never make the history books as the great American general. So we turned back." Wilson shrugged his shoulders as he expertly turned his horse away from a dome shaped rock that could cause his horse to slip.

"So you know the way to the gold." Hansen asked, moving his horse around the other side of the rock then back to Wilson's side.

"Not all the way. Just some of the way. If I'd of known the whole way I would have been down here a long time ago." was the answer.

Hansen nodded and said, "So how far do you know?"

"About ten miles ahead is a sort of monastery or big church. It is right on top of a hill that overlooks a big canyon that has a very steep entrance. Both sides of the canyon have a lot of caves in the walls. There are tunnels leading from the monastery to the caves, I guess there is some kind of tunnel that runs under the canyon floor to the other side of the canyon wall so the defenders of the monastery can get to them." The young man stopped talking and Hansen waited until he was certain Wilson was finished.

"What are they defending against?" Hansen asked.

"The local Indians consider the canyon, or some of it, holy ground. The people in the monastery keep gold hunters like us out of the canyon." Wilson answered.

"What are the guys defending this monastery, some kind of monks or something?" Hansen asked looking to his left at Wilson. He was looking straight ahead, carefully guiding his horse. "They use spears or rocks or what to keep people out of that canyon."

"They use guns, old muzzle loaders, but they are supposed to be about fifty caliber and they will kill you just as dead as a Winchester."

"So who are these monks? They Jesuits or some other order?" Hansen asked. He knew something of the Catholic Church and he figured he may be able to talk to them.

Wilson stopped his horse and looked at Hansen who also stopped his horse. Hansen waited and knew he was not going to like the answer he was going to get.

"There ain't monks in there, there are women in there, women who have been abused by either the bandits or the government soldiers. These women would just as soon kill a man as not. They don't trust men and I don't blame them." Wilson finished and spurred his horse forward so he was ahead of Hansen.

"Well I'll be damned." Hansen said aloud to himself. "A whole building full of women out here in the middle of nowhere. Hum." he finished shaking his head, then spurring his horse as he was being left behind. His hand was starting to hurt now. The shock of being shot was wearing off and Hansen knew it would hurt for weeks.

CHAPTER
14

They rode in single file for the next several hours and Muller could not believe they had gotten this far. According to the map they did not have far to go, maybe another thirty or forty miles. It was hot and she did not want to drink all her water. What she really wanted was a big drink of the whiskey she had packed on her mule. The same whiskey she had used on Hansen's hand. She had managed to sneak a big drink of it before putting it back on the mule. She wondered if maybe she had a drinking problem. The last two days had been the first time in God only knows she had not had at least a few drinks during the day or at night. Suddenly Farmer was riding at a full gallop toward her. She stopped her horse and waited, knowing the other three men would be caught up as soon as Farmer got to her. In a moment Farmer was facing the other four.

"There is some kind of big castle or fort or something ahead of us. Anybody know anything about it?" he questioned the other riders.

Hansen moved his horse forward a few feet and said, "I do."

Farmer looked at Muller and asked her, "Was this thing on your map?"

Muller hesitated and then answered ""Yes, but I wasn't sure what it was so I didn't say anything."

"Well, you should have said something because they could be using outriders and I could have met a couple of them and gotten myself shot. So let's start sharing some information around here."

Farmer was almost yelling at her. Muller just stared at Farmer and said nothing.

"Take it easy, Charlie, ain't nobody getting shot around here. That's a monastery up there and there ain't no outriders." Hansen stopped not knowing how to explain what was up there.

"Is it empty?" Farmer asked, now looking at Hansen, "And how come you didn't say something about it?"

"It ain't empty, it's got people in it and they will kill us to keep us from passing it." Hansen said quietly.

"Surprise. Surprise." Muttered Tucker to himself, but loud enough to be heard by everyone.

"So how come you didn't say something about it. I'm riding point, it's my shit hanging out in the breeze when something comes up." Farmer was angry and it showed in his voice which was almost a yell.

"Because I didn't tell him until a little while ago." Wilson said looking at Farmer. Farmer said nothing for a few seconds, then he looked at Tucker and asked, "You know about this too?"

Tucker shook his head and laughed, almost to himself, "No, Charlie, I didn't. I'm just as stupid as you are."

"What the..." Farmer started to say something and then stopped.

"It's my fault." Muller interrupted. "I should have said something. Charlie's right, it's his ass hanging out in the breeze and he has a right to know everything."

It took five minutes for Muller and Wilson to tell the others everything they knew about the monastery.

"You all know what I do and why I'm here." Farmer said looking at the others, each one in turn. "I'll kill the anybody holding back any information about this trip. I'll blow your head off I don't care."

No one said anything for maybe a minute, it seemed like an hour that the five sat there each in his or her own world. Their own thoughts kept to themselves.

Farmer broke the spell, the quiet, with a laugh.

"What?" Tucker asked.

"What we need is a battered woman." Farmer said looking straight at Muller and smiling

"Oh no. Not a chance." She answered looking back at Farmer.

"Why not? There is nothing I'd like better right now then to punch you in the face." Farmer said, still looking straight at the woman. The tone of his voice was full of anger.

Muller felt fear crawling up the back of her neck. She knew that Farmer would like to hurt her right now.

"I think there is another way." Wilson said to everyone, much to Muller's relief. "Let me go up there and try talking to them. Let's see what happens."

"How you gonna do that?" Asked Tucker, knowing his tail was almost as far out in the breeze as Farmer's and everyone else's for that matter.

"I have an idea that might work." Answered Wilson.

CHAPTER
15

Muller climbed up the side of the wash they had just passed
through. That had been the third wash, or was it the fourth.
She had lost count. She knew that it had been in the first wash
they had killed the seven bandits. She had learned a long time ago to
face her enemies and she was going to face one now. She was going
to talk to Farmer. She managed the last few feet. It was not a difficult
climb except Muller had taken a liberal dose of liquid courage from
her saddle bag before starting the climb. She saw Farmer sitting on
a flat piece of the wall, a small ledge not more then a foot wide and
three feet long. He was looking toward the monastery and she knew
he had heard her coming and knew she was no danger. She looked
up as she got within feet of the ledge.

"What do you want?" Farmer asked, his voice quiet. He looked
at Muller and wondered for the thousandth time why such a good
looking woman was not married and having babies. Her hair was
dark brown and hung to her shoulders, it was parted in the middle
and laid to both sides. Her forehead was kind of low and wide and
her eyes were brown, a real dark brown that flashed when she was
angry. Her nose was straight and her lips thin. Her teeth were almost
perfectly white and when she smiled it was like someone lighting
a lamp in a dark room. She had a great chest that she kept pretty
well covered most of the time. She had to be in her thirties and
she even though she had a big chest the rest of her body was tiny.
The narrow hips and slim legs Farmer knew must have been very

muscular. There was no fat on Muller's body, this was one helleva' good looking woman.

"I would like to talk to you about what happened earlier." She answered. Muller looked at Farmer as he looked toward the monastery and Wilson making his way there. He held the Winchester rifle upright and she knew it was ready. The black cutaway gun belt strapped around his waist that he never took off. He was wearing a tan sweat stained hat that covered his very short red hair. The wide forehead, almost white invisible eyebrows, the green eyes that were like looking into a very cold, very deep green lake. No matter how far you looked into it you only saw the green, no emotion. His nose was straight with a small bump in it where she guessed it had been broken at one time. The narrow space between the upper lip and the bottom of his nose was clean shaven as was the rest of his face, no mustache or beard. He was slim, almost gaunt, but Muller knew he was tough, like old rusty barbwire. He was wearing a light tan shirt which did not show the dust, but his dungarees did. The dark blue pants were dust covered as were the dark cherry colored boots he wore. There was a black duster folded up that Farmer was sitting on.

Muller hoisted herself up on the ledge next to Farmer and sat down. She pulled a hip flask from her coat pocket and asked. "Want one?"

Farmer shook his head no. Muller took a short pull on the flask and put the cork back in it. "You ain't a drinking man?" She asked. She knew she was feeling good, maybe almost too drunk to climb up here so she had better lay off the booze, but that was the only thing that gave her the nerve to come up here.

"Nope," Answered Farmer, "don't drink, don't smoke, and don't womanize." He added as he looked at her.

"Are you a preacher when you are not killing people?" she asked, smiling so the killer she sat next to did not get angry.

"No," Farmer answered as he shook his head, he too smiled, "I was shot in the head during the war and since then I feel nothing. It don't bother me to kill someone. Like those Mexicans today. I will sleep tonight and never have a thought about them. In a week I will have a hard time remembering them, their faces." He clarified.

Muller waited, but Farmer was done. They sat there in silence for maybe a minute and then Muller said, "I'm really sorry about not telling you about the monastery today, Charlie. I never thought about lookouts or outriders or any of that. Plus I also thought it was farther away then it was."

"Don't worry about it. It's like Hansen said, nobody got shot. No harm, no foul." The voice was quiet and the woman was pleased that the man next to her was not angry. She noticed he never took his eyes off the desert that lay between them and the monstery.

Muller leaned around Farmer and as she did she could smell the musty smell of his unwashed body. As she looked out over the flat plain that must have been two miles wide she did not see Wilson. "Where is he?" she asked, leaning on Farmer. Her right arm touching his chest.

"He's about half way there. Look just before that rise in the middle." He said.

She finally spotted Wilson moving slowly. He was dragging his saddle with his left hand and carrying his Winchester rifle in his right hand. The pistol strapped around his waist. He walked slow and unless you knew better he looked like a man who was on the point of exhaustion. His black shirt and dark blue pants were covered in dust as was the black hat he wore. "He looks like he is in bad shape." Muller commented.

"He better look like it or them woman in there are going to kill him." Farmer answered. His voice was flat, cold, like the voice of a dead man.

Muller sat back and removed the flask from her jacket pocket and took another hit, jammed the cork back and put it back in her pocket. It had been a long day and it had started at three in the morning. Muller was suddenly tired. She leaned her head back against the rock wall behind her and before she realized it she was asleep. She did not know how long she had slept when she dragged herself up from the depths of her sleep and felt, more then saw Farmer putting his coat around her like a blanket. The coat was warm and heavy and she fell back to sleep. When she woke the next time her head was resting on Farmers left shoulder and she moved closer and looked up at him. He was awake and she could see he was cold and yet he had given her his coat.

"You're cold," she murmured almost into Farmer's left ear, "This coat is big enough to cover us both." And she stretched the coat over Farmer's chest and shoulders. Without even realizing it she wrapped her left arm around Farmer's right shoulder and laid her head where his left shoulder met his chest. The coat was half way across her face. She was warm and comfortable and she could smell him. She suddenly realized she wanted him. She wanted to make love right here and now. She moved her head up slightly and kissed his neck. "Charlie." She whispered.

Farmer laughed out loud, quietly, but still out loud, "I told you I don't feel nothing and I don't. Besides we have to go. Wilson has to be in trouble. So button your pants and let's get down from here."

"My pants weren't unbuttoned and I bet I could make you feel something." She answered. Muller was disgusted with herself. She had made a fool of herself and she was angry with herself. "I feel like some dirty old whore.' She blurted out.

Suddenly Farmer grabbed her by her shirt front and slammed her against the back of the rock ledge they were sitting on. Her head bounced against the wall and it hurt. The rock face had a spur sticking out and it jammed into her back half way up in the middle. "Never call yourself that! Never! You understand that! Never! I'll kick your ass if I ever hear you say that again.' He growled, "Now get down from here. I have to go see about Harry."

CHAPTER 16

Harry Wilson was in trouble all right. He was tied to a cross and his feet were just close enough to the ground to allow him to stand on his tip toes and be able to breath. The idea of crucifixion was to slowly strangle a person. The human body was not made to breath with the arms outstretched to the sides and even with the shoulders with all the weight of the body hanging on them. His legs were cramping and he did not know how much longer he could hold out.

He remembered rolling in the sand and shale rocks by the camp with Hansen and Tucker telling him to do it some more, then laughing. He remembered unsaddling his horse and taking the rifle out of the scabbard and having Hansen tell him he had to walk like he was beat. He had drunk as much water as he could and then started toward the monastery. It had to be at least two miles and it was hot. He figured he sweated most of the water out of himself by the time he reached the main gate. He had yelled three or four times and nothing had happened. Hansen had told him that he had to act the part of being in bad shape. He dropped the saddle and the rifle and pushed on the huge doors. Nothing happened. He yelled hello and help me but nothing happened. He had knelt down in front of the doors and picked up his rifle and used it to bang on the doors then he yelled some more, still nothing. He felt the hot sun beating on the right side of his body and he felt, more then knew that someone was watching. He finally just leaned his head against the center of the doors and collapsed. He hoped he was a pitiable sight for who ever was watching, the sight of a man without water and on his last legs, dying in front of their eyes. He figured he would just rest for a while and wait and see if anyone came to his rescue. He did not know how long he had knelt there when he heard the footsteps crunching on the sand and shale behind him, he felt something poke him in the back. He did not move. A man in his weakened condition did not react fast to things. It poked again, harder this time, then again. He stirred, turned and looked up toward his right. His eyes were barely open and he made out a woman with a long barreled flint lock rifle. It had been her poking him with the rifle barrel he had felt.

CHAPTER 17

Hansen watched Farmer and Muller climb down from the rocks. He knew what was coming and he did not like it. Somebody was going have to go in and find out what happened to Wilson. His hand hurt, but not quite as bad as it did this afternoon. He had it in a sling that Muller had made and so it was not too bad. He would endure.

"Somebody has to go in and see what happened to Harry." Farmer said as he approached Hansen, and Tucker, Muller was following Farmer. It was getting dark and the two miles between themselves and the monastery was already deep in shadows.

"I could go." Muller volunteered. "At least I got the right plumbing if they look." She said laughing. Tucker and Hansen laughed along with her. Farmer just waited for an answer.

"Thanks, Alice, but they would probably just shoot the second person they see. And probably Harry too." Hansen said in reply.

"It's either Charlie or myself." Tucker said pulling out his pistol and making sure it was loaded. He had known it was loaded, it was just something to do. To keep his hands busy so he did not have to look at anyone. Tucker did not like being a leader, he had known for a long time that he was a follower, he was not smart enough to lead something like this. Guys like Hansen did that.

"I let him go, I'll go." Hansen said looking at Tucker.

"Ace is right," Farmer said, "It's either him or me. The girl ain't a gunfighter and you're shot. That leaves me and Ace." Farmer finished and looked at Tucker.

Everyone looked at Tucker and he did not know what to say. His ego told him he could go, but his common sense told him he was not as young and fast as Farmer. He was still checking his pistol, looking intently at it, not wanting to look into the faces of the people watching him.

"It's settled then." Hansen said, breaking the silence. Tucker jerked his head up and looked at Hansen. He saw Farmer looking at Hansen also, as was Muller. "Charlie you go."

"Wait." Tucker said.

"Ain't no waiting, Ace. I'm going." Farmer said.

"He's going." Hansen agreed, looking at Tucker.

The three watched as Farmer walked quickly to his horse and removed his canteen. Hansen knew it was full. Farmer was very careful about that. Always keep your canteen and gun loaded. He watched as the young man opened one of his saddle bags and removed a belt of shot gun shells. Hansen did not even know Farmer had a shotgun. Then he reached into his bedroll and removed a sawed off, double barreled, shotgun. From the tip of the barrel to the end of the stock the gun was not more then eighteen inches long.

"That's nasty looking, Charlie." Tucker said as Farmer approached the two men and the woman.

"It is nasty." Farmer said as he handed the shotgun to Tucker who had his hand extended so he could look and handle the gun.

"Ten gauge?" Tucker guessed.

"Eight." Farmer corrected.

Tucker broke it open and removed the two shells. It felt well balanced and it looked new, but it was the barrels that Tucker and now Hansen who was looking over at the gun noticed. The two barrels were slightly oval. They were perfectly even and Tucker thought the pattern from this gun must be awesome.

"That thing must have one hellva' pattern, Charlie." Hansen said.

"What's the range?" Tucker asked, the second question before Farmer had a chance to answer the first.

"It has a hellva' pattern and the range is about fifty feet." Was Farmers answer to the two questions.

"How did you figure out how much you could bend the barrels before it was too much?" Tucker asked, still looking at the gun.

"By blowing up a lot of shotguns." Farmer smiled at the thought. "We didn't even know if it could be done. But it worked in the end and now I'll take it with me." Farmer said holding out his hand towards Tucker. Tucker handed the gun back to Farmer after reloading it.

"Good luck, Charlie." Muller said and Farmer looked at her and smiled.

"See you in a little while." Hansen said, not knowing what else to say.

Farmer looked at Tucker and Tucker took Farmer's left elbow and walked with him

"I don't pretend to be too smart, Charlie, and I want to thank you for taking this job of seeing about Harry. I'm really too old and too fat to run that far, besides you're probably quicker then I am." Tucker said.

"I wanted to go anyway, Ace. I sort of like killing people." Farmer answered and Tucker looked at the young man and believed him.

"Anyway," Tucker continued. "I saw a low spot in the outside wall to the right of the gate and that is the only place I can see to get in. The problem is, there are bound to be a couple of guards. You have to know where Harry is before you go over the wall. If he's dead just come back, don't even think about trying to get to him. But the guards are the important thing. You have to get them."

"How many do you think they will have?" Farmer asked, referring to the number of guards.

"Probably only two if Harry is alive. More if he's already been killed. If you see four or five just come back, he's a goner." Tucker finished.

Farmer made a move to leave, then stopped and turned around and looked at Tucker in the darkening shadows, "Thanks, Ace, I'll remember what you told me."

Tucker did not notice the extended hand at first and then felt embarrassed about missing it. He took it and clasped Farmer's hand with both of his.

"Take care, Charlie." Tucker said, he was suddenly very fond of this young man. Maybe like he would be if he were the son Tucker never had.

Farmer turned and moved off into the shadows. There was no noise as he moved and Tucker knew they had made the correct choice about who to send to find out about Wilson.

An hour later Tucker walked unhurried back to the campfire carrying his Henry rifle. He squatted down and poured himself a cup of coffee the woman had made. She was a good looking woman and he thought to himself, I wouldn't mind taking a roll in the hay with her, discounting all the joking around.

"Anything?" Hansen asked Tucker, referring to Farmer and Wilson.

"No noise, no movement that I could see." Tucker answered. He looked down into the cup of coffee. "I'll get my canteen and go see what happened."

"I can go." Hansen said, his voice very quiet. Muller watched both men. Knowing one did not want to go, but had to, while the other wanted to go but could not.

"You can't go, your hand isn't any good." Tucker said, nonchalantly pointing the rifle barrel in Hansen's direction.

"I can go." Muller said, as quietly as the other two men had spoken.

"No!" Both men said simultaneously.

"My right hand is ok." argued Hansen.

"You go out there, you have to be able to use a rifle and I have never seen a one handed rifleman. So I go." There was no question of the finality in Tucker's voice. He stood up and walked to his horse and removed his canteen, and walked back to the small fire. He stood looking down at the man and woman sitting there.

"Two things, one apiece. Al, you first. If I'm not back by dawn and you don't see any movement out there," Tucker pointed the rifle in the general direction of the monastery, "you take Alice, the horses, and the mules and high tail it back to Texas. Me. Harry, and Charlie will be dead." He paused and smiled at Muller.

"What?" she asked, having no idea of what he wanted.

"Give me the hip flask.' He said extending his left hand.

Muller smiled, stood up and removed the flask from her coat pocket and handed it to Tucker, "Wow," she murmured, "I thought you were going to ask me to drop my draws so you could have some good bye loving before you left."

"That would be alright too." Tucker said laughing, handing the flask back to the woman after taking a long pull. Hansen laughed and so did Muller. Tucker turned on his heel and walked into the darkness.

Ace Tucker was not a brave man and more then once the thought had entered his mind to only go about a couple of hundred feet and then hide and come back just before dawn and tell Muller and Hansen that Farmer and Wilson were both dead. Tucker had been dishonorably discharged from the army for cowardice late in the war. Wilson and Farmer had to be dead. They had been gone for hours and not a sound. The only thing he had seen from the top of that rock had been the glow of a big fire inside the monastery walls. He figured somebody was having a party, probably celebrating the fact they killed Farmer and Wilson. He was jogging, the Henry hanging loosely in his right hand. He did not listen to the voice inside his head that kept telling him to stop. He had topped the first small rise and the monastery was closer than he thought, maybe another mile. He guessed he had already covered at least a mile. It was killing him to run this far half bent over. It would have killed him to run this far bent over or straight up. He had gotten fat and he could feel it now. His mind, after telling him to stop, had told him he could run that far with no trouble, maybe ten years ago, but not now was his rebuttal. His legs were on fire and his lungs burned just as bad, but he kept going. This was suicide, running like this. He could not see anything. Anyone lying on the ground could shoot or knife him and he would not even see them. He was breathing heavy and the damn canteen kept bouncing against his left hip. He knew if he stopped he would never start again. Jesus, this was killing him.

But above all Ace Tucker knew something else. He knew he was running out of nerve. He did not want to die. He was afraid of dying. He was not sure there was a God and if there was the life he had led was not saintly, too many whorehouses and saloons, too much whiskey and beer. A preacher had once told him he had better change his life style or he was going to hell. Tucker had shot the preacher dead just after he had said that.

Shot, something had broken into his thoughts, gunshots, two no three, maybe four, he was not sure. So Charlie and Harry were still alive. He ran faster, now his breath coming in great whooping gasps. He was almost to the wall next to the gate when he thought, what if the people in the monastery had just shot Farmer and Wilson and he was running into the sights of one of those flint locks. He had seen what one of those fifty caliber guns could do to a man if they hit him in the arm or leg or belly.

"They're dead, I ain't going any closer." He said to himself and Ace Tucker stopped running.

CHAPTER 19

A s Ace Tucker jogged across the shale and sand, Charlie Farmer listened and heard voices. He could not make out what they were saying, but he could make out the laughter. There was screaming, but it was the sound of women having fun. He was just outside the low spot in the wall Tucker had pointed out. He removed his hat and slowly raised his head knowing that a swift movement at night was picked up by the human eye more quickly then a slow gradual movement. He looked over the edge of the wall. There was a great glow from what must have been a huge fire. His head was clear of the wall now and he looked to both sides of the wall, nothing. He put his hat on and stood up slowly and stopped. Still he saw nothing. Whoever was inside had to have placed guards to watch this spot, he thought, but if they did the guards were well hidden, probably somewhere in the blackness of the many shadows. He automatically reached down and removed the hammer hoop that held his pistol in it's holster. Farmer had easily run the two miles from where the horses, mules, and Hansen, Muller, and Tucker were to the monastery wall where he now stood, actually he had probably run closer to three the route he had taken. He had run west and then south and then back east and only at the very end had he run directly at the wall for maybe the last hundred yards.

He held the shotgun in his right hand and stepped onto the top of the wall. The wall itself was almost four feet thick. Tucker had to be right, this must have been the spot where sometime in the past the attacker had breached this part of the wall. The rubble of the stones was scattered for twenty or thirty yards inside and outside the wall, mostly inside where he had to walk over the broken and scattered rocks. Farmer picked his way carefully over the rocks until he was on the original dirt floor. To his left was the gate house where the huge doors were anchored. He knew there was some type of support or something for the doors to hang on. He had no idea what they looked like because of the almost total darkness. To his right was another wall, maybe of a barracks or storeroom. That too was cast in deep shadows. If there was someone guarding this spot in the wall he could not see them. Maybe everybody is at the party, he thought. He was bent over again and he had taken only four steps when someone off to his left said, "Stop or I will shoot you."

It was a woman's voice and Farmer stopped. He straightened up, the shotgun hanging loosely in his right hand. He looked to his left and the woman stepped out of the shadows. She was tall and slender and held what looked like a flint lock rifle. She held it to her right shoulder and it was aimed directly at Farmer. At this thirty foot range she could not miss.

"How many more of you are out there?" She asked. Never wavering, never taking her eyes off Farmer.

"I just come looking for my friend." Farmer answered, pointing toward the fire light with the shotgun.

"Your friend is dying and now so will you." She said, adding "Drop the gun in your hand."

"Do it now." Another woman spoke from his right side. Farmer turned and looked and saw what he had hoped to see. She was directly opposite the woman to his left.

"The shotgun is cocked, I'm going to un-cock it and then drop it." Farmer lied. He took the shotgun by the barrel in his left hand and wrapped his right hand around the trigger guard and stock. He then cocked the right barrel and letting go with his left hand extended the shotgun up and out away from his body. The gun was pointing straight ahead in the direction of the unseen fire. Farmer dropped the shotgun and it, having a hair trigger went off when it hit the ground. It was relativity quiet in the small area where the two women and Farmer stood. The noise of the gun going off was deafening. When the gun went off Farmer dropped to the ground flat on his stomach and as he did so he drew the pistol from his holster with his right hand, cocking it as he rolled. He rolled onto his left side, then he shot the woman standing to his right, she was an easy target, she was only twenty feet away. The woman's flint lock rifle was cocked and she fired it when Farmer's bullet struck her in the stomach. That bullet struck the woman to Farmer's left in her left thigh. She screamed when she got hit with the fifty caliber ball, then she fired her rifle and it struck the woman to Farmer's right in the chest. Farmer rolled over to his right and shot the woman who had been on his left. He shot her in the chest. Both women were dead instantly. There was no moaning, no screaming, no noise at all. Only the glowing and crackling of the fire around the corner of what was the gate house leading into the monastery, and the echo of the gunfire.

Farmer got to is feet in one swift, smooth movement. He did not even attempt to find the shotgun. He ran to his left. The laughing and screaming had stopped as if it had been cut off with an axe.

"Cheryl!" Someone yelled, another female voice, and Farmer moved to the edge of the inset in the wall. He looked around the corner. He immediately drew is head back, knowing everyone standing there was looking in his direction.

Robin!" Again the voice. This time Farmer saw who had yelled. He also saw Wilson. He was tied to a cross and he was having a bad time. Farmer had seen what he wanted to see. There were seven woman standing around the fire. The woman who had yelled for what Farmer guessed were the two dead woman was standing just to the right of the cross holding Wilson.

"Whoever you are, you better come out or I will blow your friend's head off." Again the same woman spoke.

Farmer peeked around the corner again and the woman had a pistol pointed toward the head of Wilson.

"Come out or I will shoot your buddy here and I will shoot him right now." She sounded like she meant business and Farmer did what he did not want to do. He stepped out from behind the wall.

"Did you shoot Cheryl and Robin?" She asked. Now the pistol was pointed at Farmer. She was a good hundred feet away and Farmer wondered if she could hit him at that range with the hand gun. It looked like an old flint lock pistol. Farmer knew he could shoot her at that range. Maybe not kill her, but hit her anyway. It was the other six woman with the flintlock rifles that bothered Farmer. They were all aimed at him and there was almost a guarantee that one of them would hit it's target.

Farmer said nothing, he simply stood where he was.

"I asked you if you shot Cheryl and Robin." She said.

Farmer knew if he did not handle this just right both he and Wilson would end up being dead. He also knew if he told her the two women were dead she would shoot him. He looked at the woman who was obviously the leader. She was standing next to the cross, her legs spread apart, her left hand on her left hip. The pistol pointed directly at Farmer. He took a deep breath and exhaled.

"Lady I got six guys on the walls with Winchesters. If you and the other ladies don't put down your guns or you shoot me or Harry they are going to kill all of you."

All the women looked around at the walls, all the women but the leader.

"You, Sir, are lying." She said. The pistol still pointed at Farmer.

The whiplash crack of the rifle startled everybody, including Farmer. He recovered instantly, so fast not one of the women noticed the flinch.

"That bullet hit between your legs Ma'am. The next one will hit you between your tits."

Farmer recognized the voice of Ace Tucker. So he had followed him. It was a good thing too, because Farmer had run his bluff to the end.

"Everybody put the guns down and walk over there." Farmer said, pointing to an area to his right. The women hesitated, looking at the woman who obviously was their leader and when she put her gun down the rest followed. They put their guns down and walked as a group to the area Farmer had pointed to. He stepped away from the wall and walked to where Wilson was on the cross.

"Jesus, Charlie..." Wilson started to say when Farmer cut him off.

"Just keep your mouth shut." Farmer said it quietly, only loud enough for Wilson to hear.

"Are my two friends dead?" The leader asked. She had taken two steps toward Farmer.

"Stay right where you are lady." Tucker warned her from the wall.

Farmer opened the pocket knife he always carried and cut the rope holding Wilson's feet to the cross, then the rope holding his left arm. He walked around the back side of the cross and cut the rope holding his right arm. Wilson fell to the ground.

"Get up." Farmer said, his voice gruff and angry, he had never once taken his eyes off the women standing in a group except to see the ropes to cut. Wilson struggled, but got to his feet by holding onto to the cross.

"Please, my friends." Begged the leader, referring to the two women who had been standing guard duty.

Farmer walked over to her and looked at her. She had blue eyes, the darkest blue Farmer had ever seen, a straight nose, but it was bent slightly to the right. Her left eye was scarred and partially closed. The left side of her face was a single scar caused by a burn.

Farmer took her by her right arm and said, "Come with me." He was surprised that she came without a struggle. Maybe, he thought, because he was walking in the direction of the two dead women. They walked to the breech in the wall and the two women were lying there. The leader broke away from Farmer and ran first to one, then to the other of the two bodies. She saw the open eyed dead stare looking back at her when she looked into the faces.

She stood up and turned toward Farmer. "You son of a bitch, if I ever get the chance I am going to do to you what you did to them. You dirty little bastard." She added as an after thought. The venomous tone of her voice could not be missed. It was then that the leader broke and started to cry, partly out of sorrow for her friends and partly out of frustration that she could not kill the man who had killed them.

"I'm sorry." He lied, not knowing what else to say. He approached the woman and was standing opposite her.

The leader had bowed her head when she had started to cry, now she looked up and spit in Farmer's face. "What now? You and your friends going to rape and beat us and maybe kill us and have a real party while we..."

Faster then the leader could follow what Farmer did he clamped his left hand over her mouth.

"Shut up or I will knock your head off." The voice was cold and menacing. It struck fear into her heart, even through all the anger and frustration.

"What's your name?" Farmer asked, removing his hand from her mouth and using it to wipe his face. She knew any other man would have killed her for spitting in his face.

"Candy Carter." She answered, her voice neutral, showing no emotion.

"Let me tell you something Carter. Your two friends are dead because they made a mistake." Farmer said. "If you are going to use guns to defend yourselves you better learn how." He paused and then looked at her. "I'm going to ask you this once and if you lie to me I will kill you all." Again the cold menacing voice.

Carter looked at him through the blurred vision of the tears she had shed for her friends. He had green eyes and they showed nothing. They were just empty, the eyes of a killer, maybe even a man who liked it.

"How many more of you ladies are there?" Farmer asked.

"There are nine of us." God what a blunder, her right hand went to her mouth and she turned around, away from Farmer and vomited while sinking to her knees. She started to cry again and Farmer simply waited. The seconds ticked by and turned into minutes as Carter composed herself. She stood up and looked back at Farmer. "There are only seven of us now." She said between sobs.

"You feel better now?" He asked.

"How would you feel if your two friends were lying there shot dead?" She countered with a question, pointing at the woman known as Cheryl lying face up in the sand and shale, the dead eyes looking at the star filled, cloudless black sky.

"They're laying there shot dead because they made a mistake, and if you make a mistake in a gunfight you lose your life." Farmer said flatly.

Carter looked up at him, into those dead green eyes and said, "I hope to God you lose your soul."

I lost that in a shell hole in Mississippi a couple of years ago Farmer thought, but said instead, "I want your word that you won't try anything and I will turn you and the other ladies loose."

"And if I don't?" She asked.

"Then I tie you all up and you get a little something to eat and you piss and shit yourselves and exist like animals in a cage. Make up your mind." He answered her, again the cold, dead, hard voice.

"I will talk to the girls, but I need your word that you and your men will not hurt us. These poor women have been through enough." Carter said.

"If anybody tries anything I'll kill'em." Farmer told her. The finality in the flat cold voice convinced her immediately. There was not a doubt in her mind that this man meant exactly what he said.

Carter walked past Farmer, as she walked past she extended her left elbow and slammed it into Farmers left bicep. She hit him so hard that his whole body moved.

"I'll give you that one." He said to her back.

"Fuck you." She said loud enough for Farmer to hear, raising her left hand and extending the middle finger as she walked away. She hoped to God she did not make him angry enough to shoot her in the back, because after seeing and talking to him close up she had no doubts that he was capable of doing just that.

Farmer saw her drop her left hand and continue walking back toward the group of women. His left arm hurt. She had really hit him and he knew in a few hours there would be a huge bruise on his bicep and down his arm. He watched her walk away from him in her bare feet and the rag she was wearing that she probably called a dress. He followed her and when she reached the group of women he waited, knowing she would tell them about the two dead guards and he knew they would cry. Best let them do that and then get down to business.

Farmer walked to where Wilson was standing by himself next to the cross.

"How do you feel?" Farmer asked.

"I don't know," Wilson answered, shrugging his shoulders, "I guess I'm alright. Why? What do you need?"

"I need you to run back and get Hansen and Muller and all the horses and supplies and everything else we have managed to collect so far." Farmer said turning and looking over his right shoulder at the women.

"Sure, just let me get my gun belt and rifle." Wilson answered and walked off. He found his pistol, holster, rifle, and saddle not more then twenty feet away from the cross he had been hanging on. He would leave the saddle and ride one of the other horses when he got back to Hansen and Muller. He walked to the gate and was looking at the huge doors when Carol Landing, the girl of sixteen, approached him and was watching him.

"How do I get the doors open?" Wilson asked, looking at the girl. She was pretty in a wild sort of way. Her face was dirty as were her hands and naturally her feet were bare so they were dirty also.

"Just pull the chain." She answered simply and walked over to where the chain hung from the support column. She pulled the chain and slowly the doors opened. Wilson waited patently until the doors were fully opened and the girl stood looking at him.

"Thank you." He said as he walked past her into the dark.

Farmer walked to the group of women and as he did so the woman named Carter walked toward him. He thought of another woman he had known named Candy. Shot by a man who in turn had been shot by Farmer. She was buried and Farmer hoped the same fate was not in store for this woman.

"You got any tools?" Farmer asked her

"Why?" came the question.

"So you can bury your friends come daylight. For now just drag the bodies over by the fire so the animals don't get to them." He answered her. He watched her return to the other women and they all moved off in the direction of their two dead friends. Farmer looked up at the wall above the gate and told Tucker he could come down now. He did and in a minute was standing next to Farmer.

"Boy I got to that wall just in time." Tucker said, again out of breath from climbing down the wall and running to where Farmer stood. The Henry rifle held in his right hand.

"I have no doubts that if you had not done what you did when you did it, she would have killed Harry, then maybe me." Farmer answered.

Tucker looked in the direction of the group of women and commented, almost to himself, "There are a couple of good looking women there."

Farmer looked from the women to Tucker, "I'll tell you what I told that one named Carter who seems to be the leader. You touch one of them and I will kill you." He turned and walked toward the gate of the monastery. Just as he got to the gate one of the women called him. He turned and she ran to him. She stopped not more then three feet away and extended her hand, it held the sawed off shotgun "I found this." She said, then turned and ran back to where the other women were before Farmer could thank her. Later, the only thing Farmer could remember about her was she was wearing a bright blue bandanna around her neck. The gate stood wide open and he walked through it and out into the desert night. He walked what he figured was maybe a quarter of a mile and squatted down and waited for Hansen, Muller, and Wilson. He also looked for anyone else who might happen by. He did not think that was likely which is why he did not post other guards, besides if there were other bands out there and they got into the monastery he would hear the shots. The worst that could happen would be Tucker and the women would get killed. He shrugged and continued to squat, looking toward the northeast where the three should come from.

CHAPTER
20

The three came followed by the mules and the extra horses. It took about thirty minutes of running, tripping, falling, and stumbling over the treacherous shale and sand in the almost total darkness of the night for Wilson to get back to where Muller and Hansen were. He would have never found them except the half moon cast just enough light for him to find his way to the canyon. When he got there he thought maybe he had missed it because he expected a fire like when he had left. There was no fire, no horses, no mules, only the warm ashes from the old fire.

"Harry, that you?" He heard Muller ask from somewhere up in the rocks on the wall of the canyon to his right. He heard a noise to his left and turned to see Hansen step out from behind a boulder.

"What happened to the fire?" Wilson asked.

"After Ace left to check on what happened to you and Charlie I decided to put it out and me and Alice should each take a side of the canyon to stand guard over. Never can tell who is wandering around out here." Hansen said.

"Charlie said to bring everything and come to the monastery." Wilson answered.

"What happened?" Muller asked as she walked up to the two men.

"They had caught me and Charlie killed two guards and this one was going to kill me when Ace shot at her." Wilson said. They mounted their horses and he told the rest of the story as they rode to the monastery. They looked as they rode, but still passed Farmer without seeing him. They herded the three horses they rode. Farmer and Tuckers' horses, the seven taken off the bandits and the fifteen mules into what was once a corral. Tucker came over to where they stood and told his version of the story, naturally deleting the part where he thought about turning back.

"Where's Charlie?" Hansen asked when Tucker had finished.

"Here." Farmer said standing just inside the main gate.

"Where the hell were you?" Hansen asked.

"Out there." Farmer pointed over his right shoulder with his thumb.

"Why?" Muller asked, but Hansen already knew the answer.

Hansen thought about Farmer. He was dangerous, he maybe even deadly after they got the gold, but he had proved invaluable up to this point.

"Let me hear your version of what happened here tonight." Hansen said to Farmer.

"I snuck over the low spot in the wall, killed the two guards and Ace saved my ass by threatening Carter." Farmer shrugged his narrow shoulders as if it was no big deal.

"Who is Carter?" Hansen asked, confused.

"I think she is the leader of this group of ladies." Farmer answered.

"I want to meet this Carter woman." Hansen said.

"You're in luck. Here she comes." Farmer said nodding in the direction behind Hansen's left shoulder.

Hansen turned and saw Candy Carter for the first time. The fire lit up the right side of her face and body, the shadow hiding the scared left eye and face. Hansen lost his breath at her beauty. He wondered what she would look like in a decent dress, instead of the rags she was wearing. He looked at her feet and saw she wore no shoes.

"This the boss?" She asked Farmer, referring to Hansen. The hate in her voice unmasked as she asked Farmer the question. Farmer nodded yes. "He tell you what he told me?" She asked Hansen.

"I'm sorry, but I don't know what you're talking about." Hansen was totally lost.

"Tell him." She ordered Farmer, the same hateful tone in her voice.

"I don't know what you are talking about either." Farmer answered her, his voice quiet, almost a whisper.

"About your men and my women, and what you would do to them if they went after one of my friends." She said looking directly at Farmer, the challenge unmistakable in her voice.

Farmer looked from Carter to Hansen, "I told her I would kill anyone who touched one of the women. I already told Ace. I'm telling you the same thing," Farmer pointed at Hansen, "and I'm gonna tell Harry the same thing." Farmer paused, "You hurt the women, you die." Farmer turned on his heel and walked away.

"Hey!" Carter yelled at Farmer's back.

Farmer turned around and looked at her, his face held no expression, the blank empty stare of a killer.

"What about the rest of the men that are on the walls?" She asked, pointing her right hand toward the walls surrounding the monastery.

Farmer looked confused for several seconds, then smiled, "I was lying about the other five, only Ace was there. There are only four men and the woman in our group."

"You're lying!" Carter accused him.

"Ask him." Farmer answered, turning again and walking toward the front gate and out into the darkness beyond.

Hansen waited a few seconds and then asked Carter, "You don't like Charlie?"

Carter turned and looked at Hansen and told him how Farmer had killed the two women guards, one of whom was her closest friend. She had been looking at Hansen while telling him, then she looked at where Farmer had walked through the front gate and said, "He killed Cheryl, and someday I will kill him for doing that." As she started to walk away she felt Hansen grab her left arm by the bicep. She turned and looked at his hand and then at him. "Take your hand off me." She commanded.

"You listen to me." Hansen said quietly looking down at the ground, then back up and into the deep blue eyes, the bluest eyes he had ever seen. "Charlie is the best I have ever seen and I have been in this business for fifteen years or so. If you go after him he will kill you. Do you understand?" Hansen finished with a question.

"We'll see." She answered, defiantly, and tried to pull her arm free of his grip.

"You try and you will be dead, I'm telling you. Unless you are a lot better then I think you are you don't stand a chance." Hansen said letting go of her arm. Carter looked at Hansen and then turned and walked to the group of women standing near the fire.

CHAPTER 21

Albert Hansen had made it a point never to get entangled emotionally with a woman who was associated with the job he was on. He was sitting on the wall looking southeast toward the valley they were heading to for the gold. This Carter woman was something else. He could not stop thinking about her. She was tough and yet Hansen wanted to believe that she had a soft side somewhere. Maybe it was buried deep inside because of what had been done to her. But he believed it was there. He smiled and shook his head and said out loud to himself, "You jerk, you're making anything up just to justify getting to know her." He shook his head and then added, "You know you can't do that, you have to just walk away." He paused and then said, "If you weren't on this job you could go after her, but you are here and you got this job so you have to leave her alone. So do what you have to do." He went back to staring into the darkness, toward the valley with the gold. He could not see more then twenty feet in front of where he sat because there were no stars and the moon had disappeared behind some clouds, and yet he continued to stare. Then he spoke again, "Yea, right. You wish you knew just how to talk to talk to women. That's why you ain't got one and never had one for long because you don't know how to talk to them."

He heard someone climbing up the wall and he turned and saw Candy Carter climbing up. He held out his bandaged hand as she got close to the top and where he was sitting and she took his hand and he helped her to the top. She sat down next to him and pulled her legs up to her chest and wrapped her arms around them, locking her fingers together to hold everything in place.

He looked at her and then back out into the vast desert in front of them. The desert neither one could see because of the almost total darkness. The only light was from the ever present fire that was behind them in the court yard.

"Thanks for the hand up, who were you talking to just now?" Carter asked, it was all one sentence.

Hansen laughed a brief laugh and answered looking at the woman sitting beside him, "I talk to myself sometimes when I have to do something I really don't want to do."

"What don't you want to do?" she asked looking at him.

He shook his head and said, "Nothing, it's nothing."

She was sitting on his left side and she reached out and took his left hand and pulled it toward her. Hansen looked at her and questioned, but he did not resist.

"What happened?" Carter asked looking at the dirty bandage.

"I got shot by a bandit yesterday. It's alright, the bullet went right through." He said, his heart pounding because she was gently holding his wounded hand.

"You should get Mary to look at it. She is a doctor." Carter said looking at Hansen. She liked him since the first minute she had met him. She thought him handsome, the square jaw, the tough, hard, muscled body. She was still holding his hand when she said, looking out into the desert so he could not see her face, "I want to tell you this and I don't even know your name."

"Albert Hansen, but please just call me Al." He said, looking at her. "If you called me Albert I might think you were my Mother. She always used to call me that when I was in trouble."

Carter laughed and for the first time in over two years she felt comfortable with a man. She released his hand and relocked her fingers around her legs. Hansen tried not to look at Carter but he could not help himself.

"You know this is sort of a retreat for women who have been beaten and worse.?" She asked Hansen, who nodded. "I'm here because I thought I needed a place to go and be with other women who understood what I had been through. The difference is they got abused because they were in the wrong place at the wrong time. I was abused because of what I did. My husband nearly beat me to death." She paused just long enough for Hansen to ask why.

Carter looked at Hansen and continued. "There was this neighbor and one day I went to return a horse we had borrowed. His wife had died years ago and he was in his house and I went in and we started to talk and one thing lead to another before I knew it I wanted him to kiss me. I did not even think about my husband. He wanted me and it didn't take long for us to end up in bed. That is when my husband walked in. He just told me to get dressed and I did. He told the neighbor good bye and he lead me out the door. We rode back to our house and we went inside, we never said a word to each other all the way back. As soon as we got inside the door and he closed it he punched me in the face. I fell against the stove and came up with a frying pan to defend my self with. Jack was a lot bigger then me and he took the frying pan off me and grabbed me by the hair and slammed my face onto the hot stove. I got a mouth and so I yelled I had done it with four of the ranch hands too. He slammed my face into the stove a couple more times and told me that I was so ugly now that no guy would look at me. I don't know if he said anything after that because I had passed out. I think he hit me some more but I'm not sure. When I came to Cheryl was taking care of me. She had found me. I was lucky because I think I would have died out there. Cheryl was running away from a man that was after her who liked to beat her up. So we had sort of the same problem and we became fast friends. We heard about this place and decided it was the place for us. Other women drift in and out, there are no rules and we kill any men that try and come in. And there have been a few." She looked at Hansen. "You four are the first men to stay in here alive for more then a couple of hours." She finished.

They sat in silence for the next few minutes, Hansen asked, "How do you get your food and other stuff?" He looked at her and she looked back.

"There are a lot of superstitions down here among the local people and the Indians. One of the superstitions, especially among the Indians, is that this monastery and the people that live here are really ghosts or haunted spirits. How we get what supplies we need is easy. We trade water for them. Nobody around here has any water but us. Don't ask me why, but that is the how it is. So we trade the water for food and a couple of other things. We got the guns from the Indians, but that takes a lot of water. We have a hard time delivering it and they will not come into the monastery to get it."

"What keeps the bandits out? They are not too much on haunted places or ghosts." Hansen asked again looking at the woman beside him.

She was looking out into the darkness, the unscarred side of her face illuminated by the fire. "The Indians do. It's really pretty easy. If the bandits were to kill all of us the Indians would not be able to get the water. With no water they all perish or move on. So we have automatic bandit protection."

Again the silence that lasted minutes, both Carter and Hansen thinking the same thing. A different time and place, something might happen between them.

"I came up here Al to tell you something and now I am scared to say it because you may think I am nuts." Carter said, not looking at him.

"You might as well say it, we're all nuts for being here anyway." He said and laughed at himself.

Carter swallowed and said, "I have been down here for almost two years and I think sometimes the Indians and local people are right, that there is a curse or spell or something haunting this place. I have talked to the other girls and some woman who have come here have left right away saying there is something else here in this monastery, something we can't see, but can feel every once in a while."

Hansen looked at Carter and she looked back, "I think there are lot of places like that, places that are haunted and have ghosts living in them. I ain't felt nothing, but I have pretty tough skin and block a lot of stuff out, if you know what I mean."

Carter nodded, then said, "What I really came up here for is to tell you something, something about the gold. A legend or superstition or whatever you want to call it."

"You might as well tell me that too." Hansen said, after Carter paused.

"The Indians say that men have gotten to the gold, but that there is a spell of evil on the gold and that as soon as the men find it they get very greedy and kill each other." Carter paused and then continued, "They say that the closer you get to the gold the more bodies you will find, or skeletons or whatever." She paused again, "So what I'm trying to tell you is be careful." She looked at Hansen, but he was looking out into the darkness. She kept looking at him until he looked back at her, in that instant Hansen and Carter wanted each other as bad as two people ever wanted each other. Hansen reached out with his wounded left hand left hand turned Carter's face so he could look at the hideously scarred side. She resisted his turning her head, but he was too strong. He looked at what had once been so beautiful and now was so deformed. He said nothing, he simply looked.

"That's what happens when you're a whore, Al." Carter blurted out, knowing Hansen had taken a good look and anything he felt toward her was gone when he looked at the scars on her face, the twisted eye and nose, the droop in the corner of the mouth. "I guess this is the punishment God gave me for banging anything that would pull my pants off." Carter was crying and talking at the same time and she went to stand up. As she did so Hansen grabbed her right forearm with his wounded left hand. His hand hurt when he grabbed her, but he ignored the pain and held on.

"You're hurting me." Carter said, she was half standing and half leaning over because Hansen would not let go. "Let go."

"No." Was the simply answer Hansen said to her.

She swung with her left hand, but it was an award swing and Hansen grabbed her left hand with his right. He pulled her close to him, her face not more then a foot away, "I listened to you, now you sit down and listen to me." He then pulled her back down until she was sitting again. She noted the tinge of anger in his voice.

"Do you really want to be with someone as ugly as me. Look fellas', this is my new woman, she is ugly as sin, but she is great in bed 'cause she's a real good whore." Carter yelled into Hansen's face. All the anger of knowing that the first man she had been civil to in two long years was going to walk away.

Hansen waited until she was finished, he let go of her arms, then he said in a very quiet voice, a voice so quiet that Carter could barely hear, "You still don't know that people are beautiful from the inside, Candy, not from the outside?" She felt a warmth toward him using her first name. "Everybody ages and that is when the beauty shows. The people that stay together are the people that can see the beauty on the inside of the other person. I'm in a pretty nasty profession and I have met a lot of people. Most of them are no good. Most of them I don't trust. It's a hell of a way to live and if there is a lot of gold and I manage to get my share I am going to quit and buy some land. I'm tired of looking over my shoulder every where I go."

He was looking out into the darkness again and Carter knew he had just told her something not many other people knew. She was shorter then him and when she looked at him she had to look up, even when they were sitting. She was looking up at him now when she said, "You know I have been here longer then any other woman. Two years I have hidden here. Two years I have been helping other women straighten out their lives and go back to living like normal woman. I am afraid if I go back to somewhere, some town, that in a couple of days I would be sleeping with the first guy that came along." She laughed once, a sardonic self condemning laugh, "And any other guy that came along." She added.

"So you hide down here." Hansen finished saying what Carter had not said.

She hung her head between her knees and nodded yes. She was thinking once a whore, always a whore.

Hansen suddenly stood up, it was an easy, fluid motion that Carter almost did not see. She looked up at him, "I want you to stay."

Hansen ignored what she said, as bad as he wanted to do what she asked. He handed her the rifle, "You can stand the rest of the watch."

"Stay with me, Al." It was almost a beg, Carter realized.

She was still sitting and he squatted down in front of her, still holding the rifle, "Take the rifle and stay here. I cannot stay, if I do we will end up together and I cannot have that. I'm the leader of this bunch and I cannot do what I tell everybody else not to do. You're beautiful and you turn me on and that is why I have to go." Hansen laid the rifle down and turned and climbed down the wall of the gate tower.

Carter sat stunned, because he had said what he said. She finished the last two hours of the watch never moving, almost never blinking. Thinking only of what Hansen had said to her.

CHAPTER 22

"Hey, what do you say, Ace." Farmer said to Tucker as he walked up to where Tucker was sitting. Tucker had built a small fire and was reading an old newspaper by the light.

"Sit down Charlie, take a load off." Tucker answered.

"What are you reading about?" Farmer asked, sitting down.

"I was really just looking at the advertisements. I was looking at the new ladies styles. I don't know Charlie, the dresses are above the ankles this year." Tucker commented, shaking his head back and forth.

Farmer shrugged and said nothing.

"I'm waiting for when they get above their belly buttons." Tucker said laughing. Farmer laughed also.

"I remember what you said about leaving those women alone, but there are a couple of them I wouldn't mind seeing in a dress that is above their belly button."

"You are a dirty old man, Ace." Farmer said.

"You'd be a dirty old man too, Charlie, but you ain't old yet." And they both laughed again.

"You know Ace," Farmer began, "we got all that stuff from those bandits we killed. Maybe these ladies could use it. Kind of, like, get out of those rags."

"I thought about that too." Tucker answered, "It is alright with me if nobody else cares."

"I'll have to talk to the others." Farmer said.

"You know Charlie, unless there are a lot more women around here then those seven, there is no way for them to defend this place." Tucker said, looking around the monastery with the crumbling walls and huge parade ground, most of which could not be seen because of the darkness even with the big fire.

"What do you mean?" Asked a puzzled Farmer.

"I mean there is no way seven women, or men for that matter to defend an area this big." Tucker nodded his head in the direction of the parade ground where the rest of the people sat around talking by the fire. "When you defend a place it has to be large enough to withstand cannon fire, and yet small enough to not have to move the defenders around from wall to wall."

"Wow, Ace. That sounded real professional." Farmer said. Tucker did not miss the awe he heard in Farmer's tone of voice.

"It was." Said Tucker, "straight out of the books at West Point."

Farmer thought about what Tucker said for a minute, letting it sink in.. "You went to West Point?"

"Graduated second in my class." Tucker said, his voice so quiet Farmer could hardly hear it. "Graduated a couple of years before the war broke out. Not to brag, but I'm a pretty smart guy, Charlie."

"Tough too." Farmer said.

"What do you mean?" Tucker asked.

"Don't you have to eat a lot of shit when you go through that school?"

"Oh, I know what you mean." Tucker said, "You mean the hazing. It's all part of the training. Have you ever been in combat, Charlie?" Tucker asked, looking Farmer directly in the face.

"Yea." answered the killer.

"Then you know the confusion and fear. Well one of the things they teach at the Point is how to overcome those fears and keep your head on straight and look past the confusion into what is actually happening. In a big battle, you not only have to know what you are doing, but what the other men are doing, both your allies and your enemy. If you don't, you will make a mistake and it will cost you a lot of lives, maybe even your own." Tucker was looking at Farmer as if he was the instructor and Farmer was the student. "You will also make a wrong decision and it could cost a very smart officer his career in the army."

Farmer picked up on the hint immediately. "And that is why you ain't in the army anymore, because you didn't know what you were doing?"

Tucker laughed, but there was no humor in the laugh. "Not to brag again, but I did know what I was doing, it was my commanding officer who did not know." Tucker paused, now looking out in the direction of the dark desert. "You want to know why I am not in the army any more?" Tucker asked Farmer, looking him in the face again.

Farmer nodded yes.

"It was the battle called the wilderness. There were three companies holding a line against Lee's army. Colonel John Peck was in command of our company and I was in command of the actual line combat troops. Peck was to hold our position against any attack and help the companies on our flanks if they needed help. The Rebels came at us and Peck changed his mind and ordered me to retreat. I knew if I did the other two companies would be out flanked and would have to retreat also. For all intents and purposes the whole section of Union line would fall. I argued with Peck, but to no avail, so I ordered the retreat. We retreated, but the line held because a company of cavalry was in the area and they plugged the gap in the line. That saved the other two companies from being outflanked and the line held. After the battle the commanding general wanted to know who ordered the retreat. Peck said I did without his authorization. I said he was lying but that did not do any good. I got court marshaled. Just before I was to testify my lawyer took me into a room and told me to resign from the army, that there was no way I could prove that Peck ordered the retreat. That the court marshal board was going to find me guilty. So me, being who I am I wrote out my resignation, but still took the stand, just so I could tell my side of what happened. During the questioning the prosecuting officer, who was a Colonel, asked me a question and I answered with a nasty answer. The presiding judge asked me, "Captain do you know what insubordination is?" Tucker smiled to himself, "I looked at him and asked "Do you know what stupid is?" Tucker paused again, laughing. "That was about the end of my career in the army. That afternoon the army accepted my resignation."

CHAPTER 23

he camp fire was small, just large enough to see the twelve people sitting or squatting around it. Farmer and Tucker were on one side and Hansen, Muller, Wilson, and Carter were on the other. The remainder of the women scattered in different spots around the outside. The coffee pot sat in the middle.

"Ace you want to tell them?" Farmer began.

Tucker shook his head no. "I not any good at talking, Charlie, not in front of a lot of people." He moved his right hand to encompass the four people sitting opposite himself and Farmer.

"Well I ain't too good at this public speaking either." Farmer started nervously, poking the small fire with a stick. A few scattered sparks rose in the air, only to die a few feet above the flames. They were easy to follow because of the darkness of the night. No moon, no stars. "We killed those seven bandits back in the canyon yesterday and took everything but their long johns. Me and Ace think we should give the horses, guns and clothes to the ladies living here." This was addressed to Hansen, Muller, and Wilson.

"Oh no!" said Carter in a loud voice, "No way am I wearing some dead guys pants and shirt with a bunch of bullet holes in them." She paused, and then added, "All bloody and everything."

Farmer waited patiently for her to finish, when he was sure she was finished he continued, "Lady in six months you and your friends are going to be running around here naked if you don't do this."

"No! No way!" shouted Carter, her thinking distorted by her hatred of Farmer. "Shut up." Farmer shouted back at her.

"I'd rather run around naked, then take a hand out from you." Carter answered, pointing her finger at Farmer for emphasis, again the hatred in the voice.

"Charlie, go take a walk." Hansen said to Farmer. He could see the killer was getting angry and he did not need Farmer angry.

Farmer stood up and started to walk away, then stopped and turned and looked at Carter, who returned his stare. Farmer shook his head and said nothing.

"Why don't you go murder somebody, you're good at that." She yelled, she had lost all control of her emotions.

Hansen was on his feet in an instant standing in front of Carter, who had never moved from her squatting position by the fire. She simply looked at Farmer. The rest of the people froze, either not knowing what to do or not realizing how close Farmer was to doing something to hurt Carter. Farmer had taken two steps back toward the woman and stopped when Hansen stepped between them.

"What's the matter, you afraid when a man stands up to you. I guess you're just good at shooting women. You little..." Carter was silenced by Wilson clamping his hand over her mouth and forcing her to fall backward. He leaned on the hand and knew he was hurting her.

"Shut your mouth lady, or I will turn you loose and get Hansen out of the way and Charlie will kill you deader then hell." Wilson had no intention of turning Carter loose, he knew he just had to say and do something or Farmer would kill Carter and for some reason Wilson felt that they needed Carter.

Carter could not move and when Wilson told her he would turn her loose and Farmer loose she suddenly realized he was telling the truth. She had no doubts Farmer would kill her. She was suddenly very afraid of Farmer. She saw the dead green eyes looking at her. Then he turned and walked away, out into the inky blackness.

Hansen turned and looked at Carter and said, "And you cool off. Don't push Charlie too far. He'll go crazy and kill all of us."

Wilson released her and Carter sat up. She looked at Wilson and said nothing.

"Think what you want, Candy, but me and Al just saved your life. Now act nice, I can get mad enough for the both of us." Wilson said, then he smiled. She looked at Wilson and thought to herself he has a very disarming smile.

"I guess I should say I'm sorry, but I am not. I just can't stand Farmer, every time I am any where near him I get angry. He killed my best friend." Then she did something she hated doing, she started to cry. She felt an arm around her shoulders and knew Muller was holding her. She stopped crying and Hansen handed her his bandanna. She took it and looked around at the people looking at her.

"Well Ace, I guess you now chair the meeting.' Hansen said to Tucker. He did it so Carter would not be the center of attention, which he thought she did not want to be right now.

"I guess so." He answered. "Charlie and I were talking and we saw what a state the women were in and thought it, or they rather, could use the horses and clothes and guns. So we decided to ask." Tucker never looked up while he was talking, he looked at the fire and had picked up the stick Farmer had held and was poking the fire just as Farmer had. "There were a couple of other things too. First off this place is too big for six women to defend. It has to be smaller. A lot smaller."

"I suppose you are an expert at defending forts?" Carter asked, sarcastically.

"As a matter of fact I am. I graduated second in my class at West Point. I am the expert you need for this place." Tucker said. He looked at the shocked faces looking back at him. "Anyway, the third thing is these ladies have to be trained on how to use the guns we give them. All this will take time, two maybe three days. Me and Charlie are willing to stay here for that long before we move on, but you three have to decide if you want go along with me and Charlie. If you decide no then me and Charlie will go with you. We can leave in the morning." Tucker shrugged his shoulders and looked back at the fire. He waited to see if anyone had anything else to say before he continued. "There is one more thing." He said looking at Carter, "You have to get your water somewhere, where?"

"Don't say nothing, anything!" One of the women yelled from behind Tucker. He turned around and looked at her and stood up.

"What?" He questioned her.

"Maybe we should talk it over first." Carter said to both Tucker and the woman named Blue.

"Why don't we just look at it a different way." Said another woman from the back of the group of woman. She stepped forward and looked at the other people standing and sitting around the fire. She was a plain woman with a long face, she was thin, very thin. She was short and her voice when she spoke was very husky, like someone had used sandpaper on her vocal cords. She too was dressed in rags.

"This is Mary Thomas. She is a doctor and probably the only one of us with a really level head. Or brains if maybe you want to call it that." Carter said.

There was silence until Hansen said to Thomas, "You're on Doc, speak your piece."

"What I was just thinking was these guys have all the guns and let's face it, all the muscle. All they have to do is tie us up and they can go anywhere and do anything they want here. They have been nice and they didn't have to be. They could have just moved in and taken what they wanted. So show them whatever they want." She finished. She shrugged her narrow shoulders and sat back down.

"Ha." Muller laughed, "Maybe the Doc should speak to Charlie," She said looking at the doctor, then she looked at Carter, "And you, you should learn to keep your mouth shut, if you hate Charlie that much when he comes into where you are you should just leave."

"I live here." Carter protested.

"Only for as long as Farmer and these others say so." Commented the doctor, from her sitting position.

There was silence. No one spoke, most just looked at the fire or the beautiful night sky, carefully avoiding the eyes of someone else. No one noticed Blue walking away into the darkness only to return a moment later to her pervious spot. She stood in the shadow, so no one saw the slight smile on her face.

"Enough!" Farmer said from behind Blue. He grabbed Blue's left arm and half pulled her, half dragged her next to the fire. He had walked right up to the edge of the fire light and no one had noticed his coming. Blue was wearing a blue bandanna around her neck and her blue dress was also in rags. When they got next to the fire everyone saw the pistol pointed at her head. The pistol held by Farmer. "Tell me where the water is or I will pull the trigger, then I will go to the next one and the next until I find out where the water is or all you women are dead."

"It's in the tunnel under the road." A woman yelled from behind Carter. 'I can't tell you where it is, but I can show you, just don't pull the trigger, Mr. Farmer. Please don't." She was not more then a girl, maybe sixteen at most. She had red hair and a light complexion, which was red with sun burn, a face full of freckles, light blue eyes and thin lips. She was dressed in the usual assortment of rags. Her name was Carol Landing and she was the youngest person there. She was the one who had opened the doors of the monastery for Wilson

"Harry, go with her." Farmer said, then changed his mind, "Wait a minute." He said and pointed the pistol into the air and pulled the trigger three times, cocking it deliberately each time. The only sound was the hammer hitting on an empty chamber.

"The whole seventh cavalry could have marched up here and you would have never known it. You should have some guards." Farmer said, carefully avoiding Carter's hateful stare.

"I'll take care of that, Charlie." Tucker said and then looked at the women as a group, "How long you ladies been out here?" He asked all of them.

"A few months." The girl answered who had spoken up about the water.

"Anybody know anything about guns?" Tucker asked, the voice of a frustrated lifelong soldier asking what he considered a stupid question.

"I do." Blue answered still standing next to the fire. She held out her right hand for the pistol, Farmer had held to her head. Farmer gave it to her. "Now this here's a weapon." She said as she opened the chamber cover where the bullets were put into the pistol. She pulled the hammer back part way and expertly spun the chamber. She pulled the hammer all the way back and pulled the trigger and everyone heard the click. She closed the chamber cover and spun the pistol around her pointer finger, first forward, then backwards. Then she flipped it into the air while it was still spinning and it went maybe ten feet high and when it came down she caught it with her finger, it never stopped spinning. Then she slipped it into the rope holding the dress tight around her waist.

"I'm impressed." Muttered Wilson loud enough for all to hear. Someone started to clap and in an instant everyone was clapping. Blue bowed, then curtsied, "Than you one and all, if I had a hat I would pass it around." Then she laughed, more at herself then anything or anyone else. "Damn near dropped it when it came down." She said and laughed again. The mood of the group was suddenly much lighter.

CHAPTER 24

"**O**kay ladies, this is just like being in the army. In the army everybody is stupid until I teach you how not to be stupid." Tucker spoke with the voice of a drill sergeant. He was good at this and he was going to have a good time for the next day or two. "We, the smart ones are going to teach you, the stupid ones how to use a gun and while using it not getting yourselves shot. Some of this is easy, some is hard, but you will learn it. When we leave you will know how and what to do with your new weapons." Tucker paused and Trudy Anderson asked "What kind of gun is this?" She asked innocently holding up a Winchester lever action rifle.

"Lady that is a rifle and we are about to have our first lesson in weapons." Tucker answered, "Step out here by me and face the rest of the ladies." Anderson did as she was told. "Hold the rifle out and repeat after me." Anderson nodded looking at Tucker.

"This is my rifle." Tucker said he almost could not hold back a laugh.

"This is my rifle." Repeated Anderson.

"Louder!" Shouted Tucker.

"This is my rifle." Screamed Anderson.

"This is my gun!" Shouted Tucker, pointing at his crotch.

"This is my gun!" Anderson yelled and pointed at her crotch

"With this I kill people!" Shouted Tucker, holding up his Henry rifle.

"With this I kill people!" Yelled Anderson holding her rifle.

"With this I have fun!" Tucker yelled and could no longer contain his laughter.

"With this I have fun!" Screamed Anderson, realizing Tucker was having fun at her expense. The woman burst into fits of laughter and could not remember having such fun since anyone of them had been here.

CHAPTER
25

It was later that evening, dusk was just settling on the parade ground of the monastery and everyone had gathered around the ever present fire and the woman were still in a good mood from when Tucker had given them their first lesson in the art of shooting a modern lever action rifle. He had simply taught them how to work the lever action and how to break down, clean, and reassemble the Winchester rifle. He had told them that the rest was just keeping the gun clean and practice. There was no shortage of ammunition so they would get plenty of practice.

"Hey Harry," Tucker asked Wilson, "how did you do that beer bottle trick and win the hundred bucks off that guy?"

"It was just something I learned somewhere." Wilson was sitting next to Carol Landing and on the opposite side of the fire from Blue Bonnet. Tucker was next to Landing and next to Tucker was Hansen. Muller stood behind Hansen. She could see Bonnet by simply looking over Hansen. Linda Joyce stood to Muller's right and next to her was Trudy Anderson and next to her was Wanda Jennings. Behind Joyce and Anderson, but looking between them was the doctor. She was short, but the space in front of her was clear. Candy Carter was standing watch on the wall near the gate. She watched between looks out into the coming night blackness.

"Excuse me, Harry, but what trick did you do to win the hundred bucks." Bonnet asked Wilson.

"It was nothing." Wilson said in reply.

"It was something," Tucker continued. "He tossed a beer bottle up in the air and then shot the bottom out, and then caught the beer bottle or what was left of it and won a hundred bucks. I'll tell you, Harry, I was impressed." Tucker finished.

Thomas was glad to see the women having a good time. They needed some entertainment and this was going to be a good thing. She smiled her small smile and watched.

"Harry, if you're a catholic you better go to confession and confess stealing that mans hundred dollars." Bonnet said.

"Now listen..." Wilson started to say something, some type of protest, when Tucker cut him off.

"You know that trick, Blue?" Tucker asked Bonnet. Tucker was on a first name basis with the women since the training session.

"Can you do it?" Asked Hansen, it was the first time he had spoken all night. The question addressed to Bonnet.

"Wait just a minute." Bonnet said and ran off into the darkness. She returned a minute later carrying six empty beer bottles. The monks who had lived here sometime in the past must have bottled their own beer and when they drank it, they simply put the empty bottles in a corner of one of the rooms used as a barracks at some time. Then when they needed more bottles they just went into the barracks room and got what they wanted. "Alright here goes, ladies and gentlemen, and I tell you I use both those terms very loosely around you people." This raised a chorus of objections and boos from the people standing and sitting near the fire. "For my next trick I will throw this empty beer bottle into the air and while it is spinning, I will draw my trusty pistol and shoot the bottom of the bottle out while leaving the rest of the bottle intact." She started to toss the first bottle into the air and stopped the forward motion of her arm. "Wow, I almost forgot. I need a pistol." She looked around and Wilson said, "Here, take mine."

"Harry, I can't do that, everybody knows your pistol can shoot the bottom out of the bottle. I need someone else's. I need a real good looking one." At which time she looked at Hansen, "Al, you are wearing a good looking rig. Let me use yours."

"I may need it.' Hansen said.

"Why? You gonna shoot the beer bottle?" Bonnet asked and this brought laughter and the Doctor laughed along with the rest, even Hansen. Hansen unbuckled his pistol and handed it to Bonnet who stretched almost across the fire to get it. "This thing must be hot stuff, or it felt like it." Bonnet quipped. She strapped the holster around her waist and tied it to her right leg. "Now I look just like you, Al." She said, more laughter. She pulled the pistol from the holster and twirled it around her finger three times and slipped it back in the holster in one swift, smooth move. "Now I got your gun, it will cost you a hundred bucks to see the trick." Hansen smiled and shook his head no. "Come on Al. If I pull off the trick I get a hundred of your easy made dollars and if I don't pull it off you get your gun back. Now how does that sound?"

"Oh, that's a good deal." Hansen answered. Again everybody laughed.

"I'll tell you what, I'll bet anybody a hundred bucks I can do it. I know I'm as good as Harry with a pistol. Probably better because Harry is getting old." More laughter.

"I got a hundred says you can't do it." Farmer said. He had walked up next to Thomas and she had never heard him. She turned and looked up at him. There was something about him that she felt drawn to. She liked having him standing next to her. For the first time since that little Texas town, she liked being near a man. Not any man, this man.

"Charlie, it's a trick, I know." Wilson said quickly, turning to look at Farmer. He did it so Farmer was not fooled. Because it was Farmer who made the bet, the mood had suddenly become sober.

"I know. I just want to see it done, and how." He answered.

"Show me your hundred." Bonnet said, smiling to let everyone, including Farmer, know she was just fooling around.

Farmer took out four twenty-five dollar gold pieces and held them up for everyone to see. "Hold these, Doc." He said to Thomas standing next to him and handed her the coins. Their fingers touched as the coins exchanged hands and the Doctor felt something stir inside her, "What do you have to put up, Blue?" He asked.

Bonnet cocked her head to one side, shrugged her shoulders and said, "I have this nice gun and holster." She slapped both her hands against the buckle.

"Looks like something you would wear, Al." Farmer said to Hansen.

"Yea. It looks just like one I used to have." Hansen said. There was a scattering of laughter.

"You shouldn't give a woman a gift until after you get what you want, Al." Bonnet said. Again more laughter and again Thomas felt good about it because the mood was light again even with Farmer being a big part of it.

"Now that we have all that settled." Bonnet said, "We will do the impossible. I will toss this empty beer bottle up in the air and shoot the bottom out by shooting through the small opening you drink out of. It's all in the hands and the wrists." Bonnet twisted both her hands and wrists in different directions. She took the beer bottle in her right hand and tossed at least ten feet in the air and as it reached the top of the throw she drew and fired the pistol and the bottom of the bottle exploded and the rest of the bottle fell. She holstered the pistol and caught the bottle by the neck and held up the unbroken bottle.

For several seconds there was silence, then Wilson started to clap, followed by the others.

"Shit!" Exclaimed Farmer.

"Don't feel bad Charlie. You lost a hundred bucks. Al, there lost his pistol and holster." Bonnet said laughing.

"So how did you do it, Blue?" Tucker asked.

"It's easy. All you have to do is watch." Bonnet picked up another bottle, tossed it into the air, bang, the bottom was gone, the rest of the bottle she caught. "Nothing to it."

"I got another hundred says you can't do another one." Farmer said.

Before he could get the coins out of his pocket, Bonnet picked up another bottle, tossed it in the air and shot out the bottom, catching the remainder of the bottle when it came down.

"I bet I got more bottles then you got money." Bonnet said, turning to look at Farmer. There was an edge to Bonnet's voice that everyone picked up on. It was a challenge and it was being issued to Farmer. It was Hansen who first reacted to it. The position of Bonnet, her right hand only inches from the butt of his pistol in his holster. That was the second challenge being issued.

There was silence, the challenge hanging in the air. "That's enough!" shouted Hansen, standing up. He was an impressive figure as large as he was. Maybe even intimidating within the small area the group was gathered in.

"Don't go for it Charlie." Thomas said looking at Farmer. "Blue knows what she is doing and she will take all your money." The Doctor too was trying to defuse a possible deadly situation.

"Your pants too if you want to bet them." Bonnet quipped, again the silence. She suddenly realized that she was facing off against a man who had no sense of humor and she also realized that she had gotten irritated by his tone of voice when he told her she could not do it a third time. This is how people get themselves killed, she thought.

The tension broke when Farmer smiled, he knew when to quit, when he had been bested, "I don't know how you did it, but that is all the money you get off me." He said. He knew he could beat Bonnet at a fast draw, but now was not the time for pride. This was a money trip and if Muller was right, there was maybe millions in it for him.

"I don't care, I got this nice pistol and holster from that handsome looking gentlemen standing right over there. Now watch carefully." Bonnet said. She pulled the pistol from the holster, twirled it, and put it back in the light tan holster, she twisted her hands and wrists again, "I'm going to miss this one, but someone tell me how I did it." Then she tossed the bottle into the air and fired the pistol and caught the bottle. No one said a word so she did it again. Farmer felt the Doctor grab his left arm and jump up and down with excitement.

"I know, Charlie, I know." She yelled, still holding Farmers left arm. There was no mistaking the excitement in her voice. Like a little girl winning a prize at a fair.

"You're better then me." He said to her.

"Tell me." Bonnet said to Thomas.

"It's not the gun like you want us to believe, it's the bottle." She almost yelled.

"Tell me." Bonnet said smiling at the excited Doctor. No one had ever seen her like this in the months she had been here.

"It's the way you throw the bottle. You throw it so it only goes about fifteen feet in the air. When the bottle reaches the apex of it's height, the small opening is facing directly at you. You simply shoot through the hole, an easy shot at ten or fifteen feet and the bottom comes out."

"You are right Doc. Charlie give her another hundred dollars for figuring it out." Bonnet told Farmer, then laughed.

"What's the apex of the height?" Farmer asked, looking down at the small woman standing next to him. Most of the people sitting or standing around the fire wanted to ask the same question, but were too embarrassed to do so.

The Doctor looked up at Farmer with a look that said you don't know that?

"Charlie, you're going to have to get educated if you want to hang around us upper class people." Thomas said, then she did something, few if any people did. She laughed at Charlie Farmer. Much to the surprise of everyone Farmer laughed back. "Let me explain, Charlie. Blue does all this talking and playing with the gun. You watch that instead of the bottle. She just tosses the bottle into the air and when it reaches the apex, the very top of the toss. Just when it is no longer going up or down, the little opening is facing her. Shooting into a one inch hole at ten or fifteen feet is nothing to someone who is any kind of a shot with a pistol."

While the Doctor was explaining the bottle trick Bonnet had walked to the cross and spitting on some sand she attached three pieces of the damp sand to the cross. They were about a foot apart in a vertical line chest high. She then measured off about fifteen feet and made a line in the sand with her right foot.

"Alright Ace, you ain't done nothing tonight but look at the women, so step on up here." Bonnet ordered still using the bossy tone of a side show barker in the circus. The one she had used all night except for the one sentence challenging Farmer. Tucker liked Bonnet so he did as he was told. He got up and stood behind the line.

"Put a bullet into those three sand marks." Bonnet said to him pointing at the three sand marks on the vertical post and walking away. Tucker drew and fired three shots so fast they almost sounded like one. Bonnet walked back to the cross looked at the holes and said to Tucker. "Good man Ace. You can do that trick too."

"I have a question, Blue." The Doctor asked, the tone of her voice serious. Bonnet looked at her and said nothing. "How come the whole bottle doesn't shatter when the bullet hits the bottom?"

"That's a good question and I really don't have the answer, but it don't and I can make a lot of money so who cares." She answered smiling.

"I can't really explain why," said Wilson standing up, "I mean..." He paused trying to gather the right words. He turned to Bonnet and said, "Throw the Doctor a bottle." Bonnet picked up a bottle and tossed to the Doctor.

Thomas did not expect it and screamed, "I don't know how to catch!" putting her hands up in front of her face to protect herself. She waited to be hit by the bottle, but nothing happened.

"You can open your eyes now Doc." Farmer said.

When she did he was holding the bottle in front of her. "Thank you." She muttered taking the bottle from him.

"Now look at the bottom." Wilson said. She did. "There is a line in the glass just above the place where the bottom and sides meet. It must be some kind of molding mark. When the bullet hits the bottom of the bottle, the bottom of the bottle snaps clean off. The bottle comes down and you catch it and low and behold you have done the trick." Wilson stopped talking and saw the doctor examining the bottle.

Carol Landing was sitting next to Wilson and she started to applaud and in an instant everyone was clapping and yelling and cheering Wilson and Bonnet. Doctor Mary Thomas was very happy. Her patients were having a good time and she was a firm believer in the old adage, 'laughter is the best medicine.' She turned and looked up at

Candy Carter sitting on the gate tower and noted she was smiling and clapping also. Farmer, Muller, Hansen, Tucker, and Wilson would be leaving in the morning and this was a good last night together.

"Let me have that bottle, Doc." Tucker said to Thomas.

The Doctor looked at Tucker and did nothing. Farmer took the bottle from her and tossed it to Tucker. Tucker caught it and turned away from everyone.

Bonnet knowing what he was going to do walked up next to him and said quietly, "The doctor is right, the toss is everything. So practice it a couple of times."

Tucker did as he was told and tossed the bottle in the air a half dozen times.

"You think you got it?" Bonnet asked.

"Yea. Yea." Tucker said, nervously, "I'm ready."

"Go for it." Bonnet said.

Tucker held the beer bottle by the neck, He tossed it up in the air and decided at the last minute he did not like the way he tossed it so he did not draw and fire, instead he caught the bottle when it came down.

"I want my money back." Wilson said, teasing Tucker because he did not shoot the bottle.

Tucker turned and looked at the crowd looking at him. "You all just have to watch, don't you?" It was half statement, half question.

"Yes we do." Answered Hansen.

"It cost me two hundred bucks to see you perform, so perform." Farmer said.

"Shoot the bottle, Ace, I'm supposed to be on look out up here." Carter yelled from the top of the gate tower. Everyone started to boo and hiss.

Bonnet leaned close to Tucker and said, "Listen Ace, I've seen this before, this crowd is getting unruly. You'd better do this or we could have a lot of trouble on our hands. There is nothing worse then an unruly mob at a shooting show." Then Bonnet turned back toward the dozen people and waved her hands so they would boo and hiss more. Farmer stood calmly, but the Doctor booed and yelled at

Tucker while never letting go of Farmer's shirt sleeve. She did not notice she was holding his sleeve, but Farmer did.

Tucker tossed the bottle into the air, drew and fired, the bottle shattered. "Great." Muttered Tucker. More boos and hisses.

"You remember what the doctor said about the top of the spin." Bonnet said as she picked up the last beer bottle and moved behind Tucker. "Now I'm going to toss it, so all you have to do is shoot it, got it?" she finished with a question. She moved forward until she was touching Tucker's back with her stomach. She wrapped her left arm around his waist, "Ready?" She asked.

"Get a room!" One of the women yelled.

"Pay attention." Bonnet said to Tucker. "Here goes." She tossed the bottle and when it reached the apex she whispered to Tucker "Now." Tucker drew and fired, the bottle exploded. "You have to relax, Ace." Bonnet said

"Here Ace." Said Muller as she stood up and passed Tucker her hip flask. "Take a belt, you'll relax a little."

Tucker took the hip flask, uncorked it and took a pull. He handed the hip flask back to Muller, nodded as the whiskey burned it's way down his throat. "I'm ready to try again." He said.

"To bad," Commented Bonnet, "There are no more bottles."

This got a laugh from everyone but Tucker. He stood looking disappointed, first at the other people, then at Bonnet.

"I will find some more bottles, Ace, while you're gone. I will make sure you do the trick before you leave." Bonnet said. She liked Ace Tucker. She felt at ease with him. The first time since she had been beaten almost to death by her drunken live in boyfriend in Waco Texas almost a year ago. All the talking and comedy had been a cover for the hurt and pain she had suffered at the hands her lover. Talking about it with the other women had helped, but it was still a black memory, a memory she would never get over.

CHAPTER 26

It was dark now it had been decided that there would always be two people on watch, one by the fire and the other on the gate tower, one to watch the fire and the one on the gate tower, the other to watch for intruders and the one watching the fire. The fire had been burning since before Carter had gotten there more then two years ago and it seemed the women felt more secure with it going, so they kept it burning all the time, the wood fuel coming from the thousands of wooden beams used in building the monastery, tunnels, and caves.

Thomas moved away from the crowd and started walking toward her room in the monastery. She was almost to the door of the monastery when she turned and saw Farmer following behind her. She stopped and waited for him to catch up. But he simply stopped.

"Why are you following me, Charlie?"

"It ain't nothing. I just wanted to make sure you got here alright. Good night, Doc." And with that he turned and walked off into the dark night. Thomas waited and watched him leave. She almost called him, knowing inside her he would have come had she called, but she did not call and he did not come back. Mary Thomas turned and entered the front door of the monastery and went to her room. She did not think of her room or anything else, her mind was totally occupied by the killer to whom she felt such an attraction. Why? He was not handsome, nor was he overly intelligent. She could not put her finger on it, but there was something. She laid down on her bed fully clothed and her last thought that night before falling asleep was of their fingers touching when he handed her the four gold coins when he had made the bet with Blue about shooting the beer bottle.

CHAPTER 27

"We have to go." Hansen said to the other four riders as he turned his horse toward the monastery gate. He moved off toward the gate and saw Carter standing just inside it. He stopped his horse and the trailing mules when he was even with her.

"Good luck, Al. I hope you find all the gold you can carry." She said smiling up at him.

"You just make sure you keep a guard posted and that she stays awake." He answered, smiling down at her. He touched his horses flanks and the animal moved off through the gate, the three mules trailing behind. The next man through the gate was Wilson, she wished him good luck as he passed by. Then came Muller and Carter thanked her for everything and clasped her left hand in both of hers. "You be careful, Alice." She said.

"I will." Said Muller and she passed.

Tucker followed Muller and he said. "See you later." as he went past, not knowing what else to say.

Carter watched Farmer as he approached and she just looked at him, smiling a false smile. He was even with her and as he passed her she said, "I hope to God you get killed." She had expected him to say something, but he said nothing, he just looked at her with those dead, empty, bottomless pale green eyes. Then he looked away and was past her, the mules trailing behind him. Someday she would get her chance to kill him and she would take it.

Hansen turned and looked at Farmer as he rode up from the back of the line. "We'll take your mules, you take the point." Hansen said and Farmer handed him the rope tethered to the lead mule. "Don't get too far ahead, Charlie, I want to keep you in sight at all times. I don't want us spread out all over northern Mexico." He finished.

"I'll keep an eye on you." Farmer answered and spurred his horse into a gallop. Hansen turned in his saddle and said to Wilson, "Harry, you cover the back door." You see or hear anything give out with a yell."

Wilson gave Tucker his mules, "Don't loose these." He said smiling at Tucker.

"I'll treat them like I do my women. I'll be soft and gentle." Tucker replied, almost laughing. Wilson laughed also and fell behind the other four. It was a nervous laugh because Wilson knew the bandits always killed the last man in line first.

"I'll be second, Alice you're third, Ace, you bring up the rear." Hansen ordered.

"That's me, always the rear end of everything." Tucker muttered to himself.

Of the four men, Muller was beginning to like Tucker the most. The night with Farmer was nothing but a whiskey and sex drive thing. She'd had a couple of drinks and was feeling a little frisky. She probably would have hit on Tucker or Hansen, Farmer just happened to be standing watch, plus she had also wanted to make sure he was not angry with her about the monastery. Ace always had something funny to say. He was constantly poking fun at himself. Even the women in the monastery liked him, especially Blue.

"We have to stay on the trail," Hansen turned in his saddle and spoke to Muller and Tucker, "Candy says both sides are nothing but sand and the horses will get bogged down in it and we won't be able to get them out. It's soft and deep."

Tucker relayed the message to Wilson and the young man nodded.

Muller followed Hansen and the six mules he lead. They headed north out of the monastery, back down the trail they had come up out of the canyon the day before. It was a slight rise and Muller could feel the heat of the early morning sun beating down on her. She wrapped the rope from her mules around her saddle horn and took off her coat. It was still cold, but she knew it would warm up and pretty soon the heat would be overpowering. She laid the coat across her thighs and looked at Hansen. He and his mules were turning right to head east. They rode east for a quarter mile or so and she saw Farmer turn back south. She knew she would only see him off and on once they entered the canyon. She watched the trail, she did not want to be the one who wandered off it and needed help getting back on. She watched Farmer turn to his left and then he disappeared as he made a hard right and he was over a small bluff going down the other side. As she started up the small rise the trail turned to the left and then back to the right on the other side. Then the trail straightened out for maybe a quarter of a mile and there was a sharp left and she just saw Farmer disappear around the next turn. Up over another bluff and down through a dry wash another turn to the right and then another to the left. Never straight, never level, always up or down, turning to the left or right. She hardly ever saw Farmer after the first bluff. Every once in a while he would be there and then he was gone again, around another turn or into a wash or down the back side of a small rise. It seemed to Muller that they were headed in a generally southeasterly direction. There was no getting off the trail, there was plenty of room to turn around, but nowhere to get off, or on for that matter. She followed Hansen as he turned to the left and up another slight rise, then down into a dry wash and across the dry wash, up the other side and another turn to the left and the trail flattened out for maybe a hundred yards. She saw Farmer. They covered the hundred yards and a turn to the right and down a small hill. The sun was hot now and getting hotter. They were still going in a generally southeasterly direction, but lower and lower into a valley of some sort. None of this was on the map, but this was the only trail, she had no idea what these men would do if this trail lead nowhere. They had already gotten their five hundred dollars, but this trail was supposed to lead to millions. They did not want the five hundred, they wanted their ten percent of the millions. Another turn to the right, if the trail had not been so clearly outlined they might be headed anywhere. Suddenly they were on a straight section, maybe a mile long. The walls of the canyon fell away to both sides and she was looking into a valley of sand. The light tan color was everywhere. Both sides of the trail were nothing but the tan colored sand tunes, the wind blowing the tops of the dunes gently off and into the next low spot. She looked ahead and saw Farmer. He was stopped and waiting. She saw him pull the rifle from the scabbard and lay it across the front of his saddle. She turned and saw Tucker waving to Wilson to catch up with them. It took only a couple of minutes for the group to converge on Farmer.

"I saw a couple of Indians on the rim of the canyon and now I just saw a couple more." Farmer told them.

"Harry, what do you know about this place? What tribe is this? How they gonna try and stop us?" The questions came one after the other and Wilson could not answer them.

"Give the kid a chance, Al." Tucker said, smiling.

"I heard they rule this valley and know every inch of it. They have been here forever. I heard they let you in, but won't let you out." Wilson shrugged his slim shoulders indicating that was all he knew.

"What tribe are they?" Hansen pressed.

"I don't know." Wilson answered with a shrug of his shoulders.

There was silence for a minute, then Tucker said, "I know what tribe they are."

The other four people looked at him in surprise since he claimed to know nothing about Mexico or the people living there. "Well." asked Hansen.

"They're the Barber tribe, if you're a white man and they catch you they give you a haircut." Tucker burst out laughing, knowing he had taken them in with his joke. There was silence and suddenly Wilson burst out laughing, then Muller, then Hansen and Farmer.

"I don't know about you. Ace." Muller said.

"Candy Carter told me that the Indians considered the valley a haunted place and would not go into it. She said they waited until you came out. The reason they consider it haunted is that nobody ever comes out. I guess they are afraid if they go in they will not come out." Hansen finished.

Hansen moved forward and stopped even with Farmer. He was looking out across the valley. "Candy also said the desert out here," He pointed toward the open space before them, "Doesn't have much life in it. She says it has been dry like this for hundreds, maybe thousands of years and every living thing has left. The only noise out here will be the sound of our horses hoofs hitting the ground."

CHAPTER 28

They were walking their horses, the trail was sand covered, but still easy to follow. It had been an hour or so since Hansen had taken the point from Farmer and Tucker was now covering the back door for Wilson. Muller was slightly behind Farmer who was walking to her left. Wilson was ahead between Farmer and her. She saw the motion with her perferial vision. She turned as fast as she could, but was too late. The rattlesnake had already coiled up and had started to strike. The head was moving forward almost faster then the eye could follow. The horse had started to rear, but it would be much too late to avoid the strike. She would probably lose her horse because there was no way to stop the snake. Then Muller saw something she would never forget. She saw Wilson and Farmer draw and fire, both at the same instant. Both men were within her field of vision. There was no difference in their speed. The two bullets slammed into the snake when it was inches away from the horse's leg, Wilson's bullet striking the snake only inches below Farmers. The impact of the two bullets caused the snake to be tossed almost at Muller's feet. She screamed and let go of the horse's reins. The horse bolted and ran into the soft sand. It started to sink immediately and the more it fought the sand the faster it went down. The lead mule had stopped just short of the side of the trail and the tether rope was tight, being pulled by the sinking horse. The horse was screaming as was the mule, one fighting to get out of the sand the other fighting not to go in. Then Muller saw the rope whirl through the air and land around the horses neck. She looked and saw it had been thrown by Wilson. It landed perfectly around her horses neck. He was pulling his horse by the reins up the trail Hansen had just covered. She saw Farmer take two steps and there was a knife in his hand, he sliced through the rope holding the mules to the saddle horn of the horse in the sand. The horse was above the bottom of the stomach, half way up it's rib cage. That is when it started to turn and there was another rope swirling through the air and that one also landed around the horses neck. The second rope belonged to Farmer and he had moved his horse so he was pulling with Wilson. Now Muller's horse was coming out of the soft sand. The stomach was clear, then the top of the legs, the knees, then it was back on the solid ground of the trail. The horses eyes were wide and bulging with fear. He was ready to bolt and would probably end up back in the sand. Wilson and Farmer held the ropes tight when Hansen arrived and he dismounted while his horse was still moving forward. He ran to the side of Muller's horse, grabbing it by the main and talking to it. It seemed like a long time, but it was only a minute until the horse settled down and Farmer and Wilson slackened their ropes.

"Keep those ropes tight." Hansen ordered the two men and they immediately did as they were told. Hansen kept murmuring into the horse's ear while he held tightly to the main. The horse visibly relaxed. The tensed muscles softened and it seemed to slouch. Hansen kept talking and petting the horse on the neck.

Tucker arrived and knew better then to do anything but sit on his horse and watch. He waited and then dismounted and walked up to Muller.

"You ok?" He asked.

"Yes, other then being scared out of my wits." She answered.

Tucker bent down and picked up the snake. It had to be at least four feet long and two, maybe three inches in diameter. The two bullet holes, inches behind the head, had all but torn the head off the snake. Tucker squeezed the back of the head and the mouth opened and as it did the two deadly fangs extended. "Those are what will get you." Tucker said. He looked at Muller, "You want this?" He asked, referring to the snake.

"No thank you." She answered, sounding a lot calmer then she felt.

Tucker threw the snake into the soft sand along side the trail. It wiggled and was gone into the sand.

"It was still alive." Muller said when she saw it move.

"It was just the nerves. If it had been alive I would never have picked it up." Tucker said looking at Muller. He marveled again at what a good looking woman she was. The pale blue eyes, slight smattering of freckles high on her cheeks, almost hidden under the sun tanned skin.

Her horse was calm now and Hansen let go of the main, he removed the ropes from around the neck and he gently slapped the neck as a sign of affection and took the reins and led the horse back to Muller.

"He'll be alright now, but I don't want you to ride him just yet. Let him walk for an hour or so. You will have to ride double with somebody." He finished.

"You can ride with me, Sweetie pie." Tucker volunteered. He was still standing next to her.

"Can I ride with you, Charlie?" She asked Farmer. She knew Farmer, of all of them was only here for the money. She knew he felt no emotion, so he would not be trying anything.

"No problem.' Farmer answered.

Minutes later they were underway again, Hansen again at the point and Tucker covering the back door. Farmer, with Muller sitting behind him was in front of Wilson. Muller's mules were reattached to her horse and the four animals trailed Farmer's horse along with Farmer's three mules.

"You should have ridden with Ace, he is much more entertaining." Farmer said after they were under way.

"Charlie, the last time I rode double with a guy like Ace, he ended up sticking his dick in me for a year then took off with another woman and I don't need that." She answered bluntly.

"Ace would like it." Farmer said, Muller could not see the smile, but she knew it was there.

"Ace is one of those guys that would stick his dick in a rock pile if he thought there was a snake in there he could have sex with." Muller answered and Farmer laughed. It was the first time Muller had heard him laugh. "You sound good when you laugh, Charlie. You should do it more often."

"I suppose." Farmer stated flatly.

CHAPTER 29

The woman, four men, horses, and mules moved on along the sand covered trail. The toughest thing was staying awake. Muller kept nodding off and finding her head against Farmer's back when she woke up. It was not a feather bed, but she had slept in more uncomfortable positions. She had her arms wrapped around Farmers waist, her fingers interlocked so they would not come apart. She looked and saw Hansen just going over another small rise in the trail. She looked behind her and saw Wilson twenty feet behind the last of her mules. Tucker was just coming around a turn in the trail, a hundred yards behind Wilson. Hansen had stopped and was waiting for the others to catch up. It was late in the afternoon of the second day since leaving the monastery. Muller figured there were maybe two hours of daylight left, definitely not more then three. Then she saw why Hansen had stopped. There was nowhere else to go. A vertical wall maybe one hundred feet high was a quarter of a mile in front of Hansen. They had reached the end of the canyon.

The four riders moved to a line abreast, the trail was that wide now. They sat on their horses looking at the wall marking the end of the trail.

"It's up to you now, Sweetie Pie." Tucker said, looking at Muller. She looked to the right and then to the left. There were very few caves on either side of the walls, which were not more then one hundred feet on either side of the trail. She closed her eyes and tried to remember the map. The memory was vague at best. The picture in her minds eye seemed to indicate the cave was on the right side, but God, she was not sure.

"I think it is one of the caves on the right side." Muller knew she sounded just as unsure of herself as she felt.

"What the hell." Wilson said. "We came this far, I'm willing to walk into a couple of those caves for a pile of money."

That seemed to break the ice. They dismounted and Wilson looked at the canyon wall with what seemed to be five caves in the side.

"The map didn't show which cave it was?" Hansen questioned Muller.

"It was pretty general, no certain cave." She answered.

Wilson reached into his saddle bag and removed a second pistol, checked to make sure it was loaded and stuck it into the back of his gun belt. Hansen removed a torch from one of his pack mules and lit it.

"I think we should tie a rope around Harry's waist just in case there is a soft spot in the sand." Hansen said handing Wilson the torch.

They tied the rope around Wilson's waist and he walked towards the nearest cave.

Wilson peered into the cave and stuck the torch in as far as he could before he took the first step into the darkness. He moved the torch to his left hand and removed the pistol from the back of his gun belt. He was going to shoot anything that moved. The rope tied around his waist dragged as he moved forward. Twenty feet into the cave and it ended, just a blank stone wall. He turned and walked back out into the bright sunlight. He shrugged his shoulders and yelled, "Nothing!" He walked to the next cave and he did not even have to enter it. He saw the back wall by just sticking the torch into the mouth of the cave. He climbed up the twenty feet of wall to reach the next cave and he again looked inside. No wall so he entered and started slowly moving forward. He never saw the sidewinder rattlesnake lying on the floor next to the side wall of the cave. It struck as he stepped next to it. He was lucky. It struck just below the top of his left boot. The snake's fangs were not long enough to penetrate both his pants and his boot. The snake died of a gunshot wound to the head an instant later. Wilson extended the torch as far forward as he could and saw the snakes. There must have been hundreds of them. They were slithering all over each other and some of them were moving toward him. He turned and walked out of the cave, climbed down the wall, and walked across the hard packed sand to where the others stood.

"That last cave was full of snakes and one of then bit me." He said, looking down at the spot where the snake had struck. The pants and boot were spotted with blood.

"Sit down and get that boot off." Hansen ordered. Wilson did as he was told as Muller knelt down to look at his leg.

"I don't see anything that looks like a bite. No marks or anything." She said, standing back up.

"I didn't feel anything, but I figured I'd better check before I go back."

"You ain't going back in there?" Asked Farmer.

"Not that one, but there are still two left and I want to look into them."

"Well, wait a minute." Farmer said and walked to his horse. He unbuckled one of his stuffed saddle bags and removed a pair of chaps. He tossed them to Wilson and said, "Wear these. They will sort of give you a little protection above your boots. Wilson untied the rope and put on the chaps and then retied the rope.

"Three down and two to go. I'm off." Wilson said as he headed for the fourth cave.

One hour later he was back standing on the trail. He gave Farmer back the chaps and answered the questions about what was in the caves, which was nothing but some old wood.

"Go and get the wood and we'll build a fire and look in the other caves tomorrow. It's getting too dark now." Hansen said.

Wilson walked back to one of the caves and as he was entering the cave Tucker was heard to mumble to himself, "That boy has more balls then brains."

CHAPTER 30

Muller could see the torch still burning in the mouth of the cave Farmer had just emerged from. It was an hour after sunrise. He calmly walked up to her and looked up at her sitting in the saddle.

"I have some bad news for you, Alice." He said. Hansen, Tucker, and Wilson listened, but Farmer was talking only to Muller. "There are no gold bars in there and there is no gold dust in there." He said looking at her, he waited.

"Damn!" She said, more to herself then to anyone else. Hansen shook his head. Tucker said, "Well at least we have a place to stay tonight." Wilson threw the torch he was holding, he could feel one of his temper fits coming on.

"I did fine a couple of these, though." Farmer said, and he reached in his pocket and pulled out a gold coin and tossed it to Muller. She caught it even though she had a hard time seeing through the tears that had started in her eyes. Farmer reached back in his pocket and pulled out some more and tossed one to Hansen, then one to Tucker. Wilson was starting to swear and curse, "Harry, get your head in the game, pay attention!" Tucker yelled at the young man standing next to him. Wilson looked up at Tucker and he nodded toward Farmer who threw a coin to Wilson.

"How many, Charlie?" Hansen asked.

"I honestly don't know." Farmer answered looking at Hansen.

"Is there enough for the bags we got?" Tucker asked.

"Nobody goes in there until I tell you this." Farmer said, and Tucker stopped in the middle of dismounting from his horse. Wilson stopped as he was walking toward the path to the cave. "These coins are in a big pile in the cave. Unless I miss my guess you would need a whole wagon train to haul it all out." He paused, "Alice, I think you should be the first one in. And you ain't gonna believe what you see."

Muller dismounted and followed Farmer as he walked along the path to the mouth of the cave. Hansen, Tucker, and Wilson followed her. The three hundred feet was covered in no time. The only thing that stopped them from running was Farmer. Wilson had retrieved his torch and he kept goosing Tucker walking in front of him saying, "Hurry up Ace, hurry up." Tucker stopped half way to the cave entrance and turned to Wilson who had just goosed him again, and said, "If you touch me with that again I am going to shove it so far up your ass I'll be able to light the end that comes out your mouth." Tucker turned around and Wilson immediately goosed him again and said, "Hurry up Ace, hurry up." And the two men burst into a fit of laughter, as they kept walking.

They gathered around the mouth of the cave and Farmer turned and addressed them all, "Just don't go nuts when you see this." He turned and pulled the torch from the pile of rocks he had stuck it in and reached over and touched the torch Wilson was carrying. The two torches flared and then Farmer pulled his back and handed it to Muller. She took it with a shaking hand and Farmer said in a quiet, soft voice, "Lead the way, Ma'am."

Muller walked maybe twenty feet into the cave, the heat was stifling, and turned right. As she turned the light from the torch reflected off the pile of gold coins and lit up the entire area of the cave. Muller almost dropped the torch when she saw the pile. She was five feet five and the pile was at least two feet taller then her. The cave at this point was about ten feet wide. The pile was wall to wall, and almost to the roof of the cave. She walked the ten feet to the edge of the pile and stopped. She could not believe what she was seeing. She said nothing, just stared at the pile.

Hansen stepped next to Muller, looking at the gold. "I don't believe this." He muttered.

Tucker was the next man and he reached down and picked up a couple of gold coins. "Ace, you now have life by the balls."

Harry Wilson stepped up to the pile and looked in awe at it. He, like Muller, said nothing.

The five people stood in front of the pile for what seemed like hours, but was no longer then thirty seconds, each thinking their own thoughts. Then Tucker broke the silence, "Alice, I love you and I need your hip flask beautiful." Muller laughed and reached under her jacket and pulled out the flask and handed it to Tucker. He took it and raised it to the pile of gold. "To you, gold pile, and to the five people who are going to carry you out of here." he turned and said to the other four, "Everybody takes a belt to the gold pile." He pulled the cork and took a swig, he handed it to Wilson who took a drink and handed it to Muller who took a drink and handed it to Farmer who passed it to Hansen who took a drink and handed it back to Farmer and said, "Charlie, I know you don't drink, but this is a once in a lifetime thing. Now you can either take a drink or we can pour one down your throat while holding you down. Take your choice.' Hansen was smiling and Farmer looked at him and took a pull on the flask. The other four cheered and then let loose. Farmer took the torch from Muller who jumped into the gold pile. Hansen sat in it. Tucker picked up a handful and put it in his shirt pocket. Wilson climbed to the top and slide back down. He turned and looked at Farmer and said, "Charlie this pile goes back for as far as I can see."

CHAPTER 31

"Listen Ace, how do we know when the sack is too heavy for the mule?" Wilson asked Tucker as he staggered under the weight of the canvas bag containing the gold. Tucker, being bigger and stronger, was having no problem carrying his sack.

"Good question, Harry." Tucker answered as they approached Hansen and Muller waiting at the trail with the horses and mules. When they reached Hansen and Muller Wilson dropped his bag, grateful to be out from under the weigh of the loaded bag.

"That bag heavy, Harry?" Hansen asked Wilson, smiling.

"You know Al the kid just asked a good question." Tucker said.

"What's that?" Hansen asked in return. He opened the bag Wilson had been carrying and looked inside, he smiled when he saw all the gold coins inside.

"He asked me how much weight can the mules carry." Tucker said.

"Oh, I don't know, maybe two hundred, two hundred and fifty pounds each." Hansen answered, reaching into the bag and taking out some of the coins and looking at them, then dropping them back into the bag.

"How do we know when we have two hundred and fifty pounds?" Wilson asked Hansen. Hansen looked up from the bag, a surprised look on his face. "I mean we could have a hundred pounds on one mule and five hundred on the next." Wilson finished.

"I'll take the one with the five hundred." Muller said.

"He wouldn't last but a couple of hours under that load in this heat." Hansen said, anger edging his voice. He was angry because he had not thought of this problem and being the leader he was supposed to think of everything.

There was silence for a minute, then Tucker cleared his throat. The other three looked at him. "I may have a solution." He said, looking at Muller, eyeing her up and down, then just staring at her.

"What are you looking at, you..." Muller was at a loss for words. She took a deep breath and continued. "You sex fiend, you." She smiled to take all offense out of what she just called Tucker.

"You're right gorgeous, I am, but that is beside the point." Tucker answered, He turned to Wilson, "Harry, you remember those big wood beams we saw near the front of the cave?" Wilson nodded. "All three of them?"

Wilson looked at Tucker in disbelief, "You expect me to carry three of those, hell I couldn't even carry one."

"You stay here Harry," Hansen said, he looked at Tucker, "You and me will get them, Ace." And saying that he started walking toward the cave.

Tucker started to follow and stopped. "Wait." He said, "I almost forgot the water bag for Charlie."

Wilson walked to the nearest mule and removed a full water bag and tossed it to Tucker. Tucker caught the bag and turned and followed Hansen toward the cave.

Wilson watched the two men walking toward the cave entrance. "So how does it feel to be rich, Alice?" Wilson asked her. She was standing behind him so he turned around and looked at her. She was looking at one of the gold coins.

"A person is not rich until they are in a place or town where they can spend it." She looked around, "And this don't look like a big city to me."

"What are you going to do with your money when you get to the big city?" Wilson asked her.

Muller gave out with a short laugh, "I really don't know Harry." She answered. "I really did not think about it. I was afraid there would be no gold and you four guys would just leave me here because you were pissed off that there was no gold." She paused, "Or you would shoot me or sell me to some slave trader or something."

Wilson laughed.

"What's so funny?" She asked, puzzled.

"You sure do look at yourself different then I do." Wilson answered. "I'm not sure about Ace, but me, Al, or Charlie wouldn't let nothing happen to you. Why do you think Al sent you behind the rocks in that canyon when he got shot in the hand."

"There were two bandits back there." Muller countered, her voice rising. Her anger was aroused by this young kid.

"Nobody knew that. Had we known do you really think Charlie would have waited until you told him to go and make sure they were dead. Do you think we would have laughed at you when you said you killed two of them. Alice you have to get a better opinion of yourself. The four of us like you. We look at you like you are our sister." Wilson finished. Then thought for a second and added, "Even Ace with all his crap about him loving you and getting married and that stuff."

Muller did not know what to say, she was flabbergasted. She heard what Wilson had said, but it did not sink in. It could not, she would not let it. She had been bouncing form one saloon to another for twenty years, being manhandled by any guy that had enough money. "Harry, I have been working whore houses and saloons for twenty years, I started almost before you were born. You do that for twenty years and you sort of lose some self respect, if you had any to start with." Muller looked at her feet, ashamed of what she just admitted, yet knowing it was the truth.

"People can change, Alice. You take this gold and go somewhere where people don't know you and you start again and you force yourself to have some self respect and other people will show you the same respect. You go some place and buy a small spread and find yourself a nice guy, you get married, have a couple of babies and live happily ever after. You just tell the guy what you did before when you get to know him and if he really loves you he'll let it go. You're a real handsome woman Alice Muller and you have a sense of humor, and you are rich, you'll make out just fine." Wilson finished, he was looking directly at her.

Muller could not believe what she had been told, about respect and being liked because she was what she was and not just some drunken whore. She was overwhelmed with emotion. She did not know what else to do so she stepped up to Wilson and hugged him. She started to cry, she felt Wilson wrap his arms around her waist and hold her.

"Jesus Harry!" Tucker yelled, "I leave for five minutes and you put your move on my woman, what the hell do you call this?"

Wilson stepped away from Muller. She turned away and wiped her eyes on her sleeve, she did not need Hansen and Tucker seeing that she was crying. She was suddenly afraid that there would be trouble between Tucker and Wilson so she turned around. She heard all three men laugh as she turned. She saw Tucker carrying a wooden beam and a canvas bag, Hansen had a wooden beam that was twice as thick as the one Tucker carried.

"Don't worry about it Harry, she told me she wants to run away with me. She's wanted to run away with me since she first laid eyes on me, me being so handsome and all." The three men laughed again and this time Muller joined in. Wilson was right, she thought, these guys are like brothers to me.

"Alright this is what we do." Tucker said, "Al, put those two beams across the trail on that flat spot like that." Tucker motioned with his hand so the two beams that were nailed together laid on flat ground. Hansen did as he was told. He laid them flat on the ground,

"No. No. Stand them on edge." Tucker ordered moving his hands this way and that. Hansen again did as he was told. Tucker reached into the canvas bag and removed a big rock. He placed it against one corner of the double beam Hansen had just laid on the ground. He removed three more rocks and placed one at each corner of the beam. Then he stood back and looked. "Good job, Ace." He muttered to himself as the double beam stood by itself. He then placed his beam across the double beam and he had a crude seesaw. Once again he stood back and looked at it. Then he turned and looked at Muller. She looked back. Tucker smiled, a slow almost wicked looking smile, "Are you ready, my secret lover?" He asked.

"What are you talking about?" Muller asked.

"How much do you weight?" He asked, no longer smiling.

"What do you care?" she said, now being defensive.

Tucker turned to Hansen, "What do you think, Al, about one twenty, maybe one twenty-five."

Hansen shrugged, "Probably." He answered.

Tucker turned again to Muller and smiled that wicked smile. "Alright, I'm finally going to get to use that cute little ass of yours."

"What is with you, Ace?" Muller asked, a touch of anger in her voice.

"You weight maybe one twenty-five. You sit on one end of the board and we put a sack of gold on the other end. When the gold balances you, and you are both level, we have a one hundred and twenty-five pound bag of gold. Two bags to a mule and we have a two hundred and fifty pound load for a mule."

Muller smiled and went and sat on one end of the beam. Tucker placed one of the bags he and Wilson had brought from the mine. He sort of dropped it and Muller's end of the board shot up in the air with Muller on it.

"Ooooh!" she yelled, "Take it easy when you put the bag on there Ace. I don't mind being goosed every once in a while, but not by something like this beam."

"Listen, sweet thing, anytime you need goosing, you just call old Ace Tucker. I am the champion gooser of the world, bar none." Tucker said as he emptied some of the gold coins out of the bag. Slowly Muller's end of the board started to come down, when it got even with the bag of gold coins Tucker said, "Hold on my lover." and removed the bag. Muller was ready and she had her feet down so her end of the board would not fall to the ground.

"Who wants the first one hundred and twenty-five pounds of gold?" Tucker asked. He looked at the other three, then Hansen spoke up.

"I think it should go to Alice, after all she got the map."

"Absolutely." Agreed Wilson.

"You get the first sack, Alice." Tucker said, looking at her he sounded serious, then he smiled, "Of course you realize that the person who gets the first sack has to buy the first round of beers for the rest of us."

"Who dreamed that one up?" she asked looking at the other three, she smiled and added, "Besides I don't know if I have enough money." The four laughed again.

CHAPTER
32

"We have to do something." Wilson said as he looked back along the trail. The war party of about fifteen Indians was still there, still about a half mile behind them. They had left the cave with the gold coins and on the second day back had seen the Indians. This was the morning of the third day. They were only a few hours from the monastery. Everyone knew that sooner or later the Indians would make their move.

"I think I know what we should do." Hansen said as he stopped his horse. "Charlie." He yelled at Farmer who had the point again. Farmer turned and Hansen waved him back. Farmer trotted his horse back and they formed a circle the horses and riders looking inward.

"We leave a rear guard at that point in the trail where there is that blind turn, me and somebody else." Hansen said looking at everyone.

"You can't stay Al, your hand still isn't any good. Whoever stays is going to have to use rifles and you can't with your hand." Tucker said as a matter of fact.

"I'll stay." Wilson volunteered.

Tucker looked at Farmer, "Charlie?" He questioned.

"Harry said he'd stay." Farmer answered, the voice cold, unemotional.

"I need somebody who is not afraid to use the rifle and kill people. I don't know about Harry. And besides this is not a suicide stand. We probably only have to shoot a couple of the Indians and

the rest will back off. Then we catch up with Alice, Al, and Harry."
Tucker said.

"Ace, you have too much faith in me." Wilson said, the hurt in
his voice could not be disguised.

"I'm sorry Harry, but you just can't murder people and that is
what is going to happen here." Tucker said. He turned to Farmer,
"What do you say, Charlie?"

Farmer shrugged his narrow shoulders, "I guess." He answered,
without enthusiasm, then added, "I never have liked these rear guard
actions. They just never seem to work out and the rear guard gets
killed."

"I've got it worked out in my head, Charlie. Neither of us is
going to get killed. You know, the rich guys never get killed." Tucker
finished, he smiled knowing full well whoever stayed behind was in
serious danger.

"Alright," Farmer agreed, "I'll stay Ace. We'll see if we can't
discourage these Indians from following us." He paused, then added,
"But no last ditch stands, I ain't willing to die for six bags of gold."

What Farmer said struck home on the other four people sitting
on their horses. It was almost like a physical blow to both Wilson and
Muller. Hansen shook his head wondering how a man like Farmer
could think of such a thing and then speak it out loud. Nobody ever
did that, it was like bad luck or a curse or something. It was then
that Hansen thought about what Candy Carter had told him about
a curse. Tucker just closed his eyes.

"Alright let's move." Hansen said as he looked at everyone else.

Farmer turned his horse and galloped up to the point again.
Hansen was next, then Muller, then Tucker. Wilson simply sat and
waited for the others to move along the trail far enough, then he
would start. He turned and in the distance he could see the war party
slowly following. They must have stopped when they saw us stop, he
thought. I wonder why they are keeping their distance. I wonder why
Ace didn't trust me to stay with him. I killed one of the Mexicans and
the guy who shot Tony. I can kill people. Well, let Ace and Farmer
stay, maybe Farmer will get killed and Ace will feel guilty about it.

I could kill the Indians, they ain't nothing anyway. Wilson knew he was fast, he knew he could beat Hansen, and Muller didn't count, he was not sure of Tucker. He talked a good game and was always willing to talk about how fast he was, "I'll bet I could take him." Wilson said out loud to himself referring to Farmer.

He looked and saw the others were far enough ahead and started to walk his horse. He turned and looked back at the Indians, the distance was the same, still maybe half a mile.

ucker was lying under the outcrop of rock that was the corner of the turn. When they had gotten to the outcrop of rock in the turn he and Farmer had simply tied their horses to some brush fifty feet further up the trail, taken their rifles and walked back to the blind corner in the trail.

He was firing his pistol, his rifle leaning against the rock wall next to him. Farmer saw at least one Indian fall. Farmer fired his Winchester at a spot in the canyon wall where he thought he saw a puff of smoke from a rifle. He levered another round into the rifle. There were rifle and pistol shots, a lot of them. The bullets were ricocheting off the rock walls of the canyon. Farmer leaned out and fired another round at another spot in the wall. Several shots were returned, it was then he heard Tucker scream.

"Ace, you hit?" Farmer yelled in Tucker's direction.

"God Charlie, I'm belly shot!" Tucker yelled back.

"I'm coming over Ace, make some room." Farmer yelled back.

"No Charlie, they will just get you too." Tucker replied.

Farmer pushed two more shells into his Winchester and squatted. Then he took off running. He had fifty feet to go and he covered the first ten before a shot was fired. The bullet hit the sand near his feet, then another, but he was half way there. He felt a bullet whiz past his head and he had only ten feet to go. He dove the last five feet as two or three more bullets hit the rock around where he and Tucker lay.

"You're crazy Charlie get the hell out of here." Tucker said the pain in his voice obvious.

"Let me see." Farmer said. Tucker rolled over a little and groaned with pain. His left hand covered his shirt in the center of his stomach. The shirt was bloody and so was Tucker's left hand.

"I ain't going to make it, Charlie. I'm richer then almost anybody in the world and now I'm going to die. Ain't that a kicker." Tucker smiled, then immediately grimaced with pain.

"What do you want me to do, Ace?" Farmer asked, he felt foolish because he should have known what to do. In order to cover how he felt, Farmer fired two shots down the canyon and was answered by several return shots.

Tucker looked at Farmer and grinned again. This time there was no pain in the grin. "You take my stuff and yours and get out of here. I can last another hour or so, I hope. That will give you a good head start. These guys will never catch you. I may even get a couple before I go."

"I don't want to leave you Ace." Farmer said, his voice almost a plea.

"I'm going to die here Charlie. You try and move me and the bullet will tear me apart inside. Besides those Indians will get you before you get twenty feet carrying my fat ass." Tucker laughed at his self criticism, then cried out in pain. "So you go. Tell Alice we could have had a great time in the sack." He paused, then finished, "Tell her I love her and give her my share of the gold. Now go." Tucker turned and fired four shots down the canyon. Farmer noticed Tucker suddenly stiffen, then he seemed to relax. The pistol slipped from his hand. His mouth hung slack, his open eyes had that blank stare Farmer had seen so many times.

Farmer shook his head and he took off running along the side of the canyon. He ran up a small slope and saw the two horses tied to the rock where he and Tucker had left them. As he ran he heard pistol and rifle shots from behind him. He untied the horses and took the reins of Tucker's horse in his left hand and mounted his horse. The bullets hit the sandy floor of the canyon between the horses hoofs and Farmer let go of Tucker's horse so he could stay mounted on his as the horse bolted toward the end of the canyon. In seconds Farmer was out of the canyon and his horse was traveling at a full gallop across the open plain where the canyon had ended.

CHAPTER
34

In the sand, and the heat, and the burning sun, Farmer pushed his horse to the very limit of exhaustion. He pushed it for two long grueling hours across the flat sandy plain. He entered the next canyon and stopped around the first turn. He dismounted and pulled the rifle from the scabbard. He tied his horse to a rock outcrop and walked back to the turn in the canyon. He looked at the plain he had just ridden across and saw only the heat waves rising from the ground. The heat waves distorted his view of the trail he had just traveled. He shrugged his slim shoulders and waited. He knew he should unsaddle his horse, but he did not know if there were any bandits or Indians around here. He wanted to be able to move fast if he had to.

He waited an hour, then mounted and moved on. Through the canyon and out onto another plain, across that plain and started into another canyon. He kept a watchful eye, but saw nobody or nothing. He looked for tracks, but saw none of those either. Maybe, he thought, Hansen, Muller, and Wilson took off with all fifteen mules and the gold and he would end up with nothing. If he did not find them by the time he got to the monastery, he would hunt them down, each one of them, and kill them. He passed through that canyon and started across the next plain. He saw miles upon miles of nothing but sand and the shale rock. Farmer believed in God and he wondered for a second how God could make such a barren place. But he also saw how awesome it was, the might of the mountains and the peacefulness of the plains. He smiled as he thought, maybe

God does know what he is doing. He entered the third canyon still thinking about the awesomeness of God, daydreaming, he was tired. He turned to his left as he saw a movement and his pistol was in his hand. Hansen held up both his hands to show they were empty.

"I just wanted to make sure it was you, Charlie." He said with a smile.

Farmer put his pistol in his holster and dismounted. "I was just starting to think I was going to have to hunt you down." Farmer said.

"No Charlie, I run an honest show." Hansen answered. Muller stepped out from behind another rock and Wilson jumped down from the wall.

"Where's Ace?" Muller asked.

Farmer shook his head and answered, "Ace ain't coming. He got belly shot and I had to leave him. He was bleeding bad and he knew he was not going to make it." The voice was cold, emotionless, again the voice of the dead.

"Damn!" Muller said as her voice cracked.

"He told me to tell you, you two would have been great in the sack together and that he loved you." Farmer said.

Muller turned away and walked into the clef in the rocks where she had been hiding. She did not get in far enough and the three men could see her shake as she cried. Hansen waited a minute and then walked to her and started talking to her. She turned and buried her face in his huge shoulder and continued to cry. Wilson and Farmer simply stood rooted to the spot where they were. They waited and in another minute Muller stopped crying.

She turned to Farmer and asked, "Did you see him die, Charlie?"

"Yes, he was bleeding real bad and then he just stopped moving and was dead. The Indians must have gotten past him just after I left him because they were shooting at me when I ran." He answered, looking down at the ground. He knew what it sounded like, like he had left Tucker to die, but he knew Tucker was already dead.

The three people looked at Farmer. All had the same expression on their faces, had the Indians really killed Tucker or had this cold blooded killer done it and blamed it on the Indians.

CHAPTER
35

Wilson sat on the rock and looked out over the flat sand that stretched as far as he could see. Somebody said twenty miles. There were mountains in the distance, but they were so far away they could be in Texas as far as he was concerned. They had returned to the monastery that afternoon, tired, and hungry. Muller had given Tuckers six bags of gold to Carter to be divided evenly between the women. The women, in turn, had decided to use it to pay for whatever was needed to keep the monestary running. He looked at Farmer climbing up the rock and moved over to make room for him to sit. It must be time to change the watch. Wilson thought about Farmer. He was a strange one. Cold, he kept to himself and never had much to say. He could get angry as he did about the monastery, but that was not too bad. Mad was what Wilson got sometimes. Yelling, screaming, swearing, throwing things. His mind would just go black, not blank, but he saw black in his minds eye, he had no thoughts as he raged, just this big black thing as he raged on. He hoped he did not have one during this little trip. Afterwards he would always be ashamed of how he had acted and got depressed. He had talked to a doctor about it once and the doctor had told him to go see some other kind of doctor, some kind of doctor who dealt in how your brain works or something like that. Someone had told him he needed a woman to seduce him when he went crazy and that would calm him down. Someone else told him a couple of shots of booze would do the trick. He simply continued to get angry sometimes.

Farmer climbed up and sat down next to Wilson.

"Is it time to change watch?" Wilson asked.

"I don't think so. I don't know." Farmer said, "I couldn't sleep so I figured I'd come up here and help you watch the sand."

"Well, it's still there, nobody stole it." Wilson answered pointing out toward the vast desert in front of them.

Farmer took his hat off and scratched his head. The curly red hair would have been sticking out all over if it had been longer.

"How old are you, Charlie?" Wilson asked Farmer.

Farmer did not look at him when he answered. "Thirty, I think."

"I'll tell you, I'm pretty impressed the way you handle yourself." Wilson said, and he was impressed. He could not believe Farmer was only eight years older then himself.

"You just have to practice all the time. I ride fences a lot on these big ranches and they are always looking for guy to do out riding. It don't pay much, but you get a lot of time to yourself and you can practice all you want. There ain't nobody pushing you to go faster or work harder. Most of the time you ain't got to do nothing but ride along the fence and make sure it ain't broke. It's easy. You don't make a lot of money, but then most of the time you don't make enough money anyway so what the hell." Farmer shrugged.

"Where you from?" Wilson asked.

"Out east." Farmer answered vaguely. "You?" The question followed.

"Kansan City."

"Let me tell you something, Harry." Farmer looked at Wilson, who returned his look, "Never tell anybody where you're from. Someday they may need to get to you for something and they will go after your family to get to you."

Wilson nodded his head in understanding. He would remember the piece of advice.

They sat for the better part of an hour. They said very little, just sat looking out over the softly, ever blowing sand.

"I'm gonna take a walk around, make sure nobody is sleeping." Farmer said as he stood up.

CHAPTER 36

arol Landing was taller then any of the other women even though she was the youngest and when she walked through the tunnel leading to the other side of the pass through the canyon she had to duck her head. She skirted past the water and started up the other side knowing by walking uphill she was more then halfway to where she wanted to go. She held the food in her right hand and the torch in her left. It did not take her long to get through the tunnel and she was in a big cave with many tunnels leading away in all directions. She put the torch in one of the holders and turned to her right and walked confidently down one of the many passage ways. She walked no more then fifty feet and she saw Wilson sitting there looking at her. He put the pistol back in the holster and turned back to looking out into the darkness.

"I brought you something to eat." She said her voice shaking because she was nervous.

"Jezz, thanks,." Wilson answered reaching for the plate Landing was carrying.

She handed it to him and asked, "Do you have anything to drink?"

"No, but this is okay, I can always get some water later." He said his mouth full of food. He was pushing it in as fast as he could swallow. Landing could not help herself and she started to laugh.

He looked at her with a questioning look, his mouth still full. She had red hair and freckles around her cheek bones and she was real skinny.

"We have more food and I will get some more for you if you want it and I promise I will not take that away from you." She said, still trying, but failing, not to laugh.

"What's so funny?" Wilson asked, still pushing the food into his mouth. Then he stopped and realized what she was laughing at. He swallowed what was in his mouth and felt himself turning red with embarrassment, he was glad it was pretty dark in the cave where they sat over looking the canyon entrance.

"I did not mean to laugh at you, it is just that you eat so fast." She said.

"The last job I was on we were out in New Mexico for a month chasing a guy. We hardly slept and seemed to ride all the time. When we stopped to eat it was light the fire, cook something and we were off again." He answered her.

"You must have slept sometime?" She asked.

"In the saddle. The lawman I was with believed in pushing as hard and as fast as the horses would go, and he did just that. We finally caught the guy and I had been working for Tony for a month when Al came and told me about the gold and how he wanted to come after it. I took a bath, threw the saddle back on my horse and here I am." Wilson finished.

"Who was the bad guy?" Landing asked.

"He is a guy named Joey Small. He is small too. He is only about five feet tall, but he is as mean as a snake." Was his answer.

Wilson finished what was on the plate and looked at Landing. "Now I could use something to drink." He said and started to stand up.

"No. No. No. Stay here I have something." And saying that she handed him a bottle. Wilson looked at the bottle and then looked at Landing.

"I thought maybe you would want something a little stronger then water. So I brought you that." She said pointing at the bottle in Wilson's hand.

He pulled the cork and sniffed the open bottle, "This smells pretty strong."

"I thought maybe we could share it. It's been a while since I had something to drink."

Wilson took a drink and handed the bottle to Landing and she took a mouthful.

"I shouldn't be drinking this when I am supposed to be on watch." He said, feeling the licquor burn down his throat and into his stomach.

"Nobodies coming and I want to get drunk tonight with you. I really like you a lot Harry." Landing said as she unbuttoned her blouse.

CHAPTER 37

Al Hansen sat looking out over the canyon they had just came from early this morning. It was dark now and he could not see that well. He listened and heard something. Someone was climbing up the monastery wall. He sat where the fort part had connected to the wall. He was below and opposite where Wilson was standing watch in the cave. Farmer was on the gate tower at the front wall. He pulled the pistol from his holster and waited. The person climbing made no effort to cover the sound of their climbing. He waited and then Carter's head cleared the edge of the top of the tower. She did not see Hansen put the pistol back into his holster. She finished climbing up and sat down next to him. She had a plate of food and a canteen.

"Supper time." she said handing him the plate.

"I guess I should lie and tell you I'm not hungry, but I am not going to." He answered. "Have you eaten?" He asked her.

"Some." She answered.

He picked up a piece of meat and handed it to her. She leaned forward and took it in her mouth. She bit off half the piece and then pushed his hand to his mouth and he ate the rest. She took a piece of meat off the plate and reached to put it in Hansen's mouth. This is wrong he told himself as he leaned forward and took the meat. Her fingers were inside his mouth and she hooked her one finger behind his lower teeth and pulled him toward her. He started to lean and then stopped.

"You remember the last time you and I talked and you asked me what I was talking about to myself." He asked.

She simply nodded her head while licking the same fingers she had just taken out of Hansen's mouth.

"I was telling myself I cannot get involved with you while I'm on this job." He said. "After I'm done I will come back if you want me to." He finished.

He was watching her watching him. She put the plate down and removed the two fingers from her mouth and reinserted them into Hansen's mouth.

"Damn." Hansen murmured as he leaned forward and kissed Candy Carter. She pulled him after her as she laid down. He was leaning across her.

"Please Al, just lay on top of me. I need you bad, so bad I hurt." She said.

"Damn." Hansen said again as he did what she asked.

He watched as his men checked their weapons. All had pistols and most had rifles. The pistols as well as the rifles were the repeating type. The pistols were single action, the rifles lever action Winchesters or Henry's. The men pulled their pistols from their holsters and pulled the hammers back part way, opened the cover and spun the cylinder to make sure it was full. Some men only carried the pistol with five rounds in it, keeping the hammer on an empty chamber to make sure if the pistol was dropped it did not fire by accident. These men put a sixth round in the empty chamber. Tonight there would be no accidents, but there would be killing, deliberate and vicious killing, of both men and women.

He watched as the men checked their rifles making sure the magazines were full. He watched as they pushed the lever part way forward and made certain there was a round in the firing chamber and yet not letting the hammer cock. The hammer cocking would come later, just before attacking the monastery and the killing inside.

He continued to watch as the men replaced the pistols in the holsters and the rifles in the scabbards attached to the saddles on the horses. They were as ready now as they would ever be. It was dark and the monastery looked to be unguarded. It is time to go, thought Walt Preston.

Ramiero Gomez looked at the monastery. It was huge and the walls were high and thick. I sure hope this guy Preston knows what he's doing, he thought. Gomez was the second in command of this gang that had been assembled by Walt Preston. There were maybe thirty five men altogether. Most were simple outlaws, men who helped rob a train or a bank, none of them leaders. Leaders were hard to find because leaders were the first ones the law went after. You get the leader, you break up the gang, at least for a while. There was little or no law down here. The Mexican Federal Troops could not cover the huge amount of territory they were supposed to control. They also had to deal with all the politicians who were corrupt. Gomez smiled at the thought of the politicians. They were the biggest crooks of all. They demanded the bandits pay them so they would keep their mouths shut, then they demanded the federals pay them to tell where the bandits were. In the mean time they were stealing everything they could from the treasury. Mexico would be better off shooting the politicians the Federal Troops caught stealing or taking bribes.

Gomez heard his name called and he turned around to see Walt Preston walking up beside him. Preston had told him the story of how he had gotten this map from an old miner, Preston said he paid for it, but Gomez was willing to bet he killed the miner to get it. Preston did not pay for anything he could get by killing for it. Preston was about the same size as Gomez, close to six feet tall. He was maybe twenty pounds heavier and ten years older. Gomez doubted if he was any smarter.

Preston raised the binoculars and looked at the monastery again. He was sure the woman was in there, the one who stole his map and his four hundred dollars. He was going to kill Alice Muller for stealing the map. He did not know how much gold they had taken from the cave, but he would split it evenly between himself and the bandits. Then Muller would die a slow, painful death. He did not know how he was going to kill her yet, but she was going to die.

"They can't have more then four or five guys in there," Preston told Gomez, referring to the men Muller had hired.

"Don't forget the women, they will have guns also." Gomez added.

"Those women don't know how to fight. They'll run away screaming at the first gunshot." Preston answered, his tone of voice conveyed that he was very sure of himself. Gomez was not that sure, but he did not argue with Preston, he just made up his mind that he would be careful of the women when they got inside the monastery.

"It's dark so we can go any time." Preston said.

"How do you plan on getting in?" Gomez questioned.

"I think we will go in at two places. That low spot where the wall is crumbling, maybe somebody breached it a long time ago, and I think by where the building meets the wall where you start to go down into the canyon." Preston answered. First he pointed to the place in the wall Farmer had entered and then he pointed to the entrance to the canyon where the caves were on one side and the monastery wall was on the other.

"If someone is in the caves and someone is on the walls we will be seen long before we can get near the walls." Gomez stated flatly.

Preston thought about it for a minute. "Yea, you're right, they will be guarding the low spot. Do you think you can take a couple of men and get into the caves and find the lookout and get rid of him, or her, and then you can cover the men going over the wall."

"I think I have a solution to your problem." Said Gomez. "I think I have a man who knows the caves and he can lead four or five men into the caves, find the lookout, take him out and then cover the wall."

"Now keep in mind the most men we have to take care of is four or five." Preston commented. "We get over the wall and bang, we're in. The women, all but one, you and your men can have."

"And the gold." Said Gomez.

"The gold gets divided up evenly between those of us left alive." Preston paused, "Make no mistake about it Ramiero, some of our men are going to die. Those are professional gunmen in there and there is a terrific amount of money at stake. They are going to fight to the death. It's not going to be easy going in there." He finished.

"You know those women are protected by the Indians?" it was a statement put in the form of a question by Gomez to Preston.

Preston looked at Gomez, a questioning look on his face.

"That monastery is considered an evil place by the local Indians. They will not go in there. The women give them water, they deliver it to the gate, and in turn the Indians protect the women." Gomez finished looking at Preston.

Preston was surprised by the fact of the Indians, but he did his best not to let it show on his face. He paused, thinking. "Yes, yes, I forgot about them."

He is lying, he never knew about the Indians, Gomez thought

"This is what we will do. We will take care of the people in the monastery and then you can take your gold and I will take Muller and we can go our separate ways. It will be every man for himself." Preston finished.

"I'll get Juan and he can tell us about the caves." Gomez said, walking away. He wandered through the men until he saw Juan. They spoke briefly before he returned to Preston with Juan following him.

"Preston, this is Juan Rivera." Gomez introduced the two men. They shook hands.

"Ramiero tells me you know the caves." Preston asked, it was more a statement then a question.

Gomez translated as Rivera looked at him questioningly. He nodded and said something to Gomez, a big smile spreading across his face. "He says he can find his way around the cave system with his eyes closed, says he spent years playing in the caves as a boy."

"Good, he can spend a couple more minutes making sure there ain't nobody in there looking for us." Preston said.

"He says to go into the caves and make sure there is nobody in there looking for us." Gomez said to Rivera.

"The Gringo doesn't understand us?" Rivera asked Gomez.

"I don't think so. Maybe a couple of words here and there, but he can't talk to us." Gomez answered, then added, "Why?"

"The men don't trust him. They think he will take all the gold and kill whoever is left of us."

"I don't think so." Gomez answered. "He is after the women who made him look like a fool. He is so full of hate for her he can't see anything else." Gomez paused, "Now go and look in the caves."

Gomez watched Rivera pick three men and he started toward the caves.

"We'll have to send two or three men to silence the guard at the low part of the wall. We have to be in position to move into the monastery when the guards are silenced and if one of the guards sounds an alarm we have to move then. We don't want to give them a chance to get ready." Preston finished.

"I'll take a man and get the guard at the low spot in the wall." Gomez said. He did not like the idea, but he knew the first man in got more gold. "Then you can follow me in with the rest of the men."

"Pick ten men to go over the wall opposite the caves. Let them go in first and we will sneak in the back door, so to speak." Preston told Gomez.

That is not the way I would do it, thought Gomez, but I will just make sure I cover my ass so I get my share of the gold and at least one of the woman.

Gomez picked ten men to scale the wall when the cave was secured. Then the remaining men followed him and Preston.

CHAPTER 39

Carol Landing felt Wilson's hand caress her stomach and it started to move lower until it touched the dungarees she was wearing, both her and Wilson's shirts were lying on the floor of the cave. She was breathing heavily through her open mouth, "Harry we have to take our clothes off, we can't do anything..." She never finished what she was going to say because Wilson's hand clamped over her mouth. He raised himself up off her and put his fore finger to his lips as a sign for quiet. He started to get to his feet when the first bandit stepped around the corner of the cave and leveled his pistol at them. He was followed by a second man, then a third and fourth. The men looked at Wilson then at the half naked girl lying on the floor of the cave. Wilson saw the men look at Landing and he finished standing upright. He had put his holster with his pistol on the ledge of the cave and he was only three feet from it. All he needed was one more diversion, one more second of the bandits looking away and he would make a grab for his gun.

"Watch him." Rivera ordered the men as he looked at the half naked girl lying in front of him. He holstered his pistol and knelt down next to the girl. She is so beautiful, he thought as he reached for her. Landing screamed and that was all the time Wilson needed, that was the diversion. The other three men looked at Rivera and the girl. Wilson reached for the pistol in the holster. His right thumb flicked off the hammer holder as the last three fingers of his right hand wrapped around the handle of the pistol. He pulled and the pistol started to come free of the holster his thumb pulled the hammer all the way back and his right fore finger sliding across the trigger. The bandits were only ten feet away and for a crack shot like Wilson it was easy shooting. The first bullet he fired hit the second bandit who had entered the cave in the center of the chest, the second bullet hit the fourth man only because he was directly behind the second man, slightly to his left. That bullet too struck the man in the chest. The third bullet hit the third man who had come into the cave, this shot hit the man in the in the forehead. The forth shot hit the first man kneeling next to Landing in his right shoulder as he tried to draw his pistol. It shattered his shoulder as he screamed in pain. The scream was cut short when Wilson's fifth bullet him in the forehead. He fell backward and missed Landing by inches. It had happened so fast that Landing had not even had a chance to scream a second time.

Wilson held the pistol vertical and open the cylinder cover and emptied the five spent cartridges. He replaced them with five more and closed the cylinder cover.

"The bandits are here, we have to help cover the wall. Get your shirt on." He ordered Landing as he grabbed the rifle from where it was leaning against the wall. He stood up and pushed the lever far enough forward to make sure there was a round in the firing chamber, he cocked it.

Landing heard the gunshot and saw Wilson arch his back, she saw the blood squirt out from the upper center of his bare back. She saw Wilson sink to his knees and then fall face first onto the floor of the cave, next to one of the bandits he had killed. She knew he was dead even as she moved next to him. She gently rolled him over, his eyes were shut and he had an ever so slight smile on his face. Landing pulled him to her naked breasts and held him against her. She would go on holding him to her until someone came and separated them.

CHAPTER 40

Hansen heard the shots fired by Wilson across the canyon and was on his feet almost faster then Carter could follow, the pistol flashing out of his holster, the first bandits head clearing the top of the wall a second later. The bandit looked up at Hansen and a look of total surprise crossed his face just before Hansen shot him dead. The second bandit died a second later, then the third and fourth. The rest jumped or fell off the wall into the darkness below.

"Climb down the inside of the wall and get your women together, get your guns and kill anybody you don't know." Hansen told her.

"You be careful." Carter said as she started to move down the wall.

"You too." Hansen answered.

Carter stopped to look at Hansen one last time. Her eyes were even with his feet and as she looked at him he looked like a giant, a huge indestructible giant.

"Go, will you." He said looking back at those dark blue eyes. The eyes he was almost lost in. So near and yet so far, he thought as Carters head sank beneath the top of the monastery wall. He turned and gingerly looked over the edge of the wall and shot another bandit as he was climbing the wall. Several shots rang out from below, but they were wild and Hansen knew the bandits would not attempt to climb the wall again for a few minutes and in that few minutes he would reload his pistol and then wait. He laid down knowing that if the bandits had tried to enter the monastery here they would also try somewhere else, probably the low spot where Farmer had entered. He looked over the courtyard and knew he could cover anything this side of the fire. He saw the women running around below and hoped they remembered what Tucker had taught them.

CHAPTER 41

Muller had her rifle and had shot two bandits, she was aiming at a third, waiting for him to move into the open again. She was inside the last room of the barracks, the room furthest away from the low spot in the wall. She waited knowing the bandit would show himself in a second. She saw the movement to her left and watched as the man moved into the open not more then twenty feet away. She looked in disbelief, it was the guy she had stolen the map from. He was sober now, but that was him, not a doubt in her mind. He was looking for her, or the person doing the shooting from here, but she knew he could not see her, she had been careful not to let the end of her rifle barrel extend past the edge of the window, or what once was a window, the glass and wooden frame long gone. He may have seen a couple of muzzle flashes, but the windows were too close together and there were too many of them for him to be certain which one the firing was coming from.

The walls separating the barracks rooms had long since been knocked down so Muller moved to her left, the Winchester cocked, her finger on the trigger. She walked in the inky blackness of the rubble carefully taking each step. She moved past where Preston was and stopped as he approached the barracks. He moved slowly, the pistol extended. He walked to one of the windows and stuck his pistol and head in at the same time.

Preston looked to his left, nothing but darkness, then to his right. He blinked because not two inches away from his face was the rifle held by Muller, of all the luck. This was the woman who had stolen the map. His pistol was pointed straight ahead, but he knew she would never pull the trigger on the rifle, women did not do that. He would take her and abuse her and then sell her to some sex slave gang.

"You should have never come after me." He heard her say. Then she pulled the trigger.

CHAPTER 42

Farmer watched as the bandits approached the shattered section of the wall. He had the shotgun in his left hand and the Winchester in his right. He was going to kill a lot of men tonight and he felt nothing. He just plan did not gave a damn. It was just something to do to keep the gold they had gotten. Farmer guessed there were at least ten or twelve men approaching the wall. He may not kill all of them, but he would get most. This is exactly what Farmer had been trained for in the army after they found out what was wrong with him. It was also why Hansen had picked Farmer for the job.

He waited, lying on his stomach, his right thumb pulled back the hammer of the rifle, his finger resting on the trigger guard. He could hear the men approaching the wall, they did not seem to care they were making so much noise. Then he realized that most other people would be watching across the monastery at the shooting going on. He stayed still as he saw the head of a bandit rise slowly over the far edge of the gate tower not ten feet in front of him. The guy was good, he moved slowly. Farmer could hardly follow his movements. He was a half seen blur in the darkness. Farmer let go of the shotgun and moved his left hand slowly across in front of his until it was next to the forward grip of the rifle He move the rifle slowly as more and more of the mans head appeared over the edge of the wall. He could feel the rifle was pointed at the bandits head. The mans eyes appeared over the top of the wall and Farmer pulled the trigger of the rifle.

The man simply disappeared off the edge of the wall, the back of his skull blown out over the soft sand at the bottom of the guard tower.

Farmer reached back for the shot gun and cocked it as he grabbed it. He rolled to his left to the edge of the tower and looked over the side. He had reacted so fast after shooting the first bandit that the men moving across the shattered rubble of the wall below had no time to look or take any sort of action. Farmer pointed the little deadly weapon and holding it with both hands pulled both triggers at once. The men below were just starting to look up. They had not had time to move their guns toward the top of the guard tower. The eight gauge double oh buckshot killed four of them instantly, the buckshot hitting them in their upturned faces. Two more went screaming into the desert holding their faces as they staggered away. Farmer swiveled into a sitting position whipping the Winchester into a firing position against his right shoulder. Each of the next twelve shots fired from the Winchester model 1873 either killed another bandit or critically wounded him so badly he was helpless. Like shooting fish in a barrel, he thought. He reloaded the shotgun, then the rifle.

Farmer waited, knowing there were more bandits, how many he did not know, nor did he know where they were. He could hear the scattered gunfire from below and behind him. He saw someone run to the base of the tower from inside the courtyard and knew it must be one of the women. He crawled to the front of the tower and carefully peeked over the edge. Two men stood below at the base. Farmer pulled the pistol from his holster and shot both men. He knew that he had to get off the tower. The bandits could pin him down up here and sooner or later one of them would get a clear shot at him. He grabbed the rifle and the shotgun and climbed down the outside of the tower wall. He looked around and saw that the men he had shot were lying around, some still, some moaning and holding their wounds. None were in any condition to offer resistance. He turned left at the base of the tower and entered the monastery the way he had the first time across the shattered remains of the wall where long ago another battle had been fought.

CHAPTER
43

Carter had run to the base of the guard tower to make sure that the bandits could not get to the chain that opened the big doors. If they opened the doors however many were waiting would have an easy time getting into the monastery. She looked around as she reached the base of the tower, she stepped over the pile of rubble and made sure she was the first person inside the tower. She turned left and walked to the edge of the tower and saw the Bandit, but it was too late. He was already aiming his rifle at her. There was no way for her to get out of the way. She saw the rifle fire and at the same instant something pushed against her right shoulder with such force she staggered to her left two steps, all but falling on the rock strewn ground. At first she thought she had been shot by the bandit, but then she turned as she took the second step and heard the deafening roar of the sawed off shotgun held by Farmer. She looked and saw the bandit crumble. The same man who was going to shoot her.

"Move! Move! Move!" yelled Farmer as he pushed her again. This time she lost her balance and fell to the ground on her left side. She looked up in time to see Farmer turn to his right and fire the shotgun again, this time the bandit took the full force of the blast and he was physically moved backward about five feet before he fell to the ground dead. He was moved backwards, but not before he got a shot off that ricocheted off the stone wall just above Carter's head. She closed her eyes as the stone chips flew everywhere. Farmer had leaned down to help her up and she thought, how could it have missed him, and yet the killer simply grabbed Carter's arm and hauled her to her feet. It was black where they stood, next to the pillar which held the gate. She could only see the vague outline of the back of Farmer's head. Here is my chance to kill him for killing Cheryl, she thought as she moved her hand to the pistol in her belt. The pistol was wet, but that was not possible, it must have been sweat on the palm of her hand. She wiped her hand on the front of her shirt and that also felt wet. She did not understand. The two waited in silence that seemed to drag on, but lasted for no longer then a minute.

"I'm going up to the top of the gate tower, right above your head. Give it a couple of minutes more and if you don't hear any shots take a look. I think this is about over." He said quietly and walked out of the darkness cast by being inside the tower and turned toward the desert. In a second, he was gone. Carter waited when suddenly she heard a shot, a pistol shot, then another, followed by several more, then the silence, the silence only the dead make.

Alice Muller stood outside the end of the barracks opposite where Carter was in the deep shadows of the guard tower. She saw Farmer's silhouette as he fired the shots into any of the still living bandits. Maybe when he was shot in the war it did not kill him outside, but it sure as hell killed him inside, she thought as she watched him climb the tower.

CHAPTER 44

C arter waited for what seemed like an hour, but knew it was only minutes, before she looked out of her hiding place. Three of the girls and Hansen were standing by the fire and so she figured it was safe to come out. The women were talking and pointing excitedly to different places around the monastery. She approached the fire and when she was only about ten feet away one of the women named Linda Joyce turned and saw her. Carter saw her put her hand to her mouth to stifle a scream. In seconds a group had gathered and was looking straight at Carter. Hansen started to move towards her when the doctor cut in front of him at a dead run.

Thomas ran to Carter and looked at her and asked in a calm, quiet voice, "Where are you hit."

Carter shook her head and said, "I'm not hit, why?" it was then that she looked down and saw the blood on the front of her shirt, then the butt of the pistol stuck in her belt, her dungarees, but she felt nothing. No pain, no burning. She did not feel faint, nothing.

"You're covered in blood, you must be hit." The doctor said to her, looking closely at her.

"I'm not." She answered.

"What happened?" Asked one of the women, the one named Joyce.

"I thought I was going to get shot when Farmer pushed me out of the way." Carter stopped and then continued more slowly. "He pushed me again when a second bandit shot. It hit the rock right next to Farmer, but he seemed fine."

"Was he bleeding?" The Doctor asked.

"I couldn't see. It was dark." Carter realized that if it was not her blood, it had to be Farmer's and he must be hit pretty bad to bleed so much.

"Where is he?" The Doctor asked.

"He is on the top of the gate tower." Carter said as the Doctor started to run toward the gate. "The tower on the left." Carter yelled after the running Doctor.

"Come over here and let me clean you up. You're a mess." Joyce said, pulling Carter closer to the fire by her arm.

CHAPTER 45

Mary Thomas ran across the court yard carrying her black doctors bag and across the rock strewn rubble at the base of the gate tower. She ignored the dead bandits. She climbed up the crumbling wall and then turned and climbed up the gate tower after looking up and seeing Farmer sitting on the top. She climbed to the top, the top of the tower must have been ten feet square, plenty of room for two people.

"Turn around and face the fire." She told the gunman.

"Why?" He questioned.

"So I can see where you are shot." She said in her no nonsense doctor's voice.

"It's not bad.' He said.

"Now you listen to me. Candy is down there all covered in blood and it is not hers, so it must be yours. So do what I say and turn around." She ordered as she pulled on the sleeve of his shirt to turn him. Thomas did not know what she would do if the man refused, but he did not. He turned around and she saw the damage. He held out his left arm and she saw the torn skin where the bullet had just grazed it, grazed it enough to make it bleed a lot. But it was his face that looked horrible. It was almost entirely masked in blood from the hairline to the chin, down his throat and onto his shirt front. The blood was smeared where Farmer had tried to wipe it off his face.

"Just sit there while I look at you." She looked at his forehead first and then at his arm. His forehead had been sliced open to the bone by something. "What did this?" she asked looking closer, she was within inches of Farmers face and she shook her head. 'I am going to have to sow this up and that is going to hurt and I am sorry." She said, searching her bag.

"Just stop it from bleeding, it's getting in my eyes." He said. She could smell the coffee on his breath when he talked to her, she was that close to his face.

Thirty minutes later she was finished. Both his forehead and his arm were stitched up and she finished wiping the remainder of the blood from his face. She had opened his shirt and using the water from his canteen wiped the blood from his chest, then she had rebuttoned the blood stained shirt.

"There you are, almost like new." She said smiling at him as she wiped the last spot of blood from his chin.

"It couldn't have been too bad, I don't feel nothing, no pain I mean." He said looking at her. She was as plain as dust, but there was something about her that Farmer could not put his finger on. She had straight blonde hair and a straight thin nose and pointed chin. She was thin as were all the woman, but she was smaller, shorter in stature, not much more then five feet. Her hands, Farmer noticed, were tiny and yet she handled the instruments deftly. Never dropped one, never mislaid one. Farmer came to the conclusion that she was very good at what she did.

"You will in a couple of hours when the shock wears off. You are going to have a head ache that will make a hangover seem like an itch." She smiled at him. The smile was warm and seemed so innocent, the teeth perfectly white. "You should go and lay down, you lost a lot of blood." She finished.

"I can just sit here." He answered her. It was a statement of fact and Thomas knew he was not going to lay down.

"I suppose." She said. She made no move to go and sat down next to him, so they sat there, each thinking their own thoughts. The silence dragged on for almost a fifteen minutes then Farmer asked her, "So how come you're here with these beat up women?"

"Oh, I'm sorry, I was gathering wool so to speak." The Doctor found herself blushing. She was glad it was dark so the man sitting next to her could not see the blush in her cheeks as she looked at him.

"I asked how come you're here with these beat up woman?" Farmer asked again, not knowing why he wished to know.

There was silence and Farmer thought maybe she had not heard him again. He was about to say something when she spoke.

"You know Mr. Farmer," She said shifting her position to face him. There was not more then a foot between them. They both sat crossed legged, their forearms resting on their knees.

"Please, call me Charlie." He told her quietly. She ignored his interruption.

"Every night the girls sit around and talk and tell what happened to them. Never once have I told anyone what happened to me." Thomas said, having no idea why she was saying what she was saying to this cold blooded killer. She sat with her back to the desert and he was facing it, always watching except when he looked at her and when he did look at her she felt it disarming her. Like there was nothing she wanted to hide from this man. The moment for her was intimate and she liked it very much, it had been a long time. "I came down here about six months ago. I had been practicing medicine in a little town just north of the Texas Mexican border. One day a gang of bandits rode in and destroyed the town. Killed the men, beat and raped the women. The bandits found out I was a doctor and they left me alone. I was the only woman not beaten and raped in that town. They made me fix their wounded." She paused, "Then they beat and raped me. I don't even know how many hurt me. After the beating I was only semiconscious. Then they just tore off whatever clothes I had left on me and took turns. I finally passed out. When I woke up I was naked in the middle of the street. Someone had covered me with a blanket. I think my insides are ruined. I mean my womanly parts. Once I stopped bleeding from the rape I have never bled again. You know, every month like I am supposed to." She fell silent, not believing she had just said what she did to a man she did not know. She smiled, a sardonic smile, "And the answer is no, I am not pregnant." She added.

Again there was silence and the two sat looking past each other, Thomas into the inside of the monastery, Farmer out over the desert.

"Do you know who the gang leader was?" Asked Farmer.

Thomas looked at him, directly into his cold green eyes. "If I did Charlie, would you kill him?"

"I could go look for him when I get back to Texas and when I find him I will if you want me to." He said.

He was holding his shotgun in his right hand, so she took his left hand in hers and looked at the back side of it, holding it up close to her face. The hand was bruised from smashing into the wall during the gunfight, she wondered for an instant how it got that way, and it was dirty, but she kissed it anyway. What are you doing? She screamed at herself, but said, "I think there has been enough killing, Charlie. I took an oath as a doctor to save lives. I pray to my God everyday and he tells me to forgive those who hurt me." She was crying now, the tears falling free down the cheeks of her face and onto the back of Farmer's hand. "I try not to hate them, Charlie, but I can't help myself. I pray for them and I pray for me and I still hate them." She cried on the back of his dirty bruised hand for a long time. All the pent up, unspoken emotion spilling out onto the bruised and dirty hand. Farmer quietly laid the shotgun down and gently touched the top of her head. She was leaning forward and resting her forehead on her hands, her elbows on her knees. She held onto Farmers hand as if her life depended on it. She squeezed it until her hands hurt with fatigue and still she continued to squeeze it anyway. How ironic was it that the only thing that kept her from going crazy that night, reliving that horrible experience, was holding the hand of a cold blooded killer who felt nothing.

homas cried long and hard. She finally stopped. She felt Farmers hand resting gently on her head. She looked up, into his face hoping to see something, Some sort of emotion, but his face was in shadow.

"What about you, Charlie? How did you get to be what you are?" the Doctors tone of voice conveyed an earnestness Farmer had never heard before.

"Oh, I don't know." He answered, avoiding both her eyes and the subject.

"Sure you do. Come on. It's a good night for letting your hair down, so to speak."

There was something in the Doctors voice that struck a cord deep inside Farmer. It suddenly dawned on him there was something about this woman that stirred deep inside him, something that had not stirred since he had been shot.

"Me and my friend were in a shell hole that was half full of ice cold water, other men had pissed in and shit in. And we were laying in it. Nice huh?" He finished with a question. Thomas said nothing, she simply watched the face in the shadow. But there was no missing the emotion in the tone of voice. "We were laying there trying to get some rest. We heard some noise and we stood up. Then somebody shot both of us in the head. Andy was dead right away. The doctors worked on me. When I got better I realized I didn't really care about anything. A Doctor told me that maybe someday I would get back some form of emotion, maybe feel something, love or hate or something. All the years since I was shot I have felt nothing." He finished and fell silent. He looked at the woman holding his hand, She was asleep.

He shook his head slowly, removed his hand from the top of her head, leaned over and gently kissed where his hand had been. After all those years the heartless killer, known to the Indians as "Charlie no soul" felt something for someone. He wondered why this woman, why not Muller with the great looks and great body? Why not one of the other woman? He shook his head again, Picked up the shotgun and went back to looking at the desert. The woman is like the desert, he thought, so plain and yet so beautiful.

CHAPTER 47

onnet walked back to the fire where the others stood or sat.

"So where is she?" Carter asked her, referring to the doctor.

"I should have never listened, but she told Farmer everything about what happened to her. When I walked away she was crying her eyes out. I mean really crying and I think he was holding her. You know trying to comfort her." Bonnet said. "He even offered to find the men that hurt her and kill them."

Muller shook her head and just laughed.

"I don't think it is funny." Joyce said, the anger edging her voice.

"No. No. Don't miss understand me. I think Charlie hates," She stopped at a loss for words, "I don't know. When we were coming down here from Texas one night and I got pretty drunk and I hit on Charlie and he told me he felt nothing and I called myself a whore. He grabbed my shirt and slammed me against the rock we were sitting on. He told me to never ever call myself that again. I have never seen him as angry as that. Even when you push him, Candy, he doesn't get as angry as he was that night. I just don't know." Muller finished, shaking her head.

The silence that lasted for almost a minute was broken by Hansen. 'Well ladies I was going to relieve Charlie from his watch, but I don't think I will do that now. I think I will just go and stand watch somewhere else. And I think you ladies should stay away from that gate tower too." He stood up and added," Maybe we should leave

Harry and Carol alone too." And he walked off in the opposite direction of the gate tower.

"Maybe I should check on Carol." Said Joyce.

"No. If something was wrong, Carol or Harry would have yelled." Said Carter

The women sat silently each gazing into the fire, each with their own thoughts. After several minutes it was Carter who broke the silence. "Do you think Charlie understands what we have been through?" She asked no one and everyone.

"I don't know if he understands," Muller said, "I just think that for some reason he has a very deep respect for women. And he expects them to have that same respect for themselves."

CHAPTER 48

When Thomas woke up it was dawn. At first she did not know where she was. She sat up and realized she had been asleep, her head on Farmer's lap, her cheek had been resting on the back of his hand. She was covered by his black heavy duster. She was still holding his hand in both of hers. She looked at him and he was smiling.

"Feel better?" He asked.

Thomas nodded and smiled back at him. "Have I been holding your hand all this time?"

Farmer nodded.

"It must be numb" she said.

"Yea, for the last couple of hours." He answered.

"I'm sorry." She said, the sorrow in her voice genuine.

"Anytime." He said, smiling. "Just don't think you can cut it off and take it with you."

She looked down at his dirty and bruised hand still holding it gently in both of hers, then she looked up at him and asked, "If I let go will you let me use it whenever I need it."

He smiled down at her, "Whenever."

She raised his hand to her lips and gently kissed it and then almost afraid to, she released it. "Thank you for your coat, but most of all thank you for your hand." She said getting to her feet and picking up her bag. She hesitated for only a second and then leaned down and kissed Farmer passionately on the lips. She picked up her black bag. straightened up, turned and climbed down the gate tower, turned into the courtyard and walked to where the fire was and poured herself a cup of coffee.

"Damn." She said to herself out loud, even though the other women sitting there could hear her, "I could fall in love with that guy right now." Thomas turned and walked away carrying the coffee, wondering if maybe she had not already done so.

CHAPTER 49

I t was well after dawn when Hansen climbed down from the top of the east wall of the monastery. He walked across the courtyard to where three of the women sat around the fire. Carter stood up at his approach and he extended the empty coffee cup and smiled. She filled the cup and smiled back.

"I think we better check on everyone and make sure they are alright." Hansen said to Carter. "I'm guessing the bandits are gone and I hope they won't be back."

"Farmer is on top of the gate tower and some of the women are scattered around the walls." Carter said.

"Let's get everybody together and see what we are going to do." Hansen said, then added in a whisper, "And they don't need to know about us last night."

In less then five minutes they were all gathered around the fire. Farmer with his bandaged head, Wanda Jennings had been shot in the left shoulder and her arm was in a sling. Trudy Anderson had been shot in the right thigh, but the bullet had only grazed her so she just walked slow and with a limp favoring the leg.

"Everybody here?" Asked Hansen as he looked over the group and knew immediately that Wilson and Landing were missing. At the same time Carter realized the same thing.

"Harry!" Hansen yelled in the direction of the cave where Wilson was.

"Carol!" Yelled Carter in the same direction, "Come here we're having a meeting." The men and women waited, but no sound or movement came from the opposite side of the canyon.

Hansen looked at Farmer and both men took off at a dead run for the monastery wall where the tunnel was leading to the cave. As he ran Hansen pulled the pistol from his holster, he knew Farmer had the shotgun and he knew it would be ready when they got to the cave. They went through the entrance to the tunnel and Hansen slowed to a cautious walk. He had no way of knowing if there were any bandits left alive in this labyrinth of tunnels and caves. He knew the women were following him and he also knew they should have left some guards, but right now he was only interested in Harry Wilson. He passed the spring where the water supply was and walked on for another hundred yards or so. He passed several caves and then turned right and right again and looked into the cave where Wilson was supposed to be standing watch. In a flash he took it all in, the four dead bandits and Landing holding Wilson in her arms, slowly rocking him back and forth.

Hansen said nothing, he just walked up to Landing who looked up at him her tear stained face saying everything there was to say. Farmer stopped and Carter, none to gently pushed past him and knelt next to Landing.

"It's ok, Baby." Carter said wrapping her arm around Landings shoulder.

Landing looked up as the Doctor moved in next, "Please Mary, make Harry be all better." The body was already turning blue from the blood congealing.

Farmer looked at the half naked woman holding the half naked man. "What the hell were you two doing?" he demanded, his voice loud, almost a yell.

"Shut your mouth Farmer." Hansen answered back in a tone of voice that left no doubt that he meant to enforce his wishes on the killer.

Farmer looked at Hansen, then at the girl, then he turned away and left the cave.

It took all of ten minutes for Carter and Thomas to pry the half naked girl and the dead man apart. When they did Carter and Thomas helped Landing stand up and as Carter did so she saw someone holding out a blanket to cover Landing with. When she reached for the blanket she touched the hand holding just as she looked to see who was extending the blanket. She saw it was Farmer. She said "Thank you." automatically, not even thinking about it. For the first time since the night he killed her friend, there was no hatred in her voice or her eyes. She took the blanket and wrapped it around Landings shoulders. Blue Bonnet stepped in front of the Doctor and helped Carter walk Landing out of the cave. Just before they made the turn to exit the cave, Landing turned and looked at Wilson, then at the Doctor and said, crying, "You won't be able to fix him, will you Doctor." It was a statement, not really a question. Landing did not wait for an answer, she simply turned away and left the cave with Carter on one side and Bonnet on the other.

Hansen and Farmer looked at each other for a minute, "I guess we better bury him." Hansen said, "We'll take him outside the walls somewhere and bury him." He finished and leaned over and picked up Wilson from under his arms and placed him over his left shoulder. He did it with little or no effort as he followed Farmer out of the cave.

An hour later it was done. Harry Wilson was buried next to the two women Farmer had shot dead. Blue Bonnet had made Carol Landing smile a few times, mostly by talking about how she and Harry could have fleeced everyone out of their money by shooting bottoms out of beer bottles.

homas walked in the front door of the monastery and was startled by Farmer standing there. The bright sunlight had blinded her to anyone standing just inside the door. She blinked several times trying to accustom her eyes to the relative darkness inside the building. She was holding her bag in her left hand and she felt Farmer take her right hand with his left and begin pulling her away from the doorway. He was squeezing it tightly and she felt the grip tighten as she resisted.

"Charlie..." She almost screamed, still trying to pull away.

"Listen to me!" He said turning to face her, interrupting what she was going to say.

"Let go of my hand." She commanded, her tone of voice a mixture of fear and anger, mostly fear. For a second she remembered the little town in Texas. Farmer let go and raised both his hands in a sign of surrender.

"I... I didn't mean to scare you. I'm sorry." He stammered the apology.

She looked up into the face and saw the hurt in the eyes that were not supposed to feel anything. She waited a few seconds and then slipped her hand back in his. "You have to promise not to hurt me." She whispered, looking into the green eyes. They were cold again, the bottomless pit.

"Come with me." He said, his voice a virtual command, yet his hand was barely grasping hers. She followed him across the big dinning room. They walked between the tables covered in dust. As far as Thomas knew the dinning room had not been used since the monks had left. When Farmer stopped and started laughing, not loud, but hard, a genuine happy laugh.

He turned and she could see him plainly now. There was a question in the eyes, the crinkles spreading out from the corners because of the smile. God he was handsome in the half shadow, half sunlight of the room. "I don't want to appear stupid, or anything, but were you hinting we should..." He was at a loss for words.

Let's see if Charlie has a sense of humor, she thought, "We should what?"

"You know." He was nervous and off balance.

"Know what?" She pushed the question, smiling.

"Do it." Again the nervous voice.

"Do what?" She could not help herself and she started to laugh. She raised his hand to her lips and kissed it gently and held it against her right cheek. She looked back into is eyes and saw they were hard and emotionless, the killer eyes. "I'm sorry, I just could not help teasing you."

He smiled and said, "I owe you one." And they both laughed. "I have to ask you this and it is very hard for me." He looked into her eyes and she knew in that instant she was in love with him. "I want you come with us."

"I can't Charlie. You know I can't leave these poor woman." She paused and added as an after thought. "Plus there may be more coming."

"If you come the others will likely follow you. I have enough gold to buy you and them a ranch so big you could build a house in the middle and no one would ever be able to find you." She realized he was pleading his case.

She shook her head, "I can't Charlie. Why don't you stay here?" knowing it was a foolish question.

"Some day I'd shoot Carter or she would shoot me." He said, knowing he had failed at his attempt to get Thomas to come with him.

She raised his hand to her lips again and kissed it. She noticed the bruise was gone and it was clean. She did not want to start crying, but she did not think she could stop it. She felt a tear leak out of the corner of her right eye and then the left eye. Then they came and she shook with the sobs. She felt his other hand under her chin and she did not want to look at him, yet he forced her head up. He was much stronger then she had thought. She looked into the green eyes and again she was looking into the eyes of the killer.

"I figure it will take me, Hansen, and Muller about three days to get home. A day to turn around and three days back." Her heart jumped at the thought of his return. "Then I'm taking you, whether you want to come or not. And you know I can do it." It was simply a statement of fact. She saw him smile, "Besides, my hand is getting water logged. And I like that."

She had been crying and now she started to laugh and she tried to do both and for a second it worked. Then she let go of his hand and wrapped her arms around his neck and kissed his cheek. She slid her left cheek up his left cheek feeling the stubble of his whiskers, and when she got next to his ear she whispered softly into it, "Don't say anything. Don't do anything. Just know that I love you. Now you go and take Alice and Al home and I will be waiting for you to come back and I will go with you wherever you want to go." She slid her cheek back down his, again the scratching of the whiskers, and kissed him on the lips as passionately as she did the morning she had slept on the gate house with him. Then she released her arms from around his neck, turned, picked up her bag and walked quickly out of the room. Farmer stood rooted to the spot, not knowing what he was feeling.

CHAPTER
51

armer had the point, Muller followed him leading the twelve pack mules. Al Hansen had the back door. They were spread out for maybe a half mile. Close enough together to act as a group if they were attacked. Far enough apart so a lone gunman could not get all three.

Hansen was thinking about Candy Carter again. She had told him she was a whore, it was that plan and simple. She had slept with four or five of the ranch hands and the neighbor, and Jack her husband, naturally, and possibly a lot of other guys she failed to mention.

"It doesn't make any difference, Candy, I feel inside me that you have changed, or maybe I am just doing some wishful thinking. Whichever, after we get back and split up the money I'm coming back down here and get you." The thought of seeing Candy Carter again made Hansen smile. He shook his head and was happy at the thought of buying some land and raising horses and living with Candy. She could have anything she wanted and they could travel and see the world. He could see her dark blue eyes looking at him, her smiling and nodding her head. Her sensual look when she wanted him.

The bullet slammed into Albert Hansen, it tore through the center of his heart. His last thought was about Candy Carter. He was dead before he fell from the saddle.

At the sound of the gunshot Muller turned and looked and saw Hansen still on his horse, but sitting awkwardly, then he fell from his saddle and Muller screamed. She released the mules and turned her horse and started to race back to where Hansen lay on the ground. She dismounted and knelt next to Hansen, cradling his head in her arms. Hansen's eyes were open and staring directly at her. She did not know how long she knelt there, probably not long, maybe a minute, but it was one of those situations where minutes seem like hours. She did not know what to do, he was dead and she knew she could not bring him back, but she could not let go either. So she knelt and held his head. She never heard Farmer ride up and dismount. She only knew he was there when he grabbed her by the collar of her shirt and started to drag her toward the side of the trail away from the river.

"Let him go, he's dead!" Farmer yelled and she did as she was told. Her shirt was being pulled up over her head and she pushed with her feet trying to keep up with Farmer pulling her. He was going to pull her shirt off and all she could think was she would be bare chested. Then the second shot rang out and Farmer let go of her as suddenly as he had grabbed her. She heard him hit the ground and she rolled over and saw him lying still.

"Charlie!" She yelled, as she tried to move to do something. What, she did not know, but something, do anything.

"Get to some cover by the wall." Farmer said. It was more of a groan then anything else.

"Oh God, you're alive." She said, as she scrambled toward the wall by the side of the trail. She heard Farmer fire a round from the rifle he was carrying and when she looked back he was on his feet running after her. He fired two more rounds as he ran after her. He was not looking at where he was firing, he was looking at where he was running, he was just putting up some covering fire, hoping to buy enough time to get behind some cover. The rifle barked again and Farmer went down again. She saw his left leg move in a funny direction and that is when he fell. He rolled to the wall and muttered. "Oh shit!"

She looked at him and for the first time since making the pass at him on the way down in the canyon, she was worried. If he dies I will never make it home. Gold or no gold, a woman alone in this country does not last long by herself. Farmer looked out around the edge of the rock and she hoped he was not going to get himself shot anymore. Another shot rang out and it was then that she watched him aim the Winchester and squeeze the trigger. He levered another round into the chamber and stood looking over the rock.

"Maybe you should get down." Muller said, questioning the safety of Farmer standing exposed like he was.

"He's dead." Farmer said in answer to her question. Muller stood up and looked back down the trail and saw the Indian lying in the dirt, face down.

"What do we do now?" She asked, looking at him for some leadership.

"We take his weapons and throw him into the gorge. We do the same thing with Al. We take his guns and horse and throw him into the gorge."

"We have to bury him." She said.

"Why, 'cause he's a white man. Let me tell you something." Farmer said turning to look at Muller, "this is solid rock around here and even if we did manage to dig a grave the animals would dig him up by tomorrow morning. At least in the gorge people won't see him being destroyed."

Muller did not have time to think about it because Farmer limped out from behind the rock and walked to where Hansen lay. He stood looking at him and she walked out and stood next to him.

"Take his gun belt and then we can throw him over." Farmer said, the voice cold and indifferent, "Ill go do the Indian." And he limped off still carrying the Winchester in his right hand.

Muller looked at Hansen and then looked away, God the blood, his shirt front was completely covered in it. I wonder if he was shot from the front and if he was there was only one person in front of him. "Oh Muller, you asshole." She said aloud to herself. She looked up and saw Farmer dragging the Indian toward the edge of the gorge. He was having a hard time because of his arm and leg. Maybe Candy should have shot you, she thought. She reached down and unbuckled Hansen's gun belt and pulled it out from under him. She removed the pistol from the light tan holster and looked at Farmer not more then fifty feet away, an easy shot for her. She cocked the pistol and then thought, if it was Farmer why didn't he shoot her too. Then he could have all the gold, and nobody would ever know. She un-cocked the pistol and slid it back into the holster. She would have to think more about this as they were traveling, but she would also have to keep a sharper eye on Farmer. She saw Farmer roll the Indian over the edge and into the gorge. She laid the holster on the ground and took hold of Hansen's boots and tried to pull, but the body would not move. She tried again and again the same thing, the body would not move. She looked up and Farmer was only feet away and she suddenly thought, kill me now you cold hearted bastard, don't drag it out, but what she said to Farmer was, "I can't move him."

He grabbed Hansen's shirt collar and pulled. The body started to slide and Farmer said to her as he pulled. "You have to put a little ass into it." He stopped and looked at her, "You ain't putting none into it right now." He finished and he started pulling again. Muller took Hansen right arm and pulled. Less then a minute later Albert Hansen lay at the bottom of the gorge.

"What a way to bury somebody you knew." She said.

"It don't make no difference to him. Not in his condition." Farmer answered. "Now if it's not too much trouble maybe you can look at my arm and leg."

Twenty minutes later they were on their way, heading north again. They had lost four mules, they had run off and when Muller had wanted to go looking for them Farmer had said no. He had told her that two thousand pounds of gold was plenty. So somewhere behind them were another thousand pounds of gold tied to the back of four mules. Somebody was going to be really rich when they found those mules.

CHAPTER 52

T he man and the woman traveled the rest of that day. They followed the trail along the edge of the gorge. They hardly spoke. Muller kept thinking of Hansen. The eyes staring at her. She slept some in the saddle while the horse walked. She would wake up with a start, thinking she heard a gunshot. Then she would see Farmer ahead of her, his four mules trailing behind him and his horse, walking slowly along the trail. They stopped that night, but Farmer did not light a fire. She ate cold beans from a can and liked them. Cold beans, water, and a couple of shots of booze. The two bullets had gone through Farmers arm and leg, so she had simply poured whiskey on the bullet holes and bandaged them to keep out as much sand as possible. The next morning they broke camp and an hour later they spotted the river. God help me, this is where the whole damn thing started, Muller thought, then she heard the gunshot.

"Go! Go! Get across the bridge!" Farmer yelled at her.

Farmer watched as Muller headed for the bridge. The water was so high sometimes it washed over some of the lower boards in the center of the bridge where it sagged closest to the water.

It must have rained up north for the river to be this high Farmer thought

The horse and four mules were going at a full gallop and Farmer watched, waiting for her to slow to a walk. She was close to the bridge now, too close Farmer realized, to slow down, she was going to cross the bridge at a full gallop. Shit, thought Farmer, the bridge will never hold if she goes across at a full gallop.

"Muller!" He yelled at the top of his voice. "No! Don't! Stop! No Muller."

Alice Muller was not going to lose her nerve this time. The bridge was awash in the middle, but she did not care. She was going to cross it and the only way to do it was to run. She felt the horse step on the first boards of the bridge and heard the hoofs clatter across the boards. She heard the mules start to cross. She felt the rope pull tight as the mules tried to slow down, but it did not work. They were going at a full gallop and she guessed they were too tired to put up a lot of resistance so they simply followed the horse. The first mule, along with the horse and Muller were on the bridge when the ropes holding the bottom could no longer take the strain of the water pushing against the boards and the weight of the horse, rider, and mule running across the boards. The rope to the north of the bridge snapped causing the rope to the south to take up the strain. The southern rope only held for seconds and then it too snapped dumping the bridge. Muller, horses, and mules into the river. The rope snapped at the far end, just where they were attached to the stakes. Muller never heard the rope snap, she just felt the bridge give out from under her. She fell from her horse and as she fell her forehead slammed into one on the beams of the bridge floor. She was knocked unconscious. The second mule in line had stopped so suddenly that the leather reins broke holding it to the first mule. It's front hoofs were on the first board of the bridge which was still over dry ground.

Farmer watched the bridge give way and reacted instantly. He turned his horse and started riding full gallop parallel with the river. He outraced the river and stopped at a narrow area where a ledge extended slightly out over the river. He dismounted as the horse was still trying to come to a complete stop. He untied his rope and ran the last ten feet to the end of the ledge. He could see her floating down the river, coming toward him, within easy reach of his lariat.

"Alice!" He yelled, "Muller, over here." He watched her turn her head and he saw the blood covering her face. She was holding onto one of the beams that made up the floor of the bridge. "Grab the rope." Farmer yelled and he saw her nod her head yes as she wiped her eyes to clear her vision. Farmer tossed the rope the twenty feet and it landed directly in front of Muller. She reached out with her right hand and grabbed the rope just above the whoop.

"Got you." Yelled Farmer, the success of her getting the rope out weighted any of the other failures of this trip. He saw the fear in her face evaporate into a smile as she held onto the rope. Farmer pulled.

The wooden beam was four inches square and four feet long. The end in front was jagged from being broken and it was traveling with the speed of the current of the river. Alice Muller was being pulled ashore by Farmer and she never saw the wooden beam coming. The beam slammed into the right side of her head, the jagged end penetrating her skull. She lost her grip on the rope and her shirt sleeve became entangled with nail sticking out of the beam. Her head went under the water and she tried to get loose of the beam, but could not figure out how to untangle herself from the nail in the wood. Something was wrong, because she could not figure out why she could not untangle herself. She had been holding her breath, but could do it no longer and she exhaled, then inhaled and got only water.

Farmer watched as the beam struck Muller and he felt her let go of the rope. She never came back up and he saw her arm hanging over the beam, the rest of her body under water. He stood on the ledge and watched her being carried down stream with the beam. He watched until she was out of sight, then he watched some more. He stood there for several minutes watching until he heard a noise behind him. He turned and saw the mule with the two sacks of gold climbing out of the river. Farmer calmly walked to where the mule stood, pulled his pistol and shot the mule dead. One shot directly in the head. He turned and looked down the river where the body of Alice Muller was being carried. Shook his head and walked back to his horse.

"Shit." Was all he said as he mounted his horse and went to get the other seven mules.

CHAPTER 53

Now he was alone. Most of his adult life he had spent alone. There were times when people had been around, but, he had still felt alone. Then he had met Andy in the army, they had become best friends almost immediately. Then Andy had been shot and killed that dark night, the same night Farmer had been shot in the head. For all these years Farmer had felt nothing. He had liked Muller and the others and now they were all dead, he thought to himself, Hansen, Tucker, and Wilson, all dead. Four people dead and all he had to show for it was one horse, seven mules, and sixteen bags of gold. And he still was not out of the woods, so to speak. He still had to cross the river somewhere north of here and there were the Indians and bandits, who could make short work of a single rider.

His leg hurt as he limped back to where his horse stood. His shoulder hurt also and he poured some more whiskey over his shoulder and leg when he reached his saddle bags. Thank God Muller had made him take four bottles from her endless supply in case they had gotten separated. Muller had said she thought the bullets had gone clean through, but she was not sure, but she thought so. When he got back to Texas he would go and see a doctor.

He gathered up the seven mules and Hansen's horse and lead then to the river. They would not go near the dead mule, they refused to move when they got within about twenty five feet, so Farmer had to drag the two one hundred and twenty five pounds bags of gold to the mules and horses. He somehow managed to get the two bags of gold onto Hansen's horse

He limped to his horse and put his left foot in the stirrup grabbed the saddle horn with his right hand. He pushed with his leg and pulled with his arm. The pain was excruciating in both his leg and shoulder. He moaned aloud as he finally managed to get into the saddle. He sat for a minute just waiting for the pain to subside some. He bent over the horses neck and grabbed the reins. He was sweating, but not because of the heat, but because of the pain. He spurred the horse and it started to walk. He followed the river, leading the mules and horse, looking, always looking for bandits, or Indians, or anything hostile and he knew anything he saw south of the Rio Grande River was hostile. He traveled for miles, never losing sight of the river to his right. Sometimes he had to go some distance inland, but he always made it back to the rivers edge.

It was just starting to get dark when he saw it. There was a sand bar stretching almost all the way across the river. He knew he had been traveling northwest and he knew also that the further he traveled in that direction the closer he came to outlaw country. The mountains would flatten out into a series of plains and there the bandits and Indians would wait. He turned the horse and mules toward the sand bar. He reached the edge of the water when the horse stopped. The mules started making noise. There has to be something wrong and then he saw it, or them rather, neither Indians nor bandits, worse for the horses and mules, he saw the water mocinsins. There must have been ten of them on the sand bar. Just lying there, waiting for some poor traveler like himself to happen by. The biggest moc was eight, maybe nine feet long. They could not eat a man or a horse or mule, but they could kill a man, or a horse, or a mule. He knew he could kill the ones on the sand bar, it was the last ten feet of water he had to wade through that would also have the snakes in it. He knew the shotgun or pistol would not work in the water and there was no chance Farmer was going to do battle with God only knew how many water mocicains using his knife. That might make good reading in the dime novels back east, but it was a losing game in reality. He knew if he tried at least one of the snakes would get him and he did not need a ponious snake bite to go along with his bullet wounds.

He turned the horse and headed northwest along the rivers edge. Now the snakes worried him. What happens if the horse steps into a nest of them. He turned left following the course of the river and as soon as he turned he saw the bridge. It was the same type of suspension bridge that had fallen apart under Muller. This one was still intact and at least thirty feet above the river. His shoulders slumped as he visibly relaxed in the saddle. Now if he could just across the bridge without any more problems he would be all set.

CHAPTER 54

Farmer looked at the bridge and thought, it looked so good from two hundred feet away. It was in just as bad shape as the one that had come apart under Muller, maybe worse. At least all the boards had been in place on the other bridge, this one had spaces, some of them a foot or two wide. He knew he had to cross this bridge. He was not sure how close he was to the end of the mountain range, to when it flattened out into the plains. He knew the mountains were the only thing keeping him alive. He also knew if he reached the plains and the Indians or bandits saw him they would not think anything of chasing him. He knew if he got caught, he was a dead man, he could not out run them, his horses and mules were about spent. So his only option was to cross the bridge.

He dismounted and again moaned in pain, it felt like someone was driving a knife into his leg and shoulder. He hoped the bullet had not hit a bone or that he was not getting gangrene in one or both wounds. He had seen gangrene during the war and it seemed that no matter how much of an arm or leg the doctors cut off it was never enough and the guy died anyway.

"Let's worry about getting the gold across the bridge for now, and the gangrene and getting your arms and legs cut off later." He said out loud, to himself. Farmer talked out loud, to himself often when he was alone. He never tried to figure out why, although it was because he, like most human beings needed to hear the sound of another human voice, even if it was his own.

He tied the seven mules up to the end of the bridge, to one of the ropes that held the bridge suspended. He led the horse across the bridge. He talked to the horse constantly as he lead it across the bridge. He half pulled and half talked, but somehow managed to get the horse across the bridge. His leg and shoulder were killing him, but he knew he had to get the mules. He realized he could not carry the bags of gold in the condition he was in. He had to get the mules across the bridge. The horse had been a job and a half, talking, pulling, he did everything but get behind the horse and push. He walked back across the bridge, making a point not to look down. He was glad nobody was around to watch this show of cowardice. He was almost all the way across to get the first mule when he stepped on the board. He was getting more confident now so he walked a little faster. That is when the board broke under his weight. It was next to where two boards were missing already. Farmer would have fallen through the hole except he managed to grab the rope that supported the bridge with his right hand. He knew he would have to use his left arm and when he did the pain was so excruciating he had tears in his eyes. He thought of letting go. It would be easy, he would drown the way Muller did, he would hit the water thirty feet below and be swept away by the current. It would be all over. Then he thought of the doctor, waiting for him to come and get her and he moved. Not much at first, but he moved. He hooked his right leg over the last board he had stepped on before the board had broken under his weight. He pulled himself up and finally managed to get onto the board. He lay there for a minute then he got to his feet and looked at the opening. It had to be three feet wide. No mule in the world was going to step across that space. He thought for a minute and turned and looked at the rest of the bridge. He walked back maybe ten feet and picked up a board that was in the middle of about six that had no missing boards between them. He carried the board back and placed it across the space. It was a sturdy looking board and he placed it side ways between the two side ropes. Then he changed his mind and placed it long ways across the hole. He gingerly stepped on it and hoped it would carry the weight of the mule. He took a second board and placed it next to the first one. "I sure hope this works." He said out loud, to himself as he walked across the two boards. It did work. The first mule hesitated slightly when it reached the boards, but then walked across them. The rest of the mules never even hesitated, they simply walked across the boards as did Hansen's horse. Farmer tied the mules and horses up, then went back onto the bridge and working from the far side he picked the boards off the bridge and dropped them into the river. Nobody would be following him across the river here.

armer had to stop. He was staggering and he knew it was from exhaustion. He was walking, leading the horse and mules. He could go no further. He had walked or ridden all night and now it was almost noon. He had poured the last of the whiskey on his shoulder sometime early in the morning. His shoulder and leg no longer hurt, they were simply numb. His entire body was numb. He tied the horse to a piece of brush and did the same with the mules after he untied them from the horse and each other. He unsaddled his horse and unceremoniously dumped the saddle on the ground. He walked around the horse and dragged the saddle twenty feet away, he undid the bed roll and then lay down and pulled the black duster over himself. He put the sawed off shotgun next to his right leg. He fell into a deep sleep, the sleep of the exhausted man.

"I tell you Trent, we should just take the mules and horse and get out of here." The voice broke through the deep sleep of Charlie Farmer.

"No. We gonna have us some fun with this here man here." The voice of the man named Trent answered.

Farmer opened his eyes and saw the man standing over him looking down at him. The man looked like a giant, but Farmer knew it was a distorted view because he was lying flat on his back looking up. From the clothes and the smell, Farmer knew the man to be a buffalo hunter. Buffalo hunters were the men who simply shot buffalo as they stood grazing. They shot as many as they wanted to or before the herd realized what was going on and stampeded off. Sometimes hundreds lay dead. They took the hides and left the rest of the carcass to rot, unlike the Indians who after killing the buffalo left nothing unused, they even made use of the bones.

"Hey, Bobby, he done waked up." Trent said pointing a pistol at Farmer's head, "You move boy and I'll give you a third eye." This addressed to Farmer.

The man named Bobby walked over and looked down at Farmer. "Shoot'em." Was all he said.

"Let me get that nice duster outta' the way, on account of there's gonna be lots'a blood." And saying that Trent reached down and pulled the duster off Farmer. He whipped the duster aside and saw the sawed off shotgun pointing at him. The rustling noise of the duster being removed had covered the sound of the shotgun being cocked. Trent's mouth fell open as he understood he was about to die. Then Farmer pulled the right trigger. The blast caught Trent squarely in the stomach, but because of the upward angle and the oval shape of the shotguns pattern it reached up to his neck. The force of the blast knocked him straight over backwards. He landed with a thud that was never heard over the noise of the shotgun going off.

Farmer moved the shotgun and pointed it at the man named Bobby. "No man! I was just lying, man. I didn't want him to shoot you, honest man." Bobby pleaded. Farmer pulled the second trigger with basically the same results as the first time. Farmer pulled his pistol as he sat up and looked around for a third buffalo hunter, but there was no one.

Farmer stood up and looked at the two dead men. He stripped them of their guns, he had to hold his breath they smelled so bad. He placed their guns over their saddles when he found their horses tied a short distance away. He also found their supply horse and three horses loaded with buffalo hides. He brought the horses back and added them to the string. He saddled his horse and mounted up and lead the horses and mules away. The two dead buffalo hunters lay where they fell. The turkey buzzards had already appeared, slowly circling on the up drafts of warm bright sunny morning air.

harlie Farmer was not the smartest man walking around these parts and he knew it. He had faced that fact years ago. Maybe it was part of becoming an adult, because during the war and just afterward he had been nothing more then a boy almost. He had done a lot of things he considered dumb. Things that came back to haunt him in his thoughts. More then once he had gotten angry with himself for remembering he had done something. He was glad no one could see inside his mind for above all else, Charlie Farmer was ashamed of himself. He never thought of the good things he had done, only the bad or dumb or foolish. He continually compared himself to other people he knew and always came up short as everyone does who engages in that mental exercise. He had been told once by a preacher that God gave everyone a different burden. That each person must carry his or her own burden and one person could not carry another persons burden it would be too heavy. We each have our own demons, Charlie, and we each have to handle them as best as we can, and only with the help of God can we do it. "I sure wish God was here now, I'd ask him what the hell I should do." There was a note of anger in the voice. Then he thought of the doctor back in the monastery and the anger was gone. He smiled at the thought of her. Maybe, just maybe he was feeling something toward her. Maybe she was the one who could make him feel something.

If the buffalo hunters had found him, he knew somebody else could also find him. Maybe Indians, maybe what was left of the bandits that he figured were still chasing him from the monastery, maybe somebody else, hell he did not know. One lone man with sixteen bags of gold, half the people in Mexico and Texas would be looking for him.

"So Charlie what do you want to do?" He said out loud to himself as he sat on his horse. "There ain't no safe place around here." He took the telescope from his saddlebags and extended it and put it to his right eye. He saw the river to his left, then the brush and the rocks. He looked behind him and saw the small group of riders. It looked like four and maybe four extra horses. They were at least four or five miles back. They, like Farmer, just rode their horses at a walking pace. He shifted his gaze to the northeast and saw the desert. Two days hard traveling and he could cross it. He smiled, lowered the telescope and turned his horse towards the river.

Fifteen water bags, that was how many he had and he filled everyone with every drop they could hold. These he tied to the two horses he gotten off the dead buffalo hunters. He let the horses and mules drink their fill as did he, then he turned toward the northeast and the desert. "Let's see just how bad these guys want this gold and how tough they really are." again this out loud, to himself as he mounted his horse. He again groaned in agony as he pushed and pulled to get himself into the saddle, again the rest after the strain of mounting. The man and the animals moved slowly off in the direction of the northeast. The brush thinned out and where the rocks had dominated the landscape and the sand had been the minority it changed as he traveled further and further to the northeast. Soon the sand overtook the rock as the dominate feature of the land. Then the sagebrush disappeared, then the rocks disappeared and only the sand was left, a land ocean of sand. Huge waves of sand that unlike the ocean did not move quickly, but seemed to remain stationary. They did not, but Farmer did not know this and he did not care that the waves of sand slowly moved over the years, for he was only interested in the next two days. Two days from hell.

armer remembered little of the following two days. He had plenty of water which is the only thing that saved him. The first few hours were a living nightmare. The pain in his leg and his shoulder were extreme. He would ride the horse for a while and then dismount and walk or limp would be a better description, for a while, then he would mount up and that was painful and he would ride for a while. He did this so he would not injure the horse. True, he had five spare horses, but he liked the one he was riding.

He could not sleep at night because it seemed like every time he moved he caused the shoulder or leg to hurt and it woke him up. He had nightmares about the water moccasins he had seen at the river crawling all over him. He would wake up sweating and it was not until the second day he realized he had a fever, maybe not a high one, but a fever none the less. He also knew that having the fever meant his gunshot wounds were probably getting infected. It did not surprise him with the sand blowing around all the time. There was almost no way to keep it out of the bullet wounds.

CHAPTER 58

I t was at the end of the second day that Farmer, walking on the ridge of the sand dunes, saw the end of them. They just suddenly stopped and the land flattened out. It turned into the shale and sand covered desert floor he had seen so much of on the way down to get the gold. He turned and looked behind him. He knew the bandits were steady gaining on him. He turned back and looked at the mountains maybe twenty or thirty miles to the north. He knew the bandits would over take him in the open. There was no way he could out run them, his animals were just too tired. He had given them water, but they did not have any food for the last day or so and water kept you alive but food gave you the energy to keep going and these animals were close to the end of the line. He knew if he could make the mountains he could find food, but he also knew that the bandits would never let him get that far. So he knew this was going to be the place to kill the four of them. He figured they were just biding their time until he reached the open plain in front of him. Then they could ride him down, kill him and take the gold.

He lead the horses and mules down the side of the sand dune. They sank in about three feet and were struggling, but they made it without falling. Farmer tied the lead horse to an out crop of rock and took his rifle from the scabbard. He took the belt of bullets from the saddle bag and started back up the dune. His leg felt like it was on fire and his shoulder hurt from straining against the sand, but he knew he had to get to the top. He finally made the top of the dune by crawling on his hands and knees. He took off his hat and peeked over the edge of the dune. He did not see the bandits yet he knew they were there, he knew they were coming. He waited for over an hour and then he spotted them, all four walking their horses along the top of a dune maybe a mile away. He had taken off his shirt and shaken out the sand, then he had taken apart the Winchester rifle and cleaned the sand out of it. He had then reassembled it, loaded it and put his shirt back on. He knew what the desert sun could do to human flesh in a very short time. He had no intention of being cooked alive like a piece of meat.

He peeked over the edge of the dune again and saw the bandits moving across the top of a dune. There was one dune between Farmer and them. When they reached the next dune and they were all sitting high in the saddle he would shoot them. He could keep his hat on because it was almost the same color as the sand around him. He waited and then peeked over the edge of the dune again. The bandits were gone, no where in sight. He waited and minutes later the lead bandit appeared on the dune next to where Farmer lay in wait. He saw the second rider appear, then the third and the fourth. The fourth rider held the reins of the two rider less horses. They had had four extra horses the first time he had spotted them. He guessed that two were dead back there in the desert somewhere. He waited as the four men approached him. The first man was almost to the end of the dune when Farmer slide the rifle into position. He cocked the hammer and aimed. He felt his finger touch the trigger. He squeezed and the Winchester kicked him in the right shoulder. He saw the leader topple from his saddle as he levered another shell into the rifle. He aimed and squeezed the trigger, again the Winchester kicked and as he levered the third shell into the chamber the second man fell from his horse. The third man was a repeat of the first two, the shot, the levering of a new shell into the chamber, the man falling from the saddle. The fourth man started to get off his horse when the bullet struck him. He fell, but he crawled over the edge of the dune. Farmer moved from his ambush position and skirted the top of the dune he had been hiding behind. He moved as quick as he could with his bad leg. He climbed the second dune and passed the first bandit, the shocked look on his dead face, the blood stain on the front of his shirt. The second bandit was also dead, as was the third. Farmer carefully looked over the edge of the dune. The fourth man was lying with his head pointing toward the bottom of the dune. He was face up and Farmer could see him breathing, he could also see the blood stain on the stomach of his shirt. He also saw the pistol lying ten feet from the mans outstretched hand. His face was the picture of agony. He lay spread eagled with his arms and legs forming a crude X.

Farmer half slid, half walked down the side of the dune until he was even with the bandit.

"Please Senior, please shoot me. I am in great pain." The bandit whispered. He spoke in Spanish, but Farmer understood and spoke Spanish fluently.

"I will as soon as you tell me who you are working for." Farmer replied. He was in no hurry, men belly shot could last for hours, going insane with the pain.

"I work for Senior Gomez. He was hired by a Gringo, but I don't know his name."

"How many men are left that are following me?" Farmer asked.

"Not many, you killed a lot when we tried to take the gold at the monastery."

"How many?" Farmer repeated the question.

"Ten, maybe twelve at the most." The Bandit answered, grimacing in pain with every word.

Farmer said nothing, he just looked at the dying man lying in front of him. He suddenly thought of Tucker, lying, dying, in that canyon.

"Please, if you do not want to shoot me, just give me my pistol and I will finish what you started."

Farmer smiled and said, "I give you that pistol and you'll shoot me first."

The Bandit smiled back and Farmer shot him in the head.

Farmer took the pistols and gun belts from the four dead men and also the six horses and everything on them. He left the four dead men where they lay, the wind and sand would cover them up soon enough, if the vultures did not get to them first.

He mounted the lead horse after tying the others nose to tail. He rode across the dune until he reached his horses and mules and tied them in a string, mounted his horse, replacing the rifle in the scabbard. He lead the string out into the flatland. If he made the mountains he was probably home free.

CHAPTER 59

And so Farmer suffered and continued to press on. His biggest worry was the fact that he may get turned around. So he kept checking the direction of the sun. In the morning it was on his right, in the afternoon it was on his left. That was his compass and his guide. He hoped he would run across a town soon, a town in Texas. He crossed a river the afternoon of the second day, it was shallow and wide and he told himself it was the Rio Grande, but he did not know if he really believed that. What he did believe was that he refilled his water bags, all twelve of them, for somewhere along the way he had lost three. It was a struggle to get them back on the mules when they were full, but he managed. He rested for a couple of hours near the river and then had the thought that if he had found the river there were probably people near by who would notice something and come and see and find him. This thought, the thought of losing any more of the gold to some people and also getting killed in the process gave him the inspiration to move.

The ground after the river changed into a rocky surface and then some plants and shrubs appeared, bigger rocks and then some trees. Late in the afternoon of the third day he saw the town. He also saw between him and the town exactly what he needed, Boot Hill. He waited until dark and moved into the cemetery. He dug a hole and buried the gold, all sixteen bags except for what he needed to fill the bottom half of his saddle bags. He pushed some old clothes on top of the gold and removed an unmarked old wooden cross from a grave site and worked it into the ground above where he buried his gold. Moving the one hundred and twenty five pounds bags of gold had been an ordeal, but he had managed. He spent the part of the night circling the town so in the morning he would enter the town from the west.

CHAPTER
60

The Doctor was tall, maybe six-three and slim. He kept that way by running all over the country side delivering babies and fixing broken bones and handing out medicine for colds. He was standing on the back porch of his house looking to the west when he saw the rider. He was coming out of the badlands of southern Texas and northern Mexico. Lands that were composed of shale rock mixed with sand. Where it never rained and where men and animals died for lack of water.

The rider must have known where he was going because he was heading straight for the little town of Poker Ridge where the doctor lived. He watched as the man and horse moved slowly across the landscape. He saw the string of about two dozen horses and mules behind him. All had that beaten look, their head hung down, the man was bent over in the saddle, the black duster was almost the same color as the land he walked his horse over. It took the man almost an hour to reach the town. He rode straight for the doctor's house. The Doctor could see now that there were thirteen horses and seven mules. All were covered with the same sand as the rider. A more exhausted group he had never seen.

The rider stopped and looked at the doctor standing on the porch, "There a doctor anywhere around here?"

"You're looking at him."

"I been shot a couple of times and I think you ought to look at where I got hit." Farmer said.

"I'm Doctor Ronnie McDuff and if you can walk inside I'll take a look at you." McDuff answered.

Farmer dismounted and limped inside, his left arm hanging straight down. McDuff had come off the porch and opened the door. He helped him off with his duster and then his shirt and pants. He noted Farmer kept the pistol when he dropped the gun belt from around his waist.

"Let's take a look at these." McDuff said opening Farmer's undershirt and looking at the shoulder wound. He looked at Farmer who had his eyes closed and looked at if he was going to fall off the examining table. McDuff cut the leg of Farmers long johns and looked at the leg wound.

"I don't know what you did to these, but they look alright to me. They are closing and I'm just going to pour some alcohol on then and put a clean bandage on them." McDuff said.

"That's what I been doing for the last three, or four, or five days. Or however long it's been since I been shot." Farmer answered.

"It must have been good booze, since they wounds look clean."

McDuff looked at the pink scar on the very top of Farmers forehead, "I supposed you sowed this up too." He asked.

Farmer suddenly smiled at the thought of the tiny doctor and that night in the monastery, "No. that was done professionally, and pretty much in the dark." He answered.

McDuff nodded several times in understanding, "Well who ever she is, she's good."

"How do you know it was a she?" Farmer looked at McDuff, who started to bandage up his shoulder.

"No man gets a look on his face like you did except over a woman." McDuff said quietly, "Does she feel the same way about you?"

"What way?" Farmer asked, truly puzzled by the question.

"Don't blow smoke up my ass, mister. You love her." McDuff paused, then asked, "By the way, what's your name?"

"Just Charlie, and I only talked to her two or three times." Farmer said, smiling again, remembering.

"I'm not one of these mind doctors, but I'm telling you, you are in love with her. It does not take a lot of talking or being together, it only takes once for some people."

Farmer shook his head, confused.

"So answer my question, does she love you?" The doctor persisted.

"She said she would come away with me." Farmer answered.

"So where is she now?"

"Down in Mexico." He answered, then added for some reason he did not know, "I have some business to attend to and then I am going back and get her and we are going somewhere together."

McDuff nodded again, then said, "Take off your dirty underwear and I will send it out to get washed with your other clothes. Meanwhile what you need most is sleep."

"I have to take care of the horses." Farmer protested.

"I'll get your horses taken care of, you just get some sleep." McDuff said guiding Farmer into a little side room with a bed.

"I ain't got no money, Doc." Farmer lied.

"I don't get paid much for my services. I took care of a lady, her husband and her four kids last week and she paid me two chickens. I figure for what I did for you, you owe me one chicken." The Doctor smiled. He took the dirty underwear Farmer handed him and closed the door.

CHAPTER 61

Thirty minutes later the doctor reentered his office. Sitting on his desk was a tall, thin, beautiful Mexican woman, the straight black hair, dark eyes, thin lips and neck.

"I want you to examine me, because I am sick. But you are going to have to take all my clothes off." She said smiling at the tall handsome doctor who she was madly and passionately in love with.

"Before I take your clothes off I have to tell you something." He said.

"I know. I know. What is wrong with me? I will tell you. My problem is I cannot take off my own clothes. I think I have," She paused trying to find the right word, she shrugged her tanned shoulders, "how do you call it?" The Mexican accent was very pronounced.

"Amnesia." McDuff answered, almost laughing.

"But it is only a part case of this amnesia stuff because I can remember how to take your clothes off. Isn't that weird?" She finished and she reached out to unbutton McDuffs' shirt.

"Juanita, you have no idea how much I want to cure what ails you this afternoon, but there is a guy asleep in our room and he said he did not want me and my girlfriend making mad passionate love next to him while he was trying to get some sleep." McDuff smiled and slide his hand up her skirt and kissed her deeply and lovingly.

"We could do it on the desk." She suggested breaking away from his kiss.

"We grunt and groan too loud." He said looking into her eyes.

Suddenly Juanita burst into a fit of laughter.

"I still love you deeply." She whispered into his right ear, then bit the lob softly.

"I love you too." He answered, and turned and walked to the other side of the room.

She got off the desk and walked to the little room where they had made love so many times, quietly opened the door and looked at the man sleeping on the bed.

She looked and when her eyes became accustomed to the dark she gasped. Her mouth fell open and her hand went to her chest, her eyes bulged and she almost cried out. She took a step backwards and quietly closed the door. She turned and quickly walked across the office and stopped behind McDuff, "Do you know who that is?" She asked in a quiet voice.

The tall doctor turned around and looked down at her. "Some guy named Charlie something or other. I don't know, you know I can't remember names." He answered, slipping his arms around her tiny waist. He leaned forward to kiss this beautiful woman and she held him away, her hand on his chest.

"I know him, Ronnie. He is called The Farmer Man on the other side of the border. He takes money to kill people. Good people or bad people, it makes no difference. They say he likes to do it."

McDuff picked up immediately on the fear in the woman's voice. He nodded his head slowly in acknowledgement. That was why he would not put down the gun while McDuff examined him.

"He is a very bad hombre." She finished.

CHAPTER 62

The blacksmith looked up from shoeing the horse and saw the tall gaunt man standing in the open doorway leading into the shop. He waited as the man approached him. His clothes were clean, but worn. For some strange reason the blacksmith noted the boots were shinny, which was rare because of the dry and dusty conditions in these parts. He also noted the low hanging pistol and holster belted around the man's narrow waist.

"I got into town a couple of days ago and the doctor brought my horses and mules here." Farmer said looking around the livery stable. 'I want to sell all of them except one. That's my horse, the rest you can have."

"I don't have a whole lot of money. I do a lot of my work for free. People around here ain't got much money." The Blacksmith replied, straightening up this full height of four inches over six feet.

Farmer stood and looked at the man, he looked at the floor, then back at the blacksmith, "I'll tell you what. I give you the horses and mules, except for my horse and one other. In exchange anytime I'm near here you take care of my horses for nothing."

Buck Abbot was the blacksmith and he knew a good deal when he heard one and this was a beaut, "I can go for that." He said smiling, "I'm Buck Abbot." He said extending his hand. Farmer took the extended hand and as far as the two men were concerned the deal was sealed.

CHAPTER
63

Juanita slipped out of bed and walked softly through the open door, her bare feet soundless on the wooden floor. She would make McDuff some coffee like she always did, every morning she awoke next to him was one more morning she thanked God for giving her this wonderful man. He had just drifted into town one day and it happened that a friend of Juanita's had been ill. McDuff had looked at her friend and given her something. The next day there must have been twenty people lined up in front of the hotel where McDuff had stayed the night. He had looked at each and every one of them and then had played a game of kick ball with some boys. He stopped to have a beer before leaving town and they had started talking and he had spent the second night in town. Then the third and forth and on and on until one night he had walked her home and after that things had just gone there way. That was about two years ago. She had been spending most nights with him ever since. McDuff had nothing to speak of, no material possessions, except his doctors equipment. His office rent was paid by taking care of the property owners family for free. She had asked him once why he had stayed. He had told her that he was a doctor and there were sick people here. He had said doctors were sort of like preachers. Preachers went where there were sinners, and doctors went where there were sick people. He visited the outlying ranches and anyone else he could find within a reasonable distance of the town. Sometimes people came from far away to see him because he was the only doctor for a long distance.

As she thought about McDuff she had gotten dressed and made the coffee. Now it was time to start her chores and when the coffee was brewed she would wake up McDuff and he would start traveling wherever he had to go and she would go to work in the general store. She walked to the door of the office and opened it. Right in front of the door was a sack. It did not look very full but when Juanita tried to move it, it was very heavy. There was a note next to the sack. She picked it up and looked at it. She could speak American, but could not read it. She was learning, Ronnie was teaching her. She opened the sack and looked inside. She took a deep breath and almost yelled. She turned and ran back into the office and into the little side room.

"Ronnie! Ronnie! Wake up!" She almost screamed.

McDuff sat up, instantly awake. "You ok?" he asked, the concern in his voice easily noted.

"There is a sack and this note was by it." Juanita said, starting to calm down.

McDuff took the note and read it. It was printed in the large block type letters like a child would use, "I ain't got no chickens doc but maybe this will cover my bill farmer" McDuff noted the lack of punctuation and looked at Juanita. "Where's the sack?"

"By the door." She answered.

He got out of bed and pulled on a pair of pants and walked to the front door, he bent over and looked into the sack. The one hundred and twenty-five pounds of gold coins glinted and gleamed in the early morning sun light.

CHAPTER 64

armer looked at the little one room cabin. Unless he was mistaken it was like the rest of the thousands built in the last couple of years out here by the settlers, called squatters by the ranchers. The one room served as the bedroom, the kitchen, the living room, dinning room, and every other room you needed in the house. He approached the cabin and dismounted by the hitching post just to the side of the stairs. He tied his horse to the hitching post then the rope leading the second horse. He did not take the two bags of gold coins hanging on the horse, he simply reached into his bedroll and pulled out the shotgun. He knew it was loaded so he walked to the three steps and climbed them to the porch. He crossed the porch and stood a foot away from the front door. He knocked using the barrel of the shotgun.

"Come in." said a gruff voice from inside.

Farmer opened the door and looked inside. He had been right, the regular one room cabin. The table was in the middle of the room. It was a round table with four chairs. A man sat on the opposite side of the table, lying on the table was a .45 caliber pistol, next to the pistol was his right hand.

"You Sam Jones?" Farmer asked.

"Yea." Came the reply.

"I want to talk to you." Farmer said, "About Alice Muller."

"Come in and sit down." Jones said, nodding to the chair opposite his. Farmer did as he was told. He walked to the table and laid the shotgun on the table, the barrels facing Jones, he swiveled it around so the barrels faced himself, pushed it to within easy reach of the older man and then he sat down.

"What about Alice?" Jones asked, looking directly into Farmers eyes.

"She's dead." Farmer said in the cold, Flat voice as he sat down opposite the old lawman.

Jones reached for the shotgun with his left hand and winced with the pain of arthritis, but he took it anyway. He broke it open and the two shells popped out. He caught them in mid air with his right hand. He is fast, thought Farmer, he must be in his sixties and he is still fast. Jones put the shotgun on the table and the two shells in his shirt pocket.

"I lent Alice three thousand dollars to do this. If people knew they would say I was crazy, but I liked Alice. She had balls and I like people with balls. You got balls?" he asked, looking directly at Farmer sitting across the table.

Farmer ignored the question. "Alice told me you were supposed to get thirty percent of the gold we brought home. I get two full saddle bags, you get two full canvas bags."

"What's your name?" Jones asked.

"Charlie Farmer."

"So you are Charlie Farmer." Jones said smiling. "Charlie No Soul, Three Finger Charlie, and probably a couple more I don't know about." Jones fell silent and leaned back in his chair, looking at the young man sitting opposite him. Jones had been a lawman for forty years and he knew dangerous men when he saw them. He knew he was looking at a very dangerous man sitting at his table.

"You want the gold or not?" Asked Farmer, his voice flat, unemotional, the voice of a dead man.

"You in a hurry, Farmer?" Jones asked.

Farmer nodded his head, "I have to go back for a woman. I told her I'd be back and I am going back." It was a statement of fact.

"Rescue missions ain't no good." Jones said, "More people die trying to save the person then that person is worth."

Jones looked at the man sitting opposite him. He looked tired and Jones could see the fresh scar across his forehead. He had not shaved in days and he smelled. "You sit there boy and give me a minute." Jones said rising from the table with effort the arthritis pain making it difficult for him to move at times. He walked across the room and picked up a dirty old flint lock rifle, removed the rammer and unwound a piece of paper from the tube and replaced the rammer. He put the gun back and walked back to the table. He sat down with some effort and then he looked at Farmer. "Here's where you went, now show me where Alice died." Jones right hand was suddenly holding the .45.

Farmer opened the map and looked in awe at the drawing. It was in color, blues, greens, yellows, purple, and some colors he did not know. He looked at the burned edge that was part of Texas, followed the marked trail south until he got to the river. There was sort of an abstract drawing of the bridge. Farmer pointed to the spot where the bridge crossed the river. "We were running from some Indians. I was covering the back door and the river was high. It was washing over the center of the bridge by a couple of inches. On the way down she had lost her nerve and Hansen had to carry her across the bridge. She just kept going at a full gallop across the bridge and the weight of the horse and a mule was too much and it gave way. She drowned and took a horse with her. I ended up with seven mules and one extra horse. I had to ride an extra day along the south side of the river to fine a place to cross. She had told all of us about how you had put up the grub stake for her, and so I figured you should get your share." Farmer paused, then added, "It's hanging out there on the horse."

Jones moved to look because Farmer was sitting in his line of sight. "Let's take a walk." Jones said as he got up from the table. Jones reached into his shirt pocket and handed Farmer the two shotgun shells, "You can have these and your gun back." He said.

Farmer picked up the shotgun off the table, reloaded it and snapped it shut

Farmer led the way out the door and down the steps. He was about to cut the rope holding the bags on the horse when the old man said, "Don't do that, I'll just look inside." And he stepped up to the bag untied the rope holding the bag closed and looked inside. Farmer saw the stunned look on the old mans face. "I ain't never seen anything like that before." He said turning to look at Farmer. "The other one full too?" he asked.

Farmer laughed, "It's just about the same. We found the gold and decided the mules could probably only carry a couple of hundred pounds each. The problem was how much was a couple of hundred pounds. It was Ace Tucker who came up with the idea. He asked Alice how much she weighted and after a couple of minutes she told us and we found an old board and made Alice sit on one end while we filled the bag until it was about even and balanced her. Then we figured we had one hundred and twenty five pounds." Jones smiled along with Farmer.

"What happened to Tucker?" questioned Jones.

"When we left the canyon, the haunted place, the Indians came after us and Ace stayed behind to hold them off and got killed." Farmer finished.

"What about Al?"

"We were about thirty or forty miles south of the bridge when he was shot in the back. He was dead before he hit the ground. It was an Indian. Anyway, he shot me too and I told Alice to get out of there. I fired a lot of rounds just to cover us moving, I got one Indian. The trail from the bridge was all twisted and I'd stop every once in a while and look behind us, but there was never anybody there. Then Alice tried crossing the bridge and that's it." Farmer said. Then a puzzled look crossed his face and he added, "I could feel somebody but I could never see anybody when I looked. It had to be another Indian."

Jones nodded his head in understanding as he looked into the other canvas bag. He looked at Farmer and said in a quiet voice, "I'm old boy," Jones paused, "I guess I should call you Charlie, huh?" He shot a questioning look at Farmer.

"For as much money as is in those bags you could call me shit head and I'd still be happy." Farmer smiled, he liked this old man.

Jones burst out laughing and started walking back into the house. When he got even with Farmer he continued what he had started to say before. "As I said before I'm getting old and I don't need all that money. There is an old bucket out back by the well. You fill that up with them coins from the sacks and bring it in the house and you can have the rest." Jones finished and just kept walking, never breaking stride, he just walked up the steps and through the door. He had just given away a huge fortune and never batted an eye.

Farmer shook his head and started walking around to the back of the house to get the bucket. He could not understand how someone could give away all that money, that was the purpose of going to Mexico in the first place. That was why Jones had staked Muller the three thousand dollars. Farmer just shook his head and started walking toward the well behind the house.

Jones sat down at the table and for the first time in a lot of years he felt like he was going to cry. Alice Muller was the daughter he never had. True, she had her vices and her morals were pretty low, but Sam Jones had loved her anyway. Over the years he had received a lot of letters from her and she had never failed to tell him she had loved him. That was his girl and now she was dead. Sam Jones rested his head on his crossed arms on the rough wooden table and cried.

Farmer came back with the bucket filled with the gold coins. He saw the old man crying. He placed the bucket quietly just inside the door, turned, walked silently across the porch, down the stairs, mounted his horse, and pulling the second horse, rode away. He would bury the gold on his way to Mexico.

CHAPTER 65

armer walked leading the horse by the reins toward the front gate of the monastery. He had seen the buzzards from way back in the canyon. There was a whole flock of them, maybe fifty or sixty. He remembered shooting them during the war because they could not bury the bodies fast enough to keep them away from the dead and dying. He walked the horse slow as he looked for any signs of life. That's good he thought, the women are hiding. They must have spotted me as I came out of the canyon and not knowing who I am they are waiting to see. Or maybe they are hiding in the caves and some of the rooms of the monastery. He looked closely and saw nothing, only the buzzards. So if they are fine, why the buzzards? He questioned himself. The gate was wide open and then he saw what looked like someone lying on the ground. The closer he got, the more defined the body became, he mounted his horse, took another look and spurred the horse into a gallop for the last fifty feet, because he realized it was a body. He galloped through the open gate and pulled on the reins and the horse skidded to a stop next to the body. Farmer was off the horse and looked at what was left of whoever it was that had been lying there. Then he saw the blue kerchief and knew. It was the woman named Blue and there was not much left of her. Then he looked around and where Wilson had been tied to the cross where the fire always burned, but was out now, there were more bodies. Farmer reached into the bedroll and removed the shotgun. There were a lot of buzzards around the cross and Farmer was only fifty feet away. Some had flown away when he had approached, but most had given him one look and gone back to devouring what was left of the bodies. He removed the belt of shells from his saddlebags and hung it over his left shoulder. He looked at the remains of the woman who called herself Blue. Then faster then the eye could follow Farmer turned and fired both barrels of the sawed off shotgun into the flock of buzzards devouring the bodies by the cross. He reloaded the shotgun and walked slowly toward the bodies, the wounded buzzards screaming in pain, some trying to fly, others trying to walk. All were trying to get away from the killer with the shotgun. Farmer shot and killed the wounded buzzards. He kicked them away from the bodies they had been picking at. He looked at one of the bodies and saw the neat round hole in the middle of the forehead. Only a bullet made a hole like that. He counted the bodies, five, with Blue that made six. There had been seven, maybe somebody was still alive. Farmer was looking for something, something was missing, he had it. The black bag the doctor always carried. She never went anywhere without it. He carefully looked around the courtyard and then decided that the best chance was the entrance to the caves. If one of the women had run it would have been to the caves. He hoped the doctor was the one hiding in the caves. Maybe she was alive, maybe. Farmer walked toward the hole in the wall and looked inside. It was dark, black inside the entrance. The bright sunlight behind him made him virtually blind. He took a step into the entrance and heard the low growl. He backed up a step and the wolf was in the air coming at him. The force of the shotgun going off at such close range flipped the wolf over backwards in mid air. It's head almost torn from it's neck. Farmer retreated from the cave entrance and found a torch and lit it. The shotgun was reloaded. He entered the cave again and saw the wolf. Ten feet beyond the wolf was the seventh body. Not three feet away from the body was the black bag.

"Shit." Farmer muttered

er name is Bodean and she sat on the west wall of the monastery. She watched the man burying another body. That made seven. She sensed, rather then saw that maybe this one was special. He had carried it out and it, unlike the others was wrapped in a blanket. The others had been a hideous mess. She had looked at the first and saw what the buzzards had left. The rest she had just put the binoculars down and let the man do what he had to do. She had watched as he had brought body after body. He had laid them in grave after grave. The seven graves had been dug across the entrance to the courtyard of the monastery, just inside the open gates. Bodean did not know if they were men or women. After seeing the first body she figured there was not enough left to tell unless you knew who they were.

Bodean had watched as the man had gone inside a hole in the wall next to where the building attached to the wall on the east side. She had watched him drag a big wolf out of the hole, and then the body. She had looked away not wanting to see the details and yet she could not stop looking as the man wrapped the body in a blanket. He had laid the body gently on the spread out blanket that lay on the ground. Then just as gently covered the head and the feet and then had covered the rest of the body. She had watched as he had gone back into the hole and came out carrying a black bag. So the last body was a preacher or a doctor, nobody else carried a bag like that. He scooped up the body and the bag and walked to the last grave.

He laid the body next to the hole and climbed into the hole and then proceeded to place the body in the hole. Just before he climbed into the hole he had touched the back of his left hand against the head of the body when he had been kneeling next to the body. He had stayed there several minutes, the hand resting on the body. Maybe he was praying, but Bodean had never seen anyone pray with one hand on a corpse and the other on his pistol. Then he had climbed into the hole and lowered the body into it, he had climbed out and started to throw the dirt into the holes, all seven of them. It took an hour for him to finish, he worked non stop, and again when he finished he knelt beside the last grave for a minute. He stood up and walked slowly to his horse tied to the cross in the middle of the courtyard. There were forty or fifty buzzards lying there, along with the wolf. He reached the horse and Bodean thought, this little show is over. She started to turn away and climb down from the wall when the man removed the rifle from the scabbard on the side of the saddle. Faster then she could follow with her eyes it was pointed at her.

"Come down off that wall and walk on over here." The man ordered. There was no mistaken the fact he would shoot her if she did not do as he said. She slid off the wall and walked toward him. He was standing on the far side of his horse, the animal between her and himself. Bodean felt that this guy knew his way around a gunfight.

"What are you doing here?" He asked.

Bodean swallowed hard and nothing came out when she tried to speak. She watched as the man un-cocked the rifle and put it back in the scabbard.

Then Bodean found her voice. "I heard there was a group of women down here that had been abused and I came down here to join them."

Farmer turned and motioned to the graves. "There they are," he looked back at her. "and if you stay here you'll join them alright."

His voice was flat and cold. Bodean felt a tinge of fear crawl up her spine.

"Who killed them?" She asked.

"I don't know." Farmer answered, shrugging his narrow shoulders, "But when I find them, I'm going to kill all of them. I was coming back to get the doctor and we were going to go somewhere together." His voice trailed off, he looked down at the ground and Bodean thought maybe he was going to start crying, but he simply shook his head.

Farmer looked at the woman. Her skin was the color of dark chocolate. Her figure was slim and she was dressed in the tightest jeans Farmer had ever seen on a woman. The shirt was open half way down her chest, showing a lot of cleavage. She had black boots on and wore a black gun belt around her slim waist. The pistol rested in the holster, the safety hoop over the hammer. The black, dust covered hat, sat at a jaunty angle on her head.

"So that is what she was." Bodean said looking back at the man looking at her. She noted the green eyes were blank, empty and realized she had been wrong, there was no pain, no anger, nothing, just emptiness.

"What do you mean?" Farmer asked.

"I saw the black bag and only a doctor or a preacher carries a bag like that." She made a face and tilted her head to the right slightly. She waited and neither spoke, he just looked at the graves.

"My name is Bodean." She said.

He looked at her and said, "Charlie Farmer." and extended his right hand. Bodean hesitated, she had never been offered a handshake before by a white man. All the old hatreds found their way to her voice when she asked, "You sure you want to shake hands with an ex slave nigger woman?"

He looked her in the eye and said with a tinge of anger in his voice, "Lady there are only two colors in this world, gray and yellow. The gray is for the lead in a bullet and the yellow is for gold. No other colors count."

She took the extended hand and noted how dirty it was. But it felt safe and secure and Bodean suddenly changed her mind and decided she liked this man.

Farmer mounted his horse and Bodean walked back across the courtyard and over the breached part of the wall to her horse. She mounted and caught up with Farmer as he rode away from the monastery. He was heading north, into the canyon.

Bodean rode next to Farmer and she was not sure if she should say something, but she figured what the hell, "I didn't come this way, Farmer." To her surprise he stopped and looked at her. "I came west of the mountains. It is longer, but a lot safer if you are traveling alone. There are a lot of farms and small towns, and soldiers and not many bandits. The farmers are nice people and treat you decent. It is just a couple of days longer."

He said, as he turned his horse towards the mountains, "Lead the way."

Bodean could not believe he was going to follow her, let her lead the way. That was unheard of in her world, the world of the slave and then the world of the saloon girl. The men, especially the white men, never took heed of what the woman said, be her black or white. She smiled and turned her horse and took the lead west toward the mountains.

Farmer's plan was to ride around any small town and at night so they would not be spotted. There was always some stand of trees or woods or swamp they could hold up in during the day. They said little or nothing,

"We'll walk for a while, rest the horses." Farmer said after the first couple of hours of riding and they did for maybe half an hour. Then he mounted back up and told her to lead on.

They had been walking the horses, along a section of desert the first day when she asked, "Farmer don't you ever stop to take a piss?"

"If you gotta piss we'll stop." He said, the voice cold.

"I have to go bad." She said and handed him the reins to her horse and walked behind the horses to the other side.

"How do you know I won't peek?" Farmer asked.

She smiled and answered, "You would not be the first guy to see it all." They both laughed and her feelings of fondness for this man grew. Her grandmother had told her there were nice white people out there, you just have to look beyond the color of their skin. "They no more chose the color of their skin they you or I did, Child." She remembered her saying.

Bodean finished and walked back to the front of the horses. Farmer said nothing, he simply handed her the reins to her horse and started walking. She pulled on the reins of the horse and she walked along side him.

They had ridden the first day and through the night. Farmer had decided to ride into the second day because they had not seen any form of civilization. No towns, no farm fields, only desert and the occasional water hole. The afternoon of the second day the sun was hot and Bodean was exhausted, she just could not go on. "Farmer we have to stop. I'm going to fall out of my saddle."

Farmer stopped and dismounted. She just sat in the saddle, she did not think she had the strength to get off the horse. Suddenly he had her around the waist and he was pulling her off the horse.

"Come on and get down." He said. She just leaned into his hands and he lowered her to the ground. "Go over there about ten feet and I'll get your bedroll" She heard him say. She staggered a few feet and laid down on the dirt and was asleep instantly. Later she would have a vague memory of him gently placing her on her bedroll.

When she awoke it was dark. There was no fire, but what was worse, there was no Farmer. She sat up, almost in a panic and looked around. She threw the blanket off and got to her feet. The moon was out and the light was fairly good. She saw the two horses, unsaddled, their reins tied to some small plant or tree. She walked toward the horses and then she saw him lying on the ground on the other side of the horses. She exhaled, not realizing she had been holding her breath. She looked around and spotted the saddles. She walked to the saddles and picked up the pistol and holster she carried and started looking around for something to burn in a fire. They had supplies and she needed a cup of coffee. She had no idea what time it was or how long she had slept. She could tell by the moon being so low in the sky that it was close to daylight. She strapped the holster around her waist and checked the pistol to make sure it was loaded. She did not know about Farmer. She did not know what he might do. The pistol was loaded and she went off in search of something to burn.

Bodean was right. About an hour later the sun came up and the heat of the day started. She was watching Farmer sleep, when she suddenly realized he was fully awake, his eyes taking in everything around him. Her, the horses, the fire.

"Welcome to the world of the living." She said, smiling.

"How long have you been up?" He asked.

"Maybe an hour, I don't know." She answered.

She watched him sit up and open the black duster. He lifted a small gun from inside the duster and she saw it was a sawed off shotgun. "Is that your bed partner?" She asked, smiling and pointing at the shotgun.

"Yea, this here is my woman. She's perfect. She don't hassle me to do something and if somebody bothers me she handles them." They both laughed. He stood up and walked to the fire.

"I have to take care of some business, there's got to be another cup somewhere. Just look though my junk." He said and walked away. Bodean walked over to his saddle and looked in one saddle bag. She found a metal cup and started to stand up and go back to the fire. She could not resist the urge to look in his other saddlebag. She unbuckled the two straps and opened the flap. Inside was a dirty cloth bag. She had gone this far, she thought, why not. She opened the bag and it took her breath away. The gold sparkled, even in the half light of the coming dawn. She reached in and picked one piece up. It was like brand new. She was memorized by it, she stared at it, holding it up before her eyes. Something in her brain clicked as she looked at the gold piece.

"Take half and put them in your saddle bags." Farmer said from behind her. She dropped the coin as she turned around, he was only about five feet away. "That way if we get separated, you got some money."

"I'm sorry, I found the cup and I couldn't resist being noisy." She was embarrassed.

He held out his hand toward the cup. "Let me have the cup and put half the gold in one of your saddle bags. I'm serious." He said looking at her. She simply stood where she was. Farmer reached and took the cup and turned around and walked to the fire. Bodean picked up the coin she had dropped and took what was far less then half of the coins and put them in her saddle bags then came back to the fire and sat down.

"You just set me up in my own business, Farmer." She said. She looked at the coin she had picked up, the one she had dropped.

"No problem." He answered, looking north in the direction they would be traveling.

"I'll be darned." She suddenly said.

Farmer looked at her, across the fire, "What?" He asked.

"I have seen one of these before." She was still looking at the coin.

Farmer looked her and shook his head, "I'm the only one left alive who had anything to do with these things and I have not used any yet."

"No. No." Bodean repeated herself. "There was this guy in El Paso who had some."

"Yea, I gave some to a doctor." Farmer said.

"No. No." Repeated Bodean. "If this guy was a doctor, I am a virgin." She paused, Farmer waited. "This guy was a gunman, a pro. He knew how to use a gun. He told everybody how good he was. Some fool called him out. That is all I remember. I was so drunk I passed out before I saw or heard anything else."

"What did this guy look like?" Farmer questioned.

"Hell, I don't know. I told you I passed out."

"How many?" Farmer asked, his voice so cold it gave Bodean the chills.

"How many what?" She asked.

"How many coins did he have?"

"I don't know that either." Bodean stopped. Suddenly she felt ashamed of herself. She felt regret that she had admitted that she had a drinking problem in front of Farmer. She had the problem for years and that was part of the reason she had been going to that monastery. She had thought maybe they could help her kick her addiction.

"Never mind." said Farmer. He stood up and looked at her. "You said he was in El Paso?"

"Yea." Bodean answered, as Farmer stood up. "What are you doing?" She asked.

"I'm leaving. I'm going to El Paso. I have to see this guy." Farmer answered.

"He probably ain't even there anymore. He's probably moved on by now." She waited, but Farmer just walked toward where his saddle lay on the ground. He picked it up and after putting the blanket on the horses back he tossed the saddle on it. Bodean got up and walked to where Farmer was.

"You can't just leave." She said.

"Sure I can."

"He ain't going to be in El Paso now. You're a gunman, you know how you guys drift all over the place." She told him.

Farmer finished saddling his horse and turned around, "Look, the only place this guy could have gotten the gold was from the doctor who probably saved my life. The only way he could have gotten them off the doctor was if he killed him. I owe that doctor my life and if somebody killed him I'm going to kill them." Farmer paused, "You can come with me or you can strike out on your own, but one way or another I'm leaving." He walked past her and started to roll up his bedroll.

"Hell, I ain't leaving you. You're the first man, black or white that ever treated me decent since I started growing a set of boobs." Bodean said. She knew Farmer was cold, but he was also nice to her and she wanted more of the being nice and she liked being treated with some respect. She liked being treated like a half way decent woman, like a woman should be treated. She stood up and ran over and grabbed her saddle and blanket and ran as best she could to her horse, half dragging, half carrying the saddle and blanket. She dropped the saddle and threw the blanket over the horses back. She threw it so hard it slid over the horses back and fell to the ground on the other side. She ducted under the horse and grabbed the blanket and stood back up. Farmer was standing on the other side of the horse.

"What are you doing?" He asked calmly, his arms folded across his chest.

"I'm going with you."

"Ok." Was all he said. Bodean looked at him and he looked back. She just held the blanket and could do nothing but look into those green eyes.

Farmer smiled and said, "Look, if you want to come let me saddle your horse and you pack up all the junk and we'll move on."

CHAPTER
67

They had traveled maybe three hours. Bodean was about ready to ask Farmer if they could walk for a while. Her rear end was getting sore from sitting in the saddle so long. She looked at Farmer and he was looking off to his right. She looked in the same direction and saw the cloud of dust. It was not a sand storm, it was way too small, it could be nothing else then horses running hard.

"Who is that?" She asked.

Farmer looked back at her, "I don't know, but I don't want to meet them." He paused. "They are pushing real hard so their horses are going to start tiring pretty soon. We are going to head for the mountains. There has to be a pass through them and we can get away from those riders." and saying that Farmer spurred his horse into a gallop. Bodean followed him. Their horses were almost fresh and rested so they made good time to the edge of the mountains. The sage brush gave the sides of the mountains a gray look. They had been traveling about a mile west of the mountains. Farmer had wanted it that way so nobody could ambush them as they traveled north. Now he led them in a northeast direction. They covered the distance between themselves and the base of the mountains quickly and were maybe a half a mile ahead of the bandits when Farmer turned north. They traveled another mile or so and she saw the entrance to a pass, a canyon cutting a slice through the mountains. Bodean hoped that it was not a dead end, a box canyon. Farmer led the way into the canyon full speed. The pass was not straight and she had a hard time staying up with him through the turns as hard as they were pushing the horses. She had always prided herself on being an excellent rider, but she realized that Farmer could give her a few tips on riding.

They made a few lefts and rights and up and down a couple small hills, a straight stretch maybe one hundred yards long. Then a hard left. She pulled her horse to the left as Farmer made the hard left. Then he pulled his horse to a stop. He dismounted and pulled his Winchester from the scabbard. He looked at her, "You keep going, just follow the canyon until I catch you or you get to the other side of the mountains. If I ain't caught you by then just keep going north. Get back into Texas as fast as you can. If the bandits catch you down here they will sell you back into slavery." He did not add any of the details of what else the bandits might do to a good looking woman like Bodean.

Bodean wanted to say something, but she could think of nothing to say. Farmer looked up at her and smiled, "Go on, get the hell out of here, I'll be fine." And saying that he slapped her horse on the rump and it started to move. She rode as far as the next sharp turn. Her master had loved talking about military maneuvers. She dismounted thinking about how he had told his guests about how when you were retreating you covered your men by splitting them. Some would shoot and cover the others while they took cover and then proceeded to cover their friends as they retreated. Run and cover, run and cover. You could hold a large force at bay for a long time if you worked it right. She pulled the rifle from her scabbard and took up a position behind a large rock and waited, knowing Farmer would be coming past her. She heard the rifle fire. It had to be Farmer shooting. There was silence, then return fire, then more rifle shots. More silence, then the sound of horses hoofs pounding along the canyon floor. Farmer came around the corner and almost did not see Bodean standing behind the rock. He pulled on the reins and dismounted and ran up beside her.

"What the hell are you doing?" He whispered, looking back the way he had come.

"I'm covering your retreat." She answered, never looking at him.
"You can do this?" He asked.

"Yes I can. You move along the canyon and pick another spot.
I'll be along as soon as I show them I'm here." She turned and looked
at him.

He looked back and then said, "I won't go too far, just shoot until
they take cover then move on." and saying that he ran back to his
horse, mounted and took off at a gallop into the canyon.

Bodean waited, it seemed like Farmer had just left when one
of the bandits came riding along the straight away in front of her.
The straightaway was maybe fifty yards long and she waited until
the bandit was not more then twenty-five or thirty yards away.
She sighted the Winchester and squeezed the trigger. The bandit
fell from his horse a look of shock and surprise on his face as he
fell. A second man had appeared and was at the other end of the
straightaway. Bodean levered another round into her rifle and sighted
it and squeezed the trigger again. The second man fell from his horse,
the same shocked look on his face as he fell from his saddle. A third
man disappeared back around the turn where the first two had come
from. Bodean waited, reloading her rifle. When it was loaded she
peered from behind the rock. She saw the two men lying motionless
on the canyon floor. She knew she should feel guilty, but she felt
nothing. What were the Mexicans? They were not black or white
men. She had heard they half Indian and half Spanish, would she have
felt something if they had been black or white men. Think about that
later, she told herself. Bodean fired four more rounds just to keep the
bandits honest. Then ran to her horse, mounted and rode full speed
further along the canyon. She passed Farmer and just kept going
until she reached another sharp turn. She dismounted and reloaded
her rifle. She heard rifle shots and knew Farmer was doing what she
had done. She listened and heard the horses hoof beats coming along
the canyon. She peeked out from behind the rock and saw Farmer
coming fast. She stepped out so he could see her. He stopped his
horse and dismounted.

Joe Kinney

"We do this once more and then we get out of here. We shoot a couple more and they won't be so anxious to come through the canyon after us. That should buy us enough time to get away." He said looking over her shoulder, along the canyon.

They waited and looked for a few minutes when Farmer asked, "Where did you learn to shoot and play soldier like this?" He asked.

Bodean turned and saw he was looking down the canyon over her shoulder. "My white master taught me. We used to play this shooting game. When I won I got to walk away. When he won he got to manhandle me anyway he wanted. I learned how to get good with a rifle real fast." She looked down at the ground, ashamed at what she was going to say next, "But not fast enough to get to walk away for the first two months or so. Sometimes we would shoot two or three times a day." Bodean left the rest of her story untold.

"You should have shot the guy when you got good enough." Farmer said in his cold flat voice.

"Some Yankee did that for me in one of the battles of the war. But I did sneak out one night and piss on his grave." and saying that she could not help laughing. She looked at Farmer and saw he was smiling.

CHAPTER 68

The sand was deep and hot to the touch. Bodean followed Farmer along the top of the sand dune. She could see the mountains in the distance. They had shot twice more from cover in the canyon and then had just run. They had ridden for hours in the canyon, sometimes stopping and waiting, but they had seen no more bandits. They guessed the bandits figured the price of catching them was too high and had turned back. The canyon had opened into the vastness of the desert, the sea of hot sand, sometimes blowing, sometimes still. They rode or walked their horses from the top of one dune to the next. It was dry, so dry that Bodean did not even see perspiration on her shirt, yet she knew she was sweating. She was thirsty and she was glad Farmer had brought so much water. He had four big water bags plus two canteens. The water was hot and she had remarked about it after the first couple of drinks. Farmer had told her better hot and wet then cold and dry. The heat was almost unbearable, but it would be dark pretty soon, Bodean knew. Yea, she thought, then I can freeze, ain't that wonderful.

Bodean could not figure Farmer out. She could make him smile, sometimes even laugh, but he just never seemed to be like other men she had known. Maybe that was it, maybe he was not like any other man she had known. He had told her he knew something was wrong with him, inside his brain. The bullet had done something, he did not know what, it had hit something. Maybe a nerve or something, but it had left him different. He said a doctor he had talked to had told him he would probably never be right. He had smiled then and said a friend of his had asked him if he shook his head could he hear the bullet rattling around in there since there was nothing else in there to stop it from banging around. Bodean smiled when she thought of him saying that. He may be different and he may be strange and most of the time he was cold and remote, but Bodean liked him. What was more surprising to her was that she trusted him. She smiled again at the thought of her trusting a white man. She shook her head almost in disbelief. It had been white men who had made her life so miserable. First the man who was her owner, abusing her from the time she had started showing herself becoming a woman. Then after being freed, after the war she had found that working in a saloon was the only job she could get that gave her any money at all. That was the up side. The down side was the booze. For the last year, maybe two she had been drunk almost all the time, day after day, week after week, nothing but one long bender. Get up sometime in the afternoon, half the time next to some guy who you could not even remember going to bed with the night before. The first thing you reached for was the bottle and it started all over again. Then one of the woman had said something about a monastery in Mexico where woman helped each other. It had not been an overnight thing, it was more like a two or three month thing. It had taken her that long to decide to make the trip. She had woke up one night screaming because she had known there were ants crawling all over her, ants in her eyes and nose and everywhere else. After one of the woman had gotten her calmed down she had told her it was the liquor. The alcohol in the stuff makes you crazy after a while, after you drank too much too long. Bodean had immediately gotten drunk and the ants had returned. After the third nightmare she had taken what money she had and bought a horse and left for Mexico. She had found the monastery and Farmer and here she was. She tried not to think about the shakes, or how on the second day of the trip to the monastery she would have killed for a drink.

"It's a good thing that horse knows where he's going, because you sure don't" Farmer's voice brought her back to reality. She opened her eyes and looked around and it dawned on her she had been sleeping, or at least dozing while in the saddle. She had never done that before.

"I was just thinking." She paused, "I guess I was just wondering in my mind, thinking about stuff."

"Well think about this, about ten miles away is a river, it is wet and cold and we should be there by tonight." He said looking toward the north.

"I'm going to lay in it for a couple of days. That is how long it will take to get all the sand off me."

They were walking their horses as they talked.

"You know how to cook?" Farmer asked, a slight smile on his face. Everything they had been eating for the last couple of days had been from a can.

"Why, do you have a steak hidden in your saddle bags?" She asked, almost laughing.

"No, but that river is full of fish and there is plenty of wood to build a fire and I have a frying pan."

"Well then Mister Farmer I invite you to one of the finest fish dinners you will ever eat." She answered.

CHAPTER
69

hey went to El Paso and from there to other small towns. Every town was the same. Nobody remembered any gunman or anybody else using gold coins to pay for anything. But something unexpected did happen. In one of the towns somebody knew who Charlie Farmer was. In another town somebody knew who Bodean was and from there the story spread like a wild fire on the grassy plains blown by a strong Texas wind. "Charlie Farmer and Bodean were riding together. They were looking to put together a gang. They were going to try and take over part of Texas and make it their own country."

In the little town of Mesa, Texas they first heard the story. They heard it from a Marshall Adam Youngblood who Farmer had met a long time ago. They were in a saloon/diner in the town when Youngblood walked in. He walked up to Farmer.

"Hello Charlie, long time no see." Youngblood said, not knowing exactly what to expect from the gunman.

Farmer looked up from his plate and a smile broke across his face, "Marshall Youngblood, how are you?" He stood up and shook the lawman's hand, "Sit down, join us."

"This is Miss Bodean, This is Marshall Adam Youngblood." Farmer made the introductions

Youngblood pulled out a chair and sat down, when the waiter appeared he just ordered coffee.

"I want to know something, Charlie." Youngblood asked Farmer.

Farmer said nothing, he just looked at Youngblood.

"I have to know if the story is true that you are putting together a gang for some reason."

"Are you serious?" Farmer asked surprised at Youngblood. This was the first time he had heard the story.

"That is what I heard. There is a white man and a black woman riding together. The white man is Charlie Farmer and the black woman is Bodean, and they are trouble." Youngblood said.

"Holy cow Farmer, we're famous." Bodean said almost laughing.

"Is it true, Charlie?" Youngblood persisted.

"No." Farmer answered. "But I am looking for someone." and saying this, Farmer handed Youngblood one of the gold coins. "You ever seen anything like this before?"

Youngblood looked at the coin, flipped it over and looked at the other side, shook his head no and then answered, "No." still shaking his head and looking at the coin.

"Somebody has got some and I want to know where they got them from." Farmer told the lawman.

"I wish I could help you Charlie, but I never saw anything like this before." Youngblood said.

"Then we'll finish eating and be moving on." Farmer said. "I don't want to cause you no trouble."

"Yea, us having a big reputation and all." Bodean said.

"You best explain to your woman there about reputations Charlie." Youngblood said, standing up.

Youngblood left and Bodean looked at Farmer and asked, "Am I your woman Farmer? Do people look at us that way?" She liked the idea of being Farmers woman. She could live with that.

Farmer looked back at her and answered, "I don't know much about being somebody's woman or man. We travel together so maybe it is so." He paused to eat another mouth full. "But I will tell you this, I don't like having a reputation. That's bad business."

"Why?" asked Bodean looking directly at Farmer.

"Because a reputation brings nothing but trouble. Somebody wants to prove they are better then you. I saw a guy get shot in the back once and then the shooter claimed it was a fair fight. I don't want nothing to do with that. I think we may have to split up and go our separate ways."

Bodean was shocked by Farmers last statement. She had never thought about them splitting up. They had never made love, although she had thought about it sometimes. It was just that she had enjoyed being with this man, and she thought he had enjoyed her company.

Farmer saw Bodean stop the fork half way to her mouth when he told her about splitting up. The shocked look was a surprise to him. He had never thought about after he had found out who had the gold, if it was the doctor or the guy who killed him.

Bodean felt herself starting to loose it. She was going to cry and she was not going to do that over a man, any man, even Farmer. She had not had a drink in months and she was going to have one now. In fact she was going to have a lot of them. She pushed her chair back and stood up and said, "We can split up right now. That will save you from being shot in the back. It's been a real slice, Farmer.' She turned and walked the twenty feet to the bar. "I want a bottle and a man who can handle me." She said in a loud voice as the bartender approached her. She would show this Farmer what she was.

"Lady you don't work here and since you don't I can't serve you." He said.

"Why not?" Bodean said in the same loud voice.

"'Cause you're a nigger and we don't serve niggers in here. Go down the street and you'll get served in the nigger bar there. But you ain't getting served here." saying that, he walked away.

"You bastard!" Screamed Bodean, "you white ..." was all she got out before Farmer clamped his hand over her mouth and said quietly in her ear.

"Just shut up and come with me." He did not release his hand from over her mouth as he said to the bartender, "We're leaving, the money for the meal is on the table. Sorry for the trouble."

"Yes Sir, Mister Farmer." answered the bartender.

Farmer half dragged, half pulled Bodean outside, down the steps to their horses. "You keep your mouth shut until I finish. You just get on your horse and follow me. You understand?" He finished with a question.

"Yea." Bodean said through his hand while nodding her head yes. Farmer released his hand and waited. Bodean mounted her horse and only then did Farmer walk around her horse and mount his. He led the way out of town and they headed west toward the next town.

Bodean rode up next to Farmer and asked in a sarcastic voice, "Can I talk now?"

Farmer stopped his horse and looked at her and said, "The only reason you're still alive is because I dragged you out of there. That bartender was going to shoot you for calling him a bastard. Down here, niggers don't call white men bastards. They may be and you can think about them that way, but if you call them that they will shoot you or hang you. So watch your mouth."

"If you had not been there I would be dead, huh?" She asked after a pause, but it was really a statement.

"Most likely." He answered.

"I'm sorry. I was upset. I had not thought about us splitting up. When you said it," She paused, searching for the right words, "I ....I don't know." She shook her head, looking down at her saddle horn.

"Well I can't have you riding around southern Texas calling white bartenders bastards, so I guess we'll be together a while longer." He said smiling at her.

Bodean laughed and felt a great weight lifted from her shoulders. "If we were standing on the ground I'd kiss you Farmer." She said, still half laughing, then she got serious, she felt the tear at the corner of her eye. "Except you love that doctor you buried in Mexico. You like me, but you love her. Maybe someday you will get over her, then maybe it will be my turn." Bodean spurred her horse into a trot and left Farmer sitting there wondering if she was right.

armer stood in the gunsmiths shop. He was buying ammunition. He had just finished paying for it and the clerk was handing it to him when Bodean walked in. She walked up next to Farmer and looked in the bag.

"That a present for me?" She asked jokingly.

"That is a present for both of us." He answered her.

She grabbed his arm and said, "You have to see this Farmer. This is great"

"What?" He questioned.

"Just come with me." She said and pulled him out of the gunsmiths store.

They walked along the boardwalk and almost reached the end of it when Bodean turned left. Farmer followed her as she walked on. He heard a lot of yelling and laughing as he walked behind her. She turned right as she passed along one side of an old barn and Farmer followed. Then he stopped. He blinked and could not believe what he saw.

The man stood on a raised platform and was collecting money. Farmer watched as he finished. "Here goes." He said. He reached down and picked up a beer bottle. He tossed it into the air and drew and fired his pistol, holstered his pistol and caught the beer bottle as it came down. He handed the endless bottle to one of the men standing there and laughed as he collected the money from the bet.

"Shit." was all Farmer said as he watched Ace Tucker bend over and pick up another bottle.

"Bodean." Farmer said. She turned around as he waved her over to him. She walked over as Farmer stepped back around the corner of the barn Tucker was performing behind.

"Ain't that a great trick." Bodean said smiling and looking up at Farmer.

He reached into his pocket and removed one of the gold coins, "Take this up there and tell him you bet that coin that he cannot do the trick again."

"Huh?" she asked, totally confused.

"Just do it. Make the bet he can't do it again." Farmer repeated, "And don't say anything about me."

Bodean shrugged her slim shoulders and took the coin, turned and walked up to the platform. Halfway to the platform it struck almost like a physical blow. The way Farmer looked, the shocked look of surprise on his face. This has to be the man he is looking for. The man on the stage was trying to entice people to bet he could not do it again.

"Hey Mister, I bet you this you can't do it again." She yelled over the noise.

Tucker turned and reached down and took the coin from the black woman, noting how beautiful she was. He almost did not look at the coin because of her beauty, but when he did he stopped, stood up straight, and looked around. "Where did you get this?" He asked Bodean, the smile gone from his face, his voice dead serious.

"A man gave it to me and told me to bet you couldn't do that trick again."

"Where is this man?" Tucker asked her still looking around.

"I don't know." She said, turning to look where Farmer was. When she looked Farmer was not there.

"What's this mans name?" Tucker asked, afraid of the answer he was going to get.

"I don't know." She answered, a questioning tone in her voice because she did not know where Farmer was or why he was hiding from her. Then she realized he was not hiding from her, he was hiding from the man standing on the platform, the beer bottle shooter.

CHAPTER 71

"**W**ell. Well, Ace, how's it going?" Tucker recognized the voice instantly. It was Farmer and Tucker knew he was in trouble. It was a question of how big a lie he had to tell until Farmer made a mistake and Tucker had his chance to kill him.

"Charlie," Tucker said and started to turn around. He was just getting ready to mount his horse and leave town. He had left the stage he had been using to show off and shoot the beer bottles. He had almost run to the hotel and grabbed his belongings and had come back down stairs and paid his bill, walked out of the hotel, thrown his saddle bags over his saddle and that is when he had heard Farmer address him from behind.

"Don't turn around, Ace. Don't move, don't even breath hard. Just stay still and keep quiet." Farmer said. His voice was quiet and cold, like the voice of a dead man.

"Do me a favor, Charlie, and at least let me turn around." Tucker said.

"Just as soon as you pull your pistol and put it on the saddle of that horse in front of you." Farmer answered.

"You got a gun on me, Charlie?" Tucker asked, looking for any kind of opening that might give him a chance.

"The shotgun is cocked and the triggers are pulled, so even if you do shoot me the shotgun goes off and you die with me." He answered.

"This ain't my horse, Charlie." Tucker said.

232

"Well, we'll just borrow it for a couple of minutes." the killer answered, "My fingers are getting tired, Ace, so I think you better put the gun on the saddle."

Tucker reached for the pistol with his right hand, if he only knew where Farmer was, he could move and draw and kill him.

"Don't get any ideas Ace, I'd hate to kill you before I heard just exactly what happened down south." Farmer said. It seemed to Tucker the voice had moved to his left, but Farmer moved quietly, so Tucker was not sure where he was. "And just use your thumb and pointer finger to lift the pistol. That way I don't have to worry about you cheating and trying to shoot me."

"You can trust me, Charlie." Tucker said. He hesitated lifting the pistol.

"I'll make you a deal, Ace. I will listen to your story if you put the pistol on the saddle. Then I will give you back the pistol and we can come out in this street and draw. The winner gets all the gold and the loser gets a one way ticket to the Promised Land." Farmer finished.

Tucker thought, any chance is better then the one I got now, "Okay, Charlie, just the thumb and the pointer finger." He reached down and gingerly picked the pistol from the holster and laid it on the saddle in front of him. "I'm going to trust you, Charlie, that you aren't going to shoot me when I let go of my gun."

"You can trust me Ace." came the answer from his right.

Tucker laid the pistol sideways on the saddle, let go and waited.

"Now walk away and we will go get something to drink and be good friends." Farmer said and Tucker could almost see in his minds eye Farmer smiling.

CHAPTER
72

Five minutes later they were sitting at a table in a diner. The room had been crowded when they had walked in, but now it was almost empty. Nobody knew who the young man was with Ace Tucker. But they knew who Ace Tucker was. Ace Tucker was dangerous and the young man holding a gun on Tucker had performed a trick that no one had ever performed before. He had gotten the drop on the old, wise gunfighter. The people who had been eating had simply paid for their meal and left. A woman had protested to her husband about leaving the food and he had told her better to leave the food in the dinning room, then to leave your life in the dinning room.

"One of us ain't too popular, Charlie." Tucker said, nonchalantly, as he started to remove his hands from the table.

"Ace, the shotgun is cocked and at a foot and a half I can't miss, so your hands stay on the table." Farmer said.

Tucker moved his hands back on the table, his left hand to within inches of the barrel of the shotgun as he looked at how far he had to reach to grab the barrel.

"I bet your life you can't make it." Farmer said and Tucker looked at him and realized he was right.

"Charlie, you pull that trigger and there will be a real mess in here. Blood and guts all over the place." Tucker said smiling, moving his right hand to encompass the entire diner.

Farmer returned the smile, looking at Tucker, "Yea Ace, but they will be yours. So keep that in mind when you think about grabbing the shotgun."

The owner of the diner approached the table and asked in a nervous voice, "Can I get you gentlemen anything?" The man was short and pushing his late forties. He was bald headed and had a plumb belly that the apron he was wearing could not hide.

"How much money you got, Ace?" Farmer asked.

Tucker pulled a hand full of gold coins from his vest pocket and laid them on the table. There had to be four or five hundred dollars in the pile. "That's just in the one pocket, Charlie. I have some in the other pocket."

"Take the money." Farmer said to the waiter, never taking his eyes off Tucker.

"All of it?" he asked, not believing what he was hearing and not being able to take his eyes off the gold coins.

"All of it." Farmer said.

"Think I could at least get a steak for that much?" Tucker asked, looking at the sign on the wall which read steak and potatoes one dollar.

"We'll each take one." Farmer told the man in the apron.

"And I will have a four hundred and ninety eight dollar beer." Tucker said smiling and sitting back against the back of the bench relaxed. "And I will buy him one too." Tucker added pointing across the table towards Farmer.

"Just water." Farmer said.

"Yes Sir." The balding man said as he scooped up the coins and disappeared into the kitchen.

"So why this special visit, Charlie?" Tucker asked the killer sitting opposite him. His hands still on the table, still inches from the shotgun.

"I want you to tell me what happened after we got the gold, Ace. How you managed to kill Wilson, Muller, and Hansen. I want the truth and I want all of it." The voice was cold and Tucker knew the man sitting across from him was close to pulling the trigger of the shotgun if he wasn't told everything. The problem was Tucker did not know how much of the truth Farmer actually knew or had surmised. Tucker decided to tell almost the whole truth, almost.

"Ha," Tucker started, the laugh not being funny, "It really happened by accident. We had gotten the gold and Al was right. The Indians waited until we had it and were out of the forbidden land before they came after us. Wilson had the back door to cover us and you were on the point. Wilson came up and said there were about twenty Indians coming up behind us and Al told me and you to buy those three some time. Just hold them off for maybe an hour, then high tail it back and catch up. Al took our mules and me and you stayed behind.

"There was a sharp turn in the canyon and we decided it was a good place to buy some time. I think you really know your stuff." Tucker added as an after thought. He knew the longer he talked, the better his chances of getting the shotgun, "We got off our horses and you stood just behind the rock at the sharp turn, I was maybe twenty feet in front of you on the opposite side. The Indians came around the corner and we must have gotten ten of them before they knew what hit them. You got more then me." Tucker looked at Farmer. "The other ones took off back down the canyon. We waited and waited and I was beginning to think they had given up when they started sniping at us from inside the canyon and the top of the canyon wall. We started shooting back and all of a sudden I thought if I play my cards right, I can have all the gold. So I waited until one of them shot at me and I yelled I was hit in the belly. I told you to get out. I would hold them for as long as I could. You almost screwed things up when you came over by me. I had to think fast how to get a lot of blood, so I cut my wrist. I let it bleed all over my stomach and when you got there I looked pretty bad. I told you to leave me and you took off like a scared rabbit. I knew then I was going to get all the gold and I was going to use you four to carry it north for me. And one by one I would kill all of you one way or another."

I've seen a lot of dead men and you sure looked dead to me." Farmer said, looking at the man sitting opposite him.

Tucker smiled a knowing smile, "Practice Charlie, just practice." Tucker was relaxed, if he could get Farmer to relax he might be able to get the shotgun, "You just hold your breath and stare at a spot in the sky and don't blink. Your eyes do the rest."

Farmer nodded in understanding. He had another question, "And all the blood? How did you get that?"

"Charlie, you want me to tell you all my secrets?" Tucker asked.

"You can tell me or I can pull the trigger." Farmer did a quick glance at the shotgun pointed at Tucker.

"You pull that trigger Charlie and you'll never know." Tucker replied, still smiling.

"There are a whole lot of things I'm gonna die without knowing, Ace. One more won't make any difference one way or the other."

It dawned on Tucker that Farmer meant exactly what he said. He knew Farmer would pull the trigger without hesitation. Tucker turned his left hand over and pointed to the small scar, "Just stick yourself there. You bleed like a pig. When you want it to stop you just press on it with your other thumb for a minute."

Farmer looked but said nothing.

"Did you kill Hansen?" Farmer asked, never moving his hand from the shotgun, the voice, cold, indifferent, almost not caring, the dead green eyes looking directly at Tucker. "Yea, I did." Tucker said. He looked down at the table and smiled. "He was the easiest of all." He was still smiling when he looked back up at Farmer. "I couldn't believe it I just rode up onto you three and when I figured I was close enough I just dismounted and shot him in the back." Tucker shrugged his shoulders. "You did me a big favor, Charlie, you shot that Indian. I did not even know he was there. He would have gotten me for sure if you had not shot him first. Hansen just fell off his horse dead. I had to be careful as I was catching up to you. I had to make sure you did not see me. After I shot him I just stayed hidden until you and Muller left. I couldn't believe you two were still dragging eight mules and an extra horse. Greed is greed, but that was just not right."

"Don't talk to me about right and wrong after what you did." Farmer replied.

The two men sat facing each other for a long minute, then Farmer asked, "What about Muller, what did you have to do with her dying?"

"Nothing, I swear Charlie, I didn't do nothing. Well almost nothing. I passed you two during the night and crossed the bridge, then cut the ropes holding it together almost all the way through." Tucker paused just long enough to cough once. "Muller came up to that bridge and started across and I knew it was going to give out. It did and she went into the river. I though you were going to save her when that board hit her. Stuck her right in the head, it did. I wonder if she drowned or if the board killed her before she let go of the rope." Tucker paused, trying to figure out if he was getting to Farmer or not. Upsetting him, maybe make him make a mistake. Farmers' face showed nothing, his hand never moved by the shotgun. "I was kind of glad you shot that mule, but I saw you take the gold after you shot him. You know that rope came undone when the second mule went in the water. The last two mules didn't go in and the second mule, the one that went in, he got out because the other two wouldn't move and the rope attached to his tail kept him close enough to the riverbank so he could get to his feet and he got out of the water and the three of them just wandered off." Tucker finished and took a deep breath. Let's see just how much Charlie knows.

"I bet you just happened to find them." Farmer stated sarcastically.

"Yea, I did," answered Tucker, "I found a place to forge the river further up stream and came back and found them. Then I re-forged the river and I was free and clear. That is when I figured I had pushed my luck far enough and that is when I stopped tracking you. I figured for sure you would never make it back to Texas alive. That was a mistake, I should have tracked you and killed you too."

"Yes, you should have." agreed Farmer.

Again the two men sat in silence, Farmer waiting for Tucker to continue and Tucker waiting to be prodded by Farmer.

"What happened at the monastery?" Farmer asked.

"What do you mean?" Tucker countered.

"I mean you went back to the monastery. What happened when you got there? That's what I mean." Farmer's voice turned brutal with the last sentence.

"It's your fault, you left my share of the gold there."

"Don't blame me for what you did." Farmer stated flatly.

Tucker shrugged his shoulders again, "I waited when I saw you, Muller, Wilson, and Hansen go into the monastery. I saw the bandits sneak in and I never thought you guys would set a trap for them. I waited in the canyon all the next day after the gun battle, when I realized that you had left some gold with them. I counted the mules as you three left, you were short three and I guessed you had left them for the women. I waited that night and the next morning to make sure you three were long gone and I just rode in and Blue was standing by the gate. I remember she was so happy to see me. She was still smiling when she fell to the ground dead after I shot her. Then I shot the other ones, including your best friend, Candy. Shot her twice just to make sure she was dead."

"And the doctor?" Farmer questioned.

Tucker was surprised, why the doctor, why that skinny, ugly bitch? Now I have to mix the truth and the lie again, thought Tucker, the problem was how much truth and how much lie. "The doctor wasn't at the fire and just after I finished shooting I saw her run out from the building. She took one look, realized what happened, and headed for the cave opening to the tunnel. I shot at her once. She went into the mouth of the cave. That's all I know about her."

Tucker saw Farmer look down at the table, then back up at him, the green eyes flashing anger and hatred, the knuckles of the right hand holding the shotgun were white.

He is going to shoot me or do something else. If he does something else I will have the shotgun because he will not be paying attention thought Tucker. Maybe I will add a little fuel to the fire. Tucker reached into his shirt pocket and removed a scrap of paper and handed it to Farmer. "You might want to read this, Charlie. I found it on your Doctor friend the morning after I killed all those poor little whores in that monastery." Tucker almost spat out the last words, as he handed Farmer the note.

Farmer took the note, unfolded it and looked at the small neat printing.

"Charlie, I needed someone to talk to that night and you were that one. I want to again thank you for the use of your hand. I don't think I will be needing it anymore. I'm dying and I know I don't have much longer. I just want you to know what happened. Ace Tucker came back the day after you, Alice and Al left. I could not believe he just shot all the women. He killed them in cold blood. I was standing watch on top of the monastery and I saw him coming and I thought I will let him surprise the women. He did alright. I heard the shots as I was almost to the door leading to the court yard. When I stepped out I saw Ace sitting on his horse and all the women were dead or dying. I ran for the cave that leads to the water because that way I knew if I got inside I could lose him. Just as I got to the mouth of the cave he shot me. He hit me at the base of the spine and I cannot walk. I dragged myself into the cave and I guess he was afraid to follow me. He must have come up to the entrance and yelled something about me coming out and dying fast or staying inside and dying slow. As I write this I hope you find me, Charlie, before it is too late. I should have come with you when you asked, I will now. I know I love you and over time I could make you feel something for me.

"Please find me, Charlie.

Love,

Mary."

Tucker did not look up at Farmer he simply waited for the killer to pull the trigger on the shotgun. It took all the will power Farmer had not to pull the triggers of the shotgun and blow Tucker to kingdom come.

Farmer felt the cold he almost always felt since being shot. He did not think about the Doctor. Something was nagging in his head, something Tucker said. Then he had it.

"A couple of more questions Ace."

"You got the gun." Tucker said.

"You said you shot the Doctor, she ran into the cave and you didn't see her no more. Then you said you got the note off her. Was she still alive when you took the note?"

Tucker realized he had told too many lies. He had gotten his story mixed up.

"Forget about all that," Farmer interrupted his train of thought, "it don't mean anything. What did you do with the gold?"

Tucker could not believe Farmer had not shot him. He was so relived he told the truth. "There is a little town just over the border called Poker Ridge. There's a graveyard just to the south of town. I filled up my saddle bags and buried the rest." Tucker got a confused look on his face as Farmer laughed.

"What's so funny?" He asked.

"I did the same thing." Farmer said still smiling.

This time Tucker laughed.

CHAPTER 73

"I'm gonna put your pistol on the saddle of a horse outside, Ace. Just pick it up and walk out into the middle of the street and wait. I'll be there." Farmer finished and stood up taking the shotgun from the table. He folded the note and put it in his shirt pocket.

"So now we know where we buried the gold. It is a winner take all thing, right Charlie." Tucker said, looking up at the gunman standing opposite him.

"Yea, winner take all." Farmer answered.

He did a sort of side shuffle out of the dinning room so he could keep his eye on Tucker.

As soon as the door closed behind Farmer, Tucker was on his feet and heading for the counter. The waiter stood frozen to the spot as Tucker approached. He moved very quickly for such a big man.

"Where's the bar gun?" Tucker demanded, grabbing the waiter by his shirt. The waiter was too stunned to answer and Tucker shook him. "Where is it?" He screamed, his mouth only inches from the waiters face. He could smell the beer on Tucker's breath.

"By the cash drawer." The waiter said, pointing to the opposite end of the counter.

Tucker ran to the end of the counter nearest to the door and leaned over the counter and saw the shotgun. It was a double barrel and it had to have thirty inch barrels. This would be auckward to swing, but it would have to do. There was also a pistol there and Tucker grabbed that too. He stuck the pistol in his holster and headed for the door carrying the shotgun in his right hand. He ran for the door and never broke stride as he kicked the double doors open with his right foot. In one stride he was out on the edge of the boardwalk, he did not even look for Farmer, he simply aimed the shotgun at the door of the saloon across the street to his left and fired one shot from the shotgun. He swung the big gun to his right and when it was lined up with the door of the general store slightly to his right he fired the second round. He dropped the shotgun and drew the pistol and fired the six rounds from the pistol randomly in both directions up and down the street. When the pistol was empty he waited, knowing he probably did not hit Farmer, but he may have upset him enough to slow him down just a bit in the gunfight, and just a bit was all Ace Tucker needed in a gunfight with Charlie Farmer.

"You missed, Ace." came the cold dead voice from behind and to Tucker's left. He turned to see Farmer standing next to the corner of the diner in the alleyway. Farmer was a few inches shorter then Tucker anyway, but now Tucker was standing on the boardwalk and Farmer was on the ground in the alleyway, a good foot and one half lower then Tucker on the boardwalk.

The shooting did not bother him, thought Tucker, so I will try something else, "You know Charlie, when I rode into that monastery after you, Muller, and Hansen left Blue was standing there. She was all smiling and happy, I should have done a little dickie dunkin' the night before we left to get the gold. Anyway she was still smiling when I drew my pistol and aimed it at her head, then she got this I don't understand look. Then she got that dead look when I shot her in the forehead.

"The rest of the women, except for the doc, were sitting around the place where the fire was and I shot them. I shot that young girl first, the one Harry wanted. That left four, and they started to scramble in all directions, I guess to try and get their guns. I shot three of them in the back as they ran. Then I saw your one true love, Carter, and she was reaching for a pistol. I even let her get her hands on the pistol before I shot her. She fell down, but she wasn't dead so I got off my horse and walked to her. She tried to say something, but all that came out was a mouth full of blood, so I figured I hit her in the lungs. She was kneeling on all fours so I kicked her over on her back and she started to choke on her own blood. I said to her, "I'm going to put you out of your misery, you ugly, scar faced bitch." Then I shot her in the forehead. You should have seen how big her eyes got when I aimed the pistol at her forehead. Boy she knew she was going to die and she was scared. Then I saw the Doc running toward the cave and I shot her. She went down, but still managed to get into the cave. I was nice, I told her if she came out I would put her out of her misery, she did not come out, so I found the gold and took one of the horses and packed the gold on it and left." Here comes the kicker, thought Tucker and said looking Farmer directly in the eyes. "You know Charlie, no matter what you say to ease your conscience, if you had not left those three bags of gold there those women would still be alive today. So it is really your fault they are dead."

Tucker waited for Farmer to do or say something, but he simply stood there and looked at Tucker. How far can I push him before he gets upset, Tucker wondered.

"Go over by the horse, Ace and get the pistol and walk out into the middle of the street and stand there or I will kill you where you stand." The voice was cold and just maybe a little angry, thought Tucker, maybe even a little upset. He looked on the saddle of the horse, but the gun was gone, then he looked on the ground and there it lay. It probably fell off the saddle when the horse moved when he had fired the shotgun and pistol. He moved between the horses and bent over and picked up the pistol and as he stood up he looked back at Farmer. Farmer had stepped onto the boardwalk and Tucker could see his pistol was still in his holster. He turned and pointed the pistol at Farmer, cocking it while he was turning.

"Come on Ace, I didn't put any bullets in the gun. I ain't too bright, but I ain't that stupid." Farmer said. Tucker pulled the trigger, cocked it again and pulled the trigger again, again the click on the empty chamber.

Tucker shrugged his shoulders and said, "What the hell, Charlie, it was worth a try." Then he laughed, turned and walked to the middle of the street. When he turned around again, Farmer was standing behind the horse and himself.

"This is how this works, Ace, you put six rounds in the pistol, put the pistol in your holster, and then raise your hands. Then I come out from behind the horse and then we shoot at each other." The cold voice was there, but the anger was gone. Tucker hoped it was the voice of a soon to be dead man.

Tucker walked to the middle of the dusty street, cocked the single action pistol and looked down the barrel, it was clear. He looked at each chamber before he inserted the bullet. He put the six rounds in and holstered the pistol and looked at Farmer. Farmer was still behind the horse. "Well, Charlie." Tucker said.

"You forgot to put your hands up, Ace." Farmer answered. That had been his last play, the fact that Farmer might forget the raised hands. Tucker reluctantly raised his hands. He watched as Farmer walked into the street never taking his eyes off Tucker. He stopped in the middle of the street and turned around so he was facing Tucker.

"This is for all the gold." Tucker said.

"All the gold." Farmer repeated.

Bodean watched from the window of the saloon as Farmer walked into the middle of the street. There was maybe fifty feet between the two men. Tucker lowered his left hand. Then he lowered his right, on the way down he stopped and wiped it on his shirt front. Then faster then her eye could follow, the hand went from the shirt front to the pistol. The pistol came out of the holster and Bodean heard the shot. Tucker seemed to hesitate for an instant, then he fired his pistol.

CHAPTER 74

I t was hot that afternoon outside the city limits of the small southern Texas town. Bodean was standing next to Farmer and they were looking at the cross marking Tucker's grave on the side of boot hill.

"After you shot him and he was lying in the street you walked over to him and squatted down. What did he say to you?" She asked.

"He said, I'm sorry I shot the Doc, Charlie, forgive me."

"What did you say?" She questioned again looking up at the man standing next to her.

Farmer looked at her, the cold bottomless green eyes, and in the cold dead voice of the killer he was, Farmer answered, "Shit."

The end

Joe Kinney was born in Paterson New Jersey. He moved with his family to northern Utah where he got married. He then moved to Chicago where he spent a lot of years. He relocated to New Jersey to get a job. He then moved to Mississippi where his job took him. He lives just south of Memphis on almost three acres of land where he works on his motorcycles in his spare time.

Printed in the United States
By Bookmasters